# Cargo
# Fever

# Cargo Fever

## Will Buckingham

Tindal
Street
Press

First published in March 2007
by Tindal Street Press Ltd
217 The Custard Factory, Gibb Street, Birmingham, B9 4AA
www.tindalstreet.co.uk

A CIP catalogue reference for this book is available
from the British Library

ISBN: 978 0 9551 384 2 3

Typeset by Country Setting, Kingsdown, Kent
Printed and bound in Great Britain by Clays Ltd, St Ives PLC

*For my friends in Indonesia*

# The Island of Kenukecil

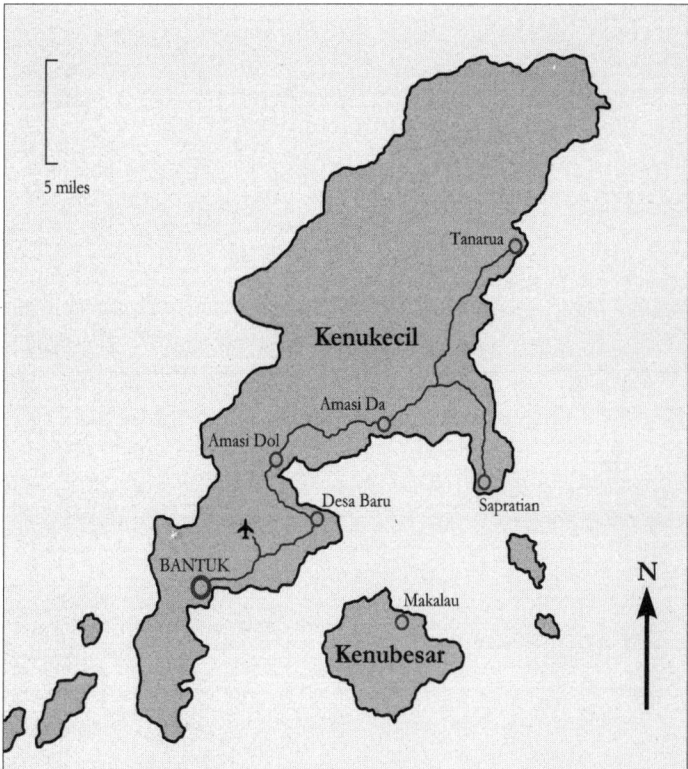

Adapted from *Life with the Kenukecilese:
A Study in the Culture of a People* by Pastor L. Kruywers
(Utrecht, 1937)

*There are accounts in pagan history*
*of certain monstrous races of men . . .*
*These accounts may be completely worthless.*
*But if such peoples exist, then either*
*they are not human; or, if human,*
*they are descended from Adam.*

St Augustine
*The City of God* XVI

# 1

At some point, Samuel Rivers realized his eyes were open. An unhappy thought took shape in his mind: *I am conscious*. The purple nylon of the bed-sheets was cold and damp against his back. His forehead trickled with sweat. Sam turned his face to the open window. The moon was up, not yet full. He could smell the sea.

Was it the sound that had woken him? Now that it had entered his stuttering consciousness, he knew it had been continuing for some time. A man's voice was calling, across the other side of the bay or down towards the harbour. Sam tried to focus; but the harder he listened, the more the voice slipped away from him. Only if he relaxed did it steal back into his awareness. Then there was his bladder. I need a piss, he thought. A piss and some chloroquine.

Wiping the clamminess from his forehead, Sam sat up. He leaned back against the wall's rough plaster. Upright, glancing round the moonlit room, he experienced a few moments of lucidity. Where was Fon now? he asked himself. What was she doing? Who was she with?

Wincing, he stretched out a hand to fumble on the bed-side table. His fingers found the bottle and closed round it. He wrestled briefly with the lid and tipped the tablets into his cupped hand: three chalky pills. He pooled a mouthful of saliva, put the tablets under his tongue and swallowed. There was a stab of bitterness. He swallowed a second time, making sure that the tablets had gone down, and returned the bottle to the table. Sam picked up his watch and held the dial at an angle so that he could read it in the moon-light. Two in the morning.

The *Pandangan Indah* – or, in translation, the Lovely Vista – was Bantuk's only hotel. A sign outside read: PANDANGAN INDAH: LUXURY, PEACE, QUITE. Sam's room was the best in the hotel: it was on the first floor, with a view of the town and the bay.

Drawn by the distant cry, Sam looked towards the window. He prepared to stand as a man twice his age might. Swinging his body round through ninety degrees, he let his legs slide from the bed. His bare feet made contact with the floor. He raised himself carefully, pushing up with his arms. On unsteady legs he shambled across the room to prop himself against the windowsill.

The main street was deserted, metal shutters pulled down to obscure the shop-fronts. From the concrete rectangle of the Hope Market, halfway down the street, the pier curved far out into the bay. Further up the coast, on a low hill to the north, he could see the silhouetted spire of Bantuk Catholic Church. The light that hung over the statue of Christ the Sacred Heart shone in the distance like a star. Due east, holding the sky and the sea apart, were the squat hills of Kenubesar. Despite its name, Kenubesar – literally Great Kenu – was the smaller of the two neigh-bouring islands while Kenukecil – Little Kenu – was the larger, an error attributable to the negligence of a Dutch cartographer in the late nineteenth century.

Sam leaned on the sill, hunching his shoulders, watch-ing the moonlight break on the surface of the sea. The breeze cooled the sweat that covered his body like a film. He shivered. He had no idea what the date was. It seemed as if he had been ill for ever. Perhaps, he said to himself, it was already Fon's birthday. Perhaps the cargo had already arrived. There was no way of telling.

Sam's mind drifted, caught up in currents and eddies and tides over which he had no control. His body rippled with the faint tremors. He closed his eyes.

When he returned to himself the shouting had stopped. The moon had inched a short distance across the sky and the breeze had fallen away. His bladder was giving him hell.

A movement down by the harbour drew his attention. He scanned the length of the pier. There was nothing there. The shadows across the bay wavered, refusing to resolve into anything clear or distinct. He glanced towards the horizon; back again to the bay. Then he saw it: a figure, a small child perhaps, stepping cautiously from the end of the pier into the Hope Market, staying out of the moonlight, half-crouching, keeping close to the cover of the buildings. Sam watched as it turned onto the main street. Then, heading up the street away from the hotel, the figure dissolved into the darkness.

Or perhaps it was nothing. The night was too dark, the layers of flickering shadow too unstable, his mind too much not his own. He could not be certain of anything. Besides, his bladder was screaming now. 'I've got to piss,' he mumbled as he turned away from the window.

Sam fumbled with the lock of his hotel room door and staggered down the corridor. His awareness of his actions was only fragmentary as he pushed open the door of the *kamar bak*, closed it behind him, emptied his bladder with gasping relief and returned to his room. He slumped exhausted onto the bed without thinking to lock the door. He was pouring with sweat and the shivering was starting again. He closed his eyes, waiting for the world to stabilize itself. There was a buzz by his ear. He lifted an ineffectual hand. The buzzing faded, then became louder again. Fucking mosquitoes, he thought. He looked at his watch. It was three.

Sam tried to remember when he had his last dose of chloroquine, but his grasp on the passage of time was weak. Better to take another load, he said to himself. Better to double up than to do nothing at all. Parasites in the blood-stream: swamp the fuckers. He leaned onto his side and opened the bottle of pills. He shook two tablets into his hand, gathered a pool of saliva in his cheeks and slid the tablets between his dry lips. Only when he tasted the bitterness did he remember his earlier dose. He spat the tablets back out into his hand and slung them across the room. They bounced into the corner: plink, plink, plink.

Sam lay back down on the bed and closed his eyes. He slipped into feverish dreams.

# 2

On the afternoon of that Sunday, 3 November 1996, Ibu Nilasera left her house by the seashore where the frigate birds circled, a clutch of plastic flowers in her hand and three sweet sago biscuits in her pocket. She climbed the hill towards the church, panting with exertion, where she intended to spend a half-hour alone in the sight of the Lord. She loved to visit the church on Sunday afternoons when the hurly-burly of the morning mass had passed, to sit in quiet contemplation and to give thanks.

Her journey took her past the seminary, where the choir was practising hymns to the accompaniment of a small Casio keyboard, and up the track past the convent, where the Sunday-school children intoned their liturgy under the unwavering gaze of the Mother Superior.

The square outside the church was deserted, except for a dog called Roki, who was resting in the shade of a bamboo bench, worrying at a small sore on his hind leg. At the top of the flagpole in the centre of the square, the *merah-putih* flapped lazily in the breeze: red for blood and white for purity.

Ibu Nilasera paused for breath by the statue of Christ the Sacred Heart on the seaward side of the square. Her right hand reached into her pocket and pulled out a sago biscuit, which she ate in three mouthfuls. Reaching down a second time, she produced another and started to eat this too. Then she glanced up at the statue of Christ and paused: his smile, she thought, had taken on a touch of severity about the edges of the mouth. She reminded herself that she had planned to offer the biscuits to the Virgin along with the flowers. 'Forgive me, Lord,' she muttered and put the half-eaten biscuit back into her pocket. One and a half biscuits would have to suffice for the Virgin today.

Ibu Nilasera straightened her dress, adjusted her hair and rearranged the plastic flowers, making sure that the tallest and most vividly coloured was in the centre. When everything was in order, she walked calmly across the square and stepped into the cool half-light of the Lord's house.

Less than five seconds elapsed before she emerged, bursting out of the church with her hands empty of offerings and her arms raised towards the skies. On her face was an expression of terror. 'The Last Days!' Ibu Nilasera was yelling. 'We are in the Last Days!'

Nobody witnessed her testimony. The people of Kenukecil were deaf to the Ibu's prophecy: the idlers too much engaged in idling; the pious too preoccupied with their pieties; the fornicators committing unspeakable acts in hidden places; the palmwine drinkers dulled by drink. Perhaps even God himself did not notice, for Kenukecil is a place easily overlooked and God has but a single pair of ears, as is confirmed by Scripture where it is written that we were made in His image. Only Roki the dog remarked on the Ibu's terror as she exploded from the church, his canine bewilderment delivering him, for a moment, from the nagging irritation of his sore.

Ibu Nilasera hurtled across the square under the watchful eyes of Our Jesus. She headed seawards down the track, careering past the convent without pause, heading towards the seminary, puffing and panting, her arms flailing. Her ears blocked by terror, she did not hear the words of the hymn the seminary choir were singing but instead continued, half-running and half-stumbling, towards the pastoran. There, on the approach to the priest's house, frantic with distress, Ibu Nilasera rounded the corner of the seminary buildings and collided with the caretaker.

Mathias was a man of many parts, few of them in anything like satisfactory working order. He had been employed at the pastoran for longer than anyone could remember and in return for his minimal labours he received a small stipend. He was tickling the path to the pastoran with his broom and singing an ungodly song under his breath when Ibu Nilasera interrupted him. The Ibu was not a small woman. In her svelte youth she had been the village beauty and by the time of her marriage she had already broken many hearts. Her husband – a kind and good man, whom nevertheless she did not love – died before the conception of a child. His demise had left Ibu Nilasera free of maternal responsibilities and uxorial duties. Thus liberated, she resolved not to remarry. Renouncing husbands, lovers and children, she systematically brought ruination on her body, indulging in a taste for sugar that led to the rapid growth of her girth and the tumbling of teeth from her mouth. Her outward beauty crumbled and she transformed herself into a creature whose loveliness was almost entirely internal: a pulchritude not of the body but of the soul. Protected from any further romantic involvements, the remainder of her life had been lived in quiet piety within the sight of God. But this piety was insufficient to protect her soul against what she saw in the church at Bantuk on that Sunday afternoon.

The collision between Mathias and Ibu Nilasera was a more severe matter for the gardener than it was for the Ibu. Mathias was a frail man, no longer as firm on his feet as in the past. When struck by the momentum of Ibu Nilasera in full flight, he came down hard on his side in the desiccated flower-beds, the profane song broken off mid-verse.

Ibu Nilasera paused and stared down with wild eyes at the caretaker sprawled out on the dry earth. 'Pak Mathias!' she hollered. 'We are in the Last Days! There is a devil in the House of the Lord!'

Without waiting for a response, Ibu Nilasera continued on her way, hitching up her dress as she ran. The cheerful blue door of the pastoran was now in sight. On the other side, the Dutch priest would be having his daily siesta. If anybody could protect her from the terror it would be Pastor Niemann.

By the time Ibu Nilasera reached the threshold, she was in a state of exhausted disarray. She hammered on the door with her fists: 'Pastor Niemann! Pastor Niemann! Get up!'

The pastor sat up in bed. He recognized the voice instantly. In the twenty-nine years he had known her, Pastor Niemann had not once seen Ibu Nilasera lose her composure. The novelty caused him to leap to his feet. With six enormous strides he left his bedroom, crossed the room he used for welcoming guests and holding meetings, and reached the door, flinging it open with such force that Ibu Nilasera, now weeping and with a trickle of blood dripping from one hand where she had beaten the rough wood too hard, came toppling into his arms.

Six feet tall, emaciated, his upper eyelids heavily hooded and with a face not given to expressions of violent emotion, Pastor Niemann looked down at the woman in astonishment, gently setting her back on her feet.

'Ibu Nilasera,' he said. 'What is wrong?'

The Ibu looked up into the priest's face. 'Pastor Niemann . . .' she said and burst into tears.

'*Masuklah, Ibu Nilasera. Duduk.*' Come, Ibu Nilasera. Sit down. The priest held open the door and led her inside. He pulled a chair back from the table and guided her towards it. Ibu Nilasera collapsed into it, sobbing and whimpering. The priest sat down opposite her, leaned forwards, hands clasped, and waited for the sobbing to subside.

'Tell me, Ibu,' he said, 'what is wrong?'

Ibu Nilasera looked up. The terror had not yet left her eyes. '*Ada setan di gereja!*' she whispered.

'A devil?' The pastor frowned. 'A devil? In the church?'

Ibu Nilasera nodded. 'Yes, Pastor. A devil.'

This was not what Pastor Niemann had anticipated for his Sunday afternoon. 'What kind of devil?' he asked, despite himself.

Ibu Nilasera sniffed a little. 'I do not know, father,' she said. 'It was sitting in the front pew and –' The woman began to weep again.

The Dutchman reached out an uneasy hand and touched her arm. 'Ibu Nilasera, calm yourself,' he said. 'Tell me what happened.'

She wiped her eyes. 'I went into the church,' she sniffed. 'I was going to pray. I had some offerings for the Virgin. I went inside and then I saw it. In the front pew.'

'Ibu,' the pastor gently interjected, 'you are mistaken. The church is dark. Perhaps it was somebody from the town.'

Ibu Nilasera shook her head. 'No,' she said. 'It was a devil and it was doing a terrible thing.'

The pastor sighed. 'Tell me, then, what was it doing?'

Ibu Nilasera lowered her head into her hands. There was a flurry of choking sobs. The priest could only just make out her words.

'Pastor,' she said, 'the devil was praying.'

Like many priests of his generation, Pastor Niemann was as much a man of science as of religion. He still held to a somewhat abstract – even vestigial – belief in God in the face of the seemingly unstoppable advance of scientific progress, but in his universe devils had no place. He had cast them out as thoroughly as Lucifer himself had been cast from the heavens. And while his faith in Ibu Nilasera's unshakeable integrity and goodness of heart was absolute, the faith he held in science and reason was still greater. Thus the Ibu's testimony did not precipitate an immediate theological crisis. The simplest explanation, he concluded, was that the Ibu, on this occasion, was gravely mistaken.

'I will make coffee,' he said, 'and then you must tell me everything.'

Up the hill, in the direction of the church, Roki the dog crawled from the shelter of the bamboo bench and scrambled to his feet. He stepped into the sun. Then he trotted over to the flagpole, where he patriotically relieved himself. A fly landed on his open sore and he shuddered, turning to nudge it away with his nose. Roki looked around once and, seeing that there was nobody around, loped over to the church doors. On the threshold he hesitated for a few moments. There was a scent on the air, something he did not recognize. He sniffed at the darkness inside with a mix of curiosity and fear. Curiosity won and Roki slunk into the building.

A few moments later, the dog came yelping and barking from Bantuk Catholic Church in wild panic. He bolted across the square and, ears pinned back, eyes bulging, plunged into the long grasses where he lay for a long time, shivering.

# 3

As she waited for the priest to return, Ibu Nilasera offered up a double prayer: half, the ancestors forgive her, to the God of Israel; and half, may God forgive her, to the ancestors. She glanced around the room. It was sparsely furnished. Before her stood a wooden table, its legs in small dishes of water to protect the sugar bowl from ants. Around the table were arranged four wooden chairs and by the wall was a cabinet with drawers and a small bookshelf. To the side of the cabinet hung a tapestry of Christ at a table, breaking bread with his disciples – a stitchwork Leonardo's *Last Supper*. Ibu Nilasera studied the silent drama: Christ's arms open wide, the disciples gesticulating, each in a different fashion. She was horribly cold. It seemed to her as if an icy breeze was blowing through the door; but when she turned her head she saw that the door was closed. She shuddered. Her whole body ached.

Pastor Niemann reappeared with two cups of coffee. When he saw how Ibu Nilasera was hunched and shivering, he nodded grimly. 'So,' he said, 'you have malaria, perhaps.' He placed the coffee down on the table and then turned to the cabinet and rummaged in a drawer, bringing out a bottle of tablets, which he placed on the table. 'You must take these,' he said. 'They will cure you. Come, Ibu, drink your coffee. Take your tablets.'

Ibu Nilasera took the coffee cup between her hands. '*Setan*,' she said.

'No,' the priest replied consolingly. 'There are no devils, Ibu.'

The woman lifted her cup. Her hand was shaking and coffee slopped over the sides as she ferried it to her lips. She took a single sip and then put it back on the table.

'*Ada banyak nyamuk di Kenukecil,*' the pastor said sadly.

He was right. There were many mosquitoes in Kenukecil. Everyone suffered from the fever at some time or other. He himself was not exempt. You cannot take chloroquine for twenty-nine years in a row. His liver too was home to seething colonies of protozoa.

Ibu Nilasera crossed her arms in front of her body. It was not clear to the priest whether this was a gesture of protest against his diagnosis, or whether she hoped that it might keep her warm and calm her shivering. '*Bukan nyamuk,*' she said. Then, as if to a child, she repeated: '*Ada setan di gereja.*'

The pastor sighed. '*Minum,*' he ordered her. Drink your coffee. He pushed the tablets towards her and then lifted his own cup, taking a large gulp. Ibu Nilasera did not respond. Tremors ran through her.

The priest scratched his head, just behind the ear, and got to his feet. He went to the door, opened it and glanced outside. The afternoon was beginning to cool. Beneath a tree a group of seminarians had gathered, fresh from their choir practice. In the centre of the group sat Benny, Pastor Niemann's assistant. He held a guitar in his lap and was strumming fat, languid chords. A little further away, Mathias stood on the path to the pastoran with his broom, either deep in thought or resting from his slight labours. Noticing the pastor emerge, the gardener began to sweep again.

The pastor beckoned to Benny. 'Benny, *ayo!*' he called.

The seminarian put the guitar down, and jogged towards the door. He was in his early twenties, uncomplicated in his convictions and with a naturally sunny temperament. There was something about him that the pastor found unnerving: the simplicity of his devotion; his easy relationship with the Lord. Although he had never spoken of the subject with him, he was certain that Benny would be as fervent a believer in devils as he was in God.

Benny stopped in front of the pastor and smiled.

'Call for Suster Elena,' the priest said. 'Ibu Nilasera is sick.'

'Yes, Pastor,' Benny replied. He turned and made his way down the path to the convent at a comfortable jog.

Benny knocked on the convent door. It was Suster Elena who answered. 'Benny!' she said. 'How hot it has been today.'

Suster Elena was one of the fortunate few for whom the life of renunciation was also one of unmixed joy. A woman of almost supernatural goodwill, she had entered her calling at the age of seventeen and since then had lived a life of service and devotion to her fellow creatures. She divided her time into thirds. The first she spent in the hospital, where she tended the sick with the application of what scant medical knowledge she had. For the second third she worked in the school. The third part was given over to quiet contemplation and prayer, a contemplation of the heart rather than of the mind, from which she arose every day refreshed and glowing.

Benny did not spend time on courtesies. 'You must come quickly,' he said. 'Ibu Nilasera is sick.'

'Ibu Nilasera is sick? What is her sickness?'

'The pastor says that it is the *nyamuk*, but I have heard that . . .' Benny tailed off and looked away.

'What have you heard, Benny?' Suster Elena's expression became serious.

'Mathias says she saw a devil in the church.'

'Benny, that is impossible!' Suster Elena said.

'You do not believe in devils?'

'Devils? Of course I believe, Benny. The Bible tells us that there are devils. Who would not believe? But surely, Benny, it would be impossible for a devil to enter a *church*.'

Benny shrugged. He did not know much about devils. He was only a seminarian, after all. 'That is what I have heard,' he said.

Suster Elena pressed her palms together in a gesture recalling that of prayer. 'Wait a moment, Benny,' she said. 'I will come.'

They arrived at the pastoran to find Ibu Nilasera lolled in a chair. Pastor Niemann was by the open door, waiting for them. 'Come in,' he said.

They stepped into the cool of the priest's house. Suster Elena laid one hand on Ibu Nilasera's shoulder and then shifted it gently to the patient's forehead. The Ibu's skin was hot to the touch.

'*Sakit?*' she asked.

'Yes,' Ibu Nilasera whispered.

Suster Elena's voice was tender. 'What is your sickness?' If voices alone had the power to heal, then Suster Elena's would have been such a voice.

Ibu Nilasera was too weak to answer.

'She has malaria,' Pastor Niemann said.

'But the devil –'

Pastor Niemann silenced Benny with a stern look before he could finish his sentence. 'There was no devil,' he said.

Suster Elena ignored the Dutchman. 'Tell me, Ibu Nilasera, what did you see?' she said.

Ibu Nilasera opened her mouth to speak; but nothing came out except a kind of croaking. Her head slumped forward onto her breast.

Suster Elena looked over at the pastor. 'I am afraid,' she said. 'Perhaps she tells the truth.'

The pastor shook his head. 'She has malaria. There are no devils. Not in the church and not anywhere else.' There were signs of strain around the corners of his mouth.

'Ah, Pastor,' Suster Elena said, smiling, 'the devils may all be gone in Holland, but here in Kenukecil things are different. Here we have many *barang aneh*.'

*Barang aneh*: strange things. Devils and curses; ancestors speaking through the mouths of lizards; children dreaming prophecies of deaths and disasters; witches who ascended over the treetops, with paraffin lamps in their hands, to fetch crates of beer from faraway Ambon.

'What do you know of our *bareng aneh*, Pastor?' the nun asked. 'You have been here for so long, but still you don't believe.'

Ibu Nilasera was now sweating a cold sweat. Her eyes were heavy and her flesh trembled. She groaned, turning her head on her neck. Her mouth gaped open, and a string of nonsense syllables poured out, not spoken so much as vomited. Suster Elena stepped back.

Horrified, Benny crossed himself. 'The devil speaks.'

The pastor made a tutting sound. 'Benny, if her mind is not her own, it is because she is suffering from the malaria. It attacks the brain.'

'But devils, Pastor, attack the soul,' Suster Elena warned. She put a protective arm around the Ibu and waited to see if she – or the devil that had taken up residence within her – would speak again. Ibu Nilasera, however, was silent.

'Suster Elena, please take these.' The priest handed her the bottle of chloroquine tablets. 'Give her a tablet every morning and every night. Make sure that she rests.'

'And if she does not recover?'

The pastor rubbed his eyes. 'Let us see,' he said. 'We can only see.'

Suster Elena helped her patient to her feet. 'I am taking you home to your bed,' she reassured the unfortunate woman. 'I will remain by your side for your protection. There is nothing to fear.'

Ibu Nilasera propped herself up on Suster Elena's shoulder and, one step at a time, the nun led her out of the pastoran and down the path back to her house.

Pastor Niemann watched the two women walking away until they turned the corner and passed out of sight. Benny turned to leave; but he hovered in the doorway as if he was expecting the pastor to make some pronouncement or other. Pastor Niemann glanced at his assistant. 'Thank you, Benny,' he said.

'Yes, Pastor,' Benny replied. He grinned and stepped out of the door. His friends were still at the foot of the tree. He went back to join them and picked up his beloved guitar. As the pastor closed the door, he could hear Benny's playing, the buzz of open strings.

Pastor Niemann finished his coffee, which he liked to drink bitter. The sugar on his table was strictly for guests. The priest's habit of drinking coffee without any sweetening agent was considered throughout Kenukecil to be a sure sign of his piety, evidence of the extent to which he had subjugated his natural desires. On those evenings when the people of the island fell to gossiping, asking, 'But does the priest, who is a man after all, relieve himself with his hand?' there was always a voice in the crowd to reply, 'Impossible! The pastor drinks coffee and tea without sugar. He is not like the rest of us.'

Outside it was growing dark. A mosquito hummed near the priest's ear. He snatched at it fruitlessly and lit a cigarette, in part to calm his nerves, hoping that the smoke would keep the irritating insect at bay. Then he closed his eyes to allow his thoughts more room to move. Somewhere up in the roof a large lizard called: *tok-eh*, *tok-eh*, *tok-eh*. He sucked in the smoke, opening his eyes every few puffs to tap the ash into the saucer of his cup. When he had finished his cigarette, he turned on the light and went over to the bookshelf. He took down a large, yellow cloth-bound volume: Kruywers's *Life with the Kenukecilese: A Study in the Culture of a People*.

He had bought Kruywers's book from a shop in Utrecht, shortly before his departure for Indonesia. It was an exemplary work of old-school ethnological description. Kruywers's collection of data was painstaking and thorough. Whole chapters were dedicated to kinship terms. One section was given over exclusively to the collection of myths, stories, folk tales and jokes. And there was a great deal of information on horticulture since Kruywers was a keen gardener. Not only this, but the book was written in the most exquisitely rendered prose. Among Dutch readers it was generally considered a masterpiece of style. No attentive reader, however, could fail to notice its inescapable tinge of melancholy. Kruywers was the first Catholic missionary to arrive on the island. By 1937, when *Life with the Kenukecilese* was published, the world of which he wrote had already been swept away, a passing for which he himself bore no small responsibility.

Leaning against the wall, Pastor Niemann opened the book and flipped through. Everything about it – the smell of the pages, the sun-faded colour of the binding, the black and white photographs, the beautiful language – spoke of the passage of time. He paused at a photograph that had always intrigued him, the image of a sculpture that had stood in the forest clearing in the village of Sapratian until 1970. It was a stone figure. The arms were flung wide from either side of the body and the face was impassive. At first glance, it could have been mistaken for a primitive image of Christ were it not for the absence of a loincloth and, in the place where the two legs met, the presence of both male and female parts. The text below the image was laconic: 'Batjameni: Culture hero of the people of Kenukecil. Maluku. Stone. Probably 19th Century.'

Pastor Niemann himself had arranged the removal of the sculpture, with the agreement of the local government authorities. It now languished in the stores of the National Museum in Jakarta and in its place on the cape at Sapratian stood an image of the Virgin. The priest allowed his eyes to flicker over the text on the opposite page, glancing over the legend that he knew well, of how Batjameni – having seeded himself – shattered the sun into a million parts, setting time in motion.

A knock at the door broke his concentration. Pastor Niemann put the book back on the shelf. 'Come in!' he called.

Suster Elena opened the door but did not enter. She stood anxiously on the threshold, unsmiling. 'Ibu Nilasera is resting. We must go to the church. We must see if there is anything there.'

'There is no devil, Suster Elena.'

'I wish to look. It is not right that I go alone.'

Pastor Niemann's voice was soft. 'Suster Elena, if you wish it, I will come with you to put your mind at rest.'

'Thank you, Pastor,' said the nun. 'Thank you very much.'

Pastor Niemann stepped out into the twilight. 'Let us go,' he said.

They left the pastoran side by side and walked in silence up the hill to the church. Old Mathias watched them from a distance. They climbed the path through the grounds of the seminary and up past the convent. The wind had fallen and in the square outside the church the flag was hanging limply from its pole. Christ was smiling inscrutably, as little perturbed by the presence of a devil in his house as he was by the raw wound in his flesh and his exposed, beating heart. As the priest and the nun walked across the square, the light suspended above Christ's head flickered into life, as it did every evening at exactly this time.

They entered the church. The pastor went first. He flicked a switch and the strip lights hummed into life. Lizards, surprised by the burst of light, scuttled through the eaves. He glanced round the pews. Nobody. The crucified looked down in sorrow from the wooden cross above the altar. In her niche the Virgin tilted her head mournfully. The air was thick with dust. Suster Elena stood just inside the door, wringing her hands anxiously. But there was nothing at all to see: no god, no devil, no villagers at prayer. Pastor Niemann glanced down and vaguely noted a clutch of plastic flowers scattered around his feet.

'There is nothing here,' he said.

The nun was about to mutter her agreement when something made her turn her head: a faint noise, a scuffling by the door. She turned round sharply. A strange, animal sound came from outside. 'Pastor,' she gasped, pulling at the man's sleeve.

Pastor Niemann stepped out into the porch of the church. Roki was cringing in the entrance, cowering and whimpering. His ears were turned back, laid flat against his skull, and he was letting out a succession of pathetic growls.

'Stupid dog,' muttered the pastor indulgently, and with uncharacteristic affection he reached down to scratch him behind the ears. 'Come on, Suster Elena, let us have no more to do with devils.'

# 4

On that same Sunday afternoon, around the time that Ibu Nilasera entered the church to discover a devil offering up prayers in the front pew, Samuel Rivers propped himself on one elbow on his sick bed to see Pak Wim standing before him like an angel come to collect his soul and ferry it to the beyond.

'Mr Samuel,' the visitor said, 'how are you, Mr Samuel?'

'Pak Wim,' Sam murmured, looking at his visitor through half-closed eyes. 'You are here. How long have you been here?'

Pak Wim shrugged. '*Tuan masih sakit?*'

Sam smiled weakly. Was he still sick? '*Sedikit,*' he said. Yes, a little. He lay back down on the mattress and stared at the ceiling.

'I have been every day, tuan, but still you are sick,' Pak Wim said sadly. 'I have been many times.'

Sam glanced over at his visitor. 'And what about the cargo?' he asked. 'Is the cargo here?'

Pak Wim hesitated, his eyes sliding evasively towards the window. 'You must rest, tuan,' he said soothingly. 'Do not worry about the cargo. First you must rest. You need strength for your journey.'

Sam felt his mind beginning to slip away again, the fragile unity of his thoughts starting to dissolve.

Pak Wim waved a hand in the air in vague and courteous apology. 'You are very sick, tuan,' he said. 'But do not worry. Soon you will be well. You will recover.'

No response came from the bed. Sam was sinking. The air smelled of sweat and illness. Pak Wim looked once more at the prone figure of the Englishman, then crept out of the room.

Sam's illness had started on the Kakatau flight from Ambon to Bantuk. As they flew south, he gazed out of the starboard window of the tiny ten-seater – half-empty of passengers, the spare seats piled high with cargo and packing crates – and the tendrils of fever began to extend through his body. He took a sarong from his bag and wrapped it around his shoulders, wondering why it was so damn cold. As the plane began its descent to Kenukecil, he looked down and caught his first glimpse of land, the cape at Sapratian. After a minute or two more, the rolling hills of Kenubesar and patchwork roofs of Makalau came into view. The plane banked westwards and the land below pitched and reeled. Sam closed his eyes at the unexpected swell of nausea. Beads of sweat broke out on his forehead. The plane skimmed over the channel separating Kenubesar from Kenukecil and then came the unnerving crunch of the landing gear being lowered. They touched down at the end of the tarmacked landing strip to the north-east of Bantuk. Sam closed his eyes as the plane bumped and lurched to a halt in front of the airport building, no more than a low concrete shack.

The remainder of his arrival in Bantuk was something of a blur. The fever had taken hold surprisingly quickly. By the time of his disembarkation Sam was running with sweat, his head spinning. He remembered crowds, a Chinese man dressed in a soiled sarong and string vest who was overseeing the unloading of various crates and packages, a jovial policeman with an impressive moustache who checked his passport and – could it be true, or was it his feverish imagination? – a gaggle of singing nuns.

Thomas, the owner of the Lovely Vista Hotel, saw the white man standing bewildered and sweating in the airport and took charge of the situation. Making his way through the crowd, he introduced himself, courteously took Sam's case and steered him out of the building and into a waiting Suzuki van.

At the hotel, Sam filled out the register and stowed his bag in his room. Then, at Thomas's invitation, he headed out to the jetty at the back of the hotel. It was a beautiful spot, looking out over the bay. Thin columns of smoke rose up into the sky across the other side of the water, where local people were burning the land in preparation for new plantations. *Cocok tanah* they called it. Two other guests were seated at a table, drinking beer. They looked an unlikely couple. One of them was dressed in a suit and tie, his hair immaculately neat. His companion was younger, stockier and angrier looking, wearing a straw sun hat and a vest top that showed off his muscular arms. From the wrists to the shoulders, his arms swirled with blue-black tattoos. Neither of the men looked Indonesian.

Seeing Sam approach, the older of the two stood up and smiled, offering a hand in greeting. 'Hello,' he said. 'My name is Mr Liao. I am a fisherman from Taiwan.' He indicated his companion. 'And this is Mr Tan. Welcome to Kenukecil. Please, join us.'

Sam drank half a beer with the two fishermen, exchanging small-talk, before complaining of a headache and retiring to his bed. He slept for twenty hours, waking at noon the following day. He picked at lunch, ate almost nothing, took a short stroll up and down Bantuk's only street – a desolate strip of small concrete shops – and returned to his room. From that point onwards, he remained pinned to his bed by fever, breaking his malarial confinement only once or twice to order food that he did not have the will to eat.

*

Samuel Rivers had been in Indonesia for several years and he knew what it was to suffer from fever. Malaria was part of the deal: *a touch of fever*, the expats liked to say casually to each other, congratulating themselves on their imagined stoicism. 'Where is Albert today?' 'Oh, Albert is in bed. A touch of fever, I'm afraid . . .' But never before had he been struck so severely as with this bout. Never before had his body so comprehensively sweated out every drop of vitality, hour after hour, day after day. Never before had he been so thoroughly robbed of his mental functions. He was too weak even to feel sorry for himself, too weak for regret, too weak to wonder what the hell he was doing there in Bantuk at all, too weak to mourn the mess he had made of things with Fonny.

Sam had arrived in Indonesia shortly after his thirty-first birthday, in the wake of his parents' deaths. A reluctant engineering student during his university years, he had fallen in love, shortly before graduation, with a girl called Vanessa. Vanessa was forceful and impassioned, naturally entrepreneurial and a student of fine arts. Sam had been sucked into her orbit almost against his will. There he had whirled around for several years before being painfully flung back out into space. It was Vanessa who suggested that they move into a flat together. It was Vanessa who told Sam to get a proper job. Her career as a printmaker was beginning to take off, while Sam was drifting from one part-time post to another. He found employment at the city council in the kind of worthy nine-to-five existence that swallows up entire lives. It was Vanessa who suggested they get married. There was nothing in the way of a proposal, just Vanessa saying, 'We should get married,' and Sam saying, 'Yes, I suppose we should.' And once married – Vanessa's prints now gaining favourable reviews in all the art magazines and Sam earning a decent salary in his Faustian bargain with the city council – it was Vanessa who proposed that they should buy a house. Finally, it was Vanessa who suggested that they should have children. Sam acquiesced.

Vanessa stopped taking the pill, but the hoped-for pregnancy did not happen. Having the monopoly on vigour, Vanessa believed the cause of this fruitlessness to be Sam: first because it was unthinkable that she might be responsible for anything that had about it the whiff of failure; secondly because despite his repeated seedings of the furrow, she sensed he was not trying hard enough; and thirdly because it was clear Sam simply didn't *want* a child enough – as if wanting ever made a difference. But Vanessa wanted. During those evenings poring over books and calendars and charts; those nights when she would pull him towards her and whisper, 'Now, I think it's a good time'; those trips to the chemist in search of ovulation kits and other paraphernalia the precise mechanics of which Sam never understood: all that was sown was bitterness. The hurts and recriminations and miseries of those final two years of their marriage were manifold; and then, six months after their divorce, Vanessa wrote to Sam to tell him that she was pregnant by her new partner, another artist.

Sam slipped into his thirties, and accepted a further promotion at work without enthusiasm. Anticipating the remaining portion of his life, he increasingly saw it following the arc of a curve that had risen insufficiently high and that was already, too soon, on the downturn.

Then Sam's parents died; first his mother, of cancer, and three weeks later, his father, of that most old-fashioned of complaints, a broken heart. Although Sam's grief was genuine, as he stood beside the grave and watched the earth fall on the coffin for the second time in a single month, he was overtaken by a curious lightness of spirit, an unfamiliar freedom so intense that he was forced to suppress an unseemly smile. At the reception that followed his father's burial, he maintained the appearance of sobriety, speaking in hushed tones with the other mourners; but as he rode in the taxi back to his hotel, he found himself planning what to do with the modest inheritance his parents had left. It would have been prudent, of course, to invest the money, but – Sam asked himself – what was the point in prudence if the end of everything was a box in the ground and the sound of cold earth falling on wood? That weekend, he responded to an advertisement in a Sunday newspaper for English teachers in Indonesia. He was accepted for the job without an interview. Soon after, he handed in his notice to his manager at the city council. Less than three months after his parents had been buried, he was on a plane from Singapore to Jakarta, crossing the equator on the final leg of a long-haul flight, passing between tall stacks of golden cloud.

The institution in which Sam was contracted to teach was not the kind of place in which he felt naturally at home. The Catholic-run Francis Xavier Language College in Jogjakarta provided supplementary education, largely in languages, to students over the age of eighteen. The college was ruled over by a director whose excessive moral rectitude almost exactly counterbalanced his extreme shortness of stature. While the atmosphere of the college was not entirely to Sam's liking – the crucifixes that hung on the wall of every classroom were oppressive, the shabby tobacco-smoke of the dingy staffroom was depressing and he had to suppress a childish urge to giggle during the compulsory prayers every morning – it was more than compensated for by his discovery of an unexpected flair for teaching. Until Jogja, Sam had always imagined that it was to be his vocation to be without vocation; but from the first morning he stood in front of his class, this changed. After working within the confines of a council office cubicle, to be faced with real flesh-and-blood human beings was exhilarating. When his end-of-year results came in they were the best the college had ever seen.

He spent his first month in Jogja in a hotel. Then he moved into a neat two-room apartment a short bus journey from the city centre. In his spare time he developed a passion for reading – the college had a set of Dickens novels, which he read in its entirety. He ate his evening meals at the *warung* of Jogja, picking up, through his conversations with other customers, an excellent knowledge of Bahasa Indonesia and a colourful command of street slang. Within a year he was almost fluent, despite having always believed himself to be hopeless at languages. In his first weeks he had dabbled in the expatriate community. Before long, however, he had learned to avoid their terrible tea parties, their warbling English choirs doggedly singing Christmas carols through the sweltering heat of December – *In the bleak mid wiiiiin-ter* – their muted, excruciating cocktail evenings and their embarrassing flag-saluting, anthem-singing, Queen-toasting patriotism. He was more at home chatting with the *becak* and *bajaj* rickshaw drivers, with the owners of the street stalls, or with the old man responsible for cleaning his apartment block. Solitary, free, satisfied in his work: for the first time in his life, Samuel Rivers was happy.

Fon came into Sam's class at the beginning of the first term of his third teaching year. She was twenty-three and attractive in an angular way, but quiet and diligent in her work, polite, even shy. Sam wasn't exactly sure why she made an impression on him. She did not flirt like some of the other girls; she did not make eyes at him or compliment him on the colour of his skin; she did not hang around after class to chat and joke. But, at the same time, there was something about how she spoke to him, a kind of knowing solicitude in the way she occasionally smiled as if they were not teacher and student but somehow allies. By the end of her first morning in his classroom, a curious thought entered Sam's mind: *I will marry her.* He was at a loss to explain why. It was a thought so unsettling, so unexpected and so entirely unbidden that, for the remainder of the year, Sam conducted himself with uncommon coolness towards this student of his; and she reciprocated in kind. Thus their strange, inverted courtship was expressed entirely in terms of formalities and courtesies.

The college policy on fraternizing between staff and students was rigorous and Sam had no difficulty in brushing off the advances of his more amorous students. The one exception he made was that, at the end of each term, in contravention of all the college rules, he liked to organize a class gathering in a local café for a drink – coffee, not alcohol, for many of his students were Muslim. To Sam's disappointment, Fon did not join the others on these occasions. She worked hard, her English improved rapidly, she did well in her exams. After her graduation, she shook his hand with grave formality. 'Thank you, Samuel Rivers,' she said. 'You are a good teacher. Thank you.'

As she left the room, Sam felt a tug of sadness. He did not expect to see her again.

Several weeks after she had graduated, Sam was sitting in his classroom, preparing a lesson for the coming afternoon, when Fon came through the door. She was wearing jeans and a black blouse. Her hair was down. It was the first time he had seen her wearing make-up. She looked ravishing.

'Hello,' she said, in English.

'Fon, come in. How are you? Take a seat.'

She didn't come in, but she leaned against the door post and smiled. 'I am not staying long. I just came to ask you a question. Have you ever been to the *wayang kulit*?'

'The shadow play?' Sam smiled. 'You are not going to think much of me, Fon, but I have to confess: after three years in Indonesia, no, I haven't. Not yet.'

'In that case –' Fon smiled '– I will take you. Are you free tonight?'

Sam was so surprised that for a few moments he was incapable of saying anything. 'Of course,' he said.

'Let us meet at six in the Kafe Kopi. OK?' Fon asked.

'OK.'

'One question, Mr Sam: do you have a girlfriend?'

'Well . . .' Sam stammered.

Fon frowned and looked at him with a critical air. 'I think that perhaps you do not,' she observed.

Sam laughed. 'Fon,' he said, 'is it that obvious? No, I don't have a girlfriend.'

'Good,' Fon said. 'Perhaps then I will be your girlfriend. We will see. I will meet you tonight, yes?'

Sam nodded. The girl turned and left the room. Sam returned to his lesson plan.

# 5

Fon was there already when Sam arrived at the Kafe Kopi at six. He had expected her to be late – *jam karet*, they call it, rubber time – but she was early, already holding a cappuccino between her cupped hands.

She smiled to see him enter. Sam, for whom sartorial matters were always something of a mystery, had made an effort. He was dressed in a loose short-sleeved shirt and linen trousers that he had, for once, taken the trouble to iron. Rising to her feet, Fon kissed him on the cheek. He blinked, astonished by such forwardness in a public place. As he sat down, he was conscious that he was beaming stupidly. Fon gestured to the waiter, who brought another cappuccino.

They drank their coffee and chatted. The first few minutes were awkward, but by the time Sam had finished his coffee the awkwardness had faded. Outside the classroom, Fon was very different. She seemed lighter, somehow easier. Sam was more aware than before of her quick intelligence and the humour he had only rarely seen during the year that he had been her teacher.

They conversed in a strange mix of Indonesian and English, their jokes cutting first from one language to the other, then in the opposite direction. They ordered platefuls of *gado-gado*, which they ate with chopsticks. After the meal they caught a rickshaw to the royal palace, where the show was due to start at nine. As the rickshaw careered through the heavy traffic spluttering acrid fumes,

Fon slipped an arm around Sam's waist. Sam leaned into her and rested his head against hers.

That night at the *wayang* was the sweetest Sam had ever known: Fon's hand in his, her fingers interlocking with his own; the flickering of the shadows as Rama voyaged to rescue his beloved Sita from the kingdom of the ogres in Lanka; Fon whispering translations and explanations into his ear, clarifying this or that nuance of the story; the not-quite full moon overhead; the night insects competing with the clatter of the gamelan; slapping at the mosquitoes buzzing around his ankles; and then the first signs of dawn, the sky becoming pale, the delicious tiredness of morning as the crowds dispersed and Fonny drew him into a doorway and kissed him on the mouth.

Unkempt, unrested, happy, in the early dawn light they meandered through the streets of Jogja, already clamorous with cars, *becaks*, rickshaws and motorbikes. They were making their way back to the Kafe Kopi, which opened for breakfast at seven, walking hand in hand, avoiding potholes in the pavements, when they were overtaken by a neat little man with a small moustache gracing his upper lip, a conscious attempt to offset the boyishness of his face.

The man turned to glance at them as he passed. 'Good morning, friends!' he said. 'Have you been at the *wayang kulit*? I believe I saw you in the crowd.'

Sam and Fon stopped. The man put out a hand. 'Hello,' he said, switching into English. 'Are you an Englishman?'

Sam shook the proffered hand. 'I am. Sam Rivers,' he said. 'From the Francis Xavier College.'

'Pak Suryono,' said the man. 'Pleased to meet you.' He turned to Fon and asked in Indonesian, 'And you?'

'Fon,' she said. 'Fonny.'

'Do you mind if I walk with you a while?' He must have been in his early forties, his age betrayed only by the traces of wrinkles around his eyes and the weary undercurrent to his speech.

'No, you are welcome,' said Sam.

The three of them walked on. 'Did you enjoy the *wayang*?' asked Pak Suryono.

'Very much,' Sam replied. 'It was my first time. But we're not used to all-night performances over in England, so I'm a little tired.' He gave a theatrical yawn.

Pak Suryono chuckled. 'It is indeed very tiring,' he said. 'This staying up all night is hard, particularly for a man like me who has to work. But there is nothing like the *wayang*. It is important to maintain *tradisi*, don't you think?'

'What is your work?' Sam asked.

'I am a businessman. Transport of goods. Cargo. Throughout Indonesia.' Pak Suryono hesitated. 'I'm sorry,' he said, 'do forgive me. I've interrupted your morning walk and it is no time for making new acquaintances. Please, take my card.'

He stopped and reached into his pocket. Sam and Fon waited for him to take out his wallet. Pak Suryono smiled, his face illuminated by a perfect set of teeth. 'My card,' he said, handing it to Sam. It was simple and elegant, slightly embossed: PAK MUS SURYONO, BUSINESSMAN. The name was followed by a Jakarta address and a telephone number.

'One moment,' Sam replied. He took out his own wallet and extracted a card of his own, stowing Pak Suryono's at the same time. 'It's been good to meet you,' he said.

'Yes, very good,' Pak Suryono agreed. 'I must go. Thank you for your company. Get some sleep, yes?'

'Good night,' Sam said.

Pak Suryono inclined his head. 'Good night? It is already morning, my friend. Look – the sun.'

The sun was spilling red over the rooftops through the mist and the pall of exhaust fumes. 'Good morning, then,' Sam said.

Pak Suryono and Sam shook hands. The businessman offered his hand to Fon, who shook it while looking just to one side, over his shoulder.

'Goodbye, Sam. Goodbye, Fon. *Selamat jalan*.' Pak Suryono turned and walked away briskly, taking a side street that led away from the main road.

When he had gone, Fon turned to Sam. 'That man – he was strange. I did not like him. Maybe you should be careful. You should not give everybody your card.'

'He seemed friendly,' Sam replied, because that morning everything seemed perfect to him, even the stench of exhaust fumes from the passing traffic and the itching of his ankles where mosquitoes had feasted on his blood as he watched the shadow-play. 'Anyway, I won't hear from him again. It's always the same when you are a foreigner – you meet people, they take your address, they give you theirs, they say that they want to be your friend for life, that they will come to visit you, that they will never forget you . . . and then you never hear from them again.'

Fon lowered her eyes. 'I hope so, Sam.' Then she smiled. 'Come on, it is not long to seven o'clock. The Kafe Kopi will soon be open.' She tugged at his hand.

'Breakfast,' Sam said, 'here we come.'

A year later, Fonny and Sam were engaged to be married. Sam proposed in the back of a rickshaw. Jolted by the potholes, above the noisy buzz of the engine, Fonny clutched his hand. *Yes*, she said. *Yes*.

They agreed later that day that they would wait before announcing the good news, so they could sort out a few bureaucratic matters. Sam needed to send for copies of the documents confirming his divorce from Vanessa – to his annoyance her name was still entered as his wife in the section of his passport reserved for next of kin. Meanwhile Sam renewed his contract for another two years.

They set a date for the announcement. As Fon had already begun to organize the celebrations for her birthday, which was on 5 November, they decided that they would tell their friends and Fon's family then. Sam returned to the college for the beginning of his fifth year.

That October, several weeks after the start of his new term, Sam was interrupted during breakfast by a telephone call from Pak Suryono. He was alone in his flat and had just finished frying some rice. He was piling it onto his plate when the telephone rang. Thinking it would be Fonny, he was surprised to hear a man's voice.

'Mr Sam? It is me, Pak Suryono. Remember?'

Sam didn't remember. Only when Pak Suryono reminded him of their dawn encounter after the *wayang* the year before did Sam recall their meeting. 'Hello,' he said. 'It has been a long time.'

'That is true, Mr Sam. How are you?'

'I am well, thank you.' Sam paused. This phone call from out of nowhere made him anxious. 'And you?' he asked.

'I am very well, thank you for asking.' There was a brief silence before Pak Suryono continued: 'Please, let me be direct. I am looking for a business partner and I need some investment. When I met you, I knew that you were a trustworthy man. Now a business opportunity has come up. I thought of you immediately.'

'Business?' Sam asked, and laughed. 'Pak Suryono, I'm not a businessman. You should probably ask somebody else.'

'No, Mr Sam, I have to disagree. You are the perfect person for this business.'

'What business would that be?'

'Trade in goods,' Pak Suryono replied. 'I know that you will be able to help, because you are English. The English are a trustworthy nation.'

Sam glanced over at his fried rice, which was rapidly cooling. 'I am sorry, Pak Suryono,' he said. 'It is very good to hear from you, but I am going to turn you down. I already have a job. I'm a teacher, not a businessman.'

There was a pause at the other end of the line. 'Let me explain,' Pak Suryono said, his voice measured. 'I am asking for an investment of around thirty thousand dollars. Do you have thirty thousand dollars?'

Other than the price of the flight from Heathrow, Sam had hardly touched his inheritance money. It was set to one side in a bank account so that he and Fon could buy a house after their marriage.

'I have a little money,' Sam said, trying to sound non-committal. 'But –'

'If you have thirty thousand dollars to invest,' Pak Suryono cut in, 'then I can offer you perhaps one million in return.'

Sam paused. His mouth went dry. 'One million?' he asked.

'Yes,' Pak Suryono confirmed.

'Dollars?'

There was a laugh at the other end of the line. 'Mr Sam, I am not talking about rupiah. In this country of ours, before long you will not be able to buy a cup of coffee for one million rupiah. I am talking about dollars. US dollars. One million dollars. Look, Mr Sam, I understand that we met only briefly. Perhaps you should come and visit me in Jakarta and we can talk face to face. It would be much better. I will even pay for the flight. There is nothing to lose. Do you have a day off soon?'

'Saturday,' Sam said. 'I am off on Saturdays and Sundays.'

'Good. Come to my offices on Saturday. That would be 12 October, yes? You still have the address?'

'One moment.' Sam took his wallet from his pocket and pulled out a sheaf of cards, riffling through them. He came to Pak Suryono's, somewhat dog-eared. 'Yes,' he said, 'I still have the address.'

'Good. Come at three in the afternoon, straight to the office. No, even better, there is a flight with Mandala Airlines that arrives at two. I can meet you at the airport. Then we can discuss further. I'll purchase the ticket. All you have to do is go to the airport and tell the people at the airline check-in desk that you are Samuel Rivers. Everything will be organized.'

Sam hesitated. 'Pak Suryono,' he asked, 'this business: is it legal?'

Another laugh. 'Do you think I am a criminal, Mr Sam?'

'No,' said Sam. 'No. Of course not.'

'Good. We can talk on Saturday.' There was a click as Pak Suryono rang off.

Sam returned to his rice. He balanced a lump between his chopsticks and then he remembered: he had arranged with Fon to go to Ratu Boko that weekend. They had planned a picnic. 'Shit,' he muttered, putting down his chopsticks. He dialled Pak Suryono's number, reading from the card. The phone at the other end rang for a long time without an answer, then the line went dead. He tried again. Same thing.

The following day, Sam tried Pak Suryono's number several times, but the telephone went unanswered. By the Thursday, he realized that he would have to postpone the picnic.

Fon did not take the news well. They met on the Thursday night in the Kafe Kopi.

'Fon,' Sam said. 'I must go to Jakarta on Saturday.'

'I thought we were going to Ratu Boko.'

He smiled awkwardly. 'I know,' he said. 'Perhaps we can go next weekend. I have to go to Jakarta for business.'

'Sam, what business do you have in Jakarta?' Fon looked puzzled.

So Sam told his fiancée about the phone call from Pak

Suryono, the thirty thousand dollars, the possibility of a million.

As he spoke, Fon removed her hand from his, turning her head to look out of the window and watch the endless procession of traffic outside. A muscle was twitching in her cheek. When he had finished, she looked at him coldly. 'Sam, are you *mad*?'

'I am only going for a meeting. I have not made any commitment. I can always say no, Fon. He's even paying for the flight. There is nothing to lose. It's just a few hours in Jakarta. That's all.'

Fon clutched her coffee cup. 'I am not worried about money, Sam. I do not care about money. Maybe you will lose thirty thousand dollars and we will live in a hut for the rest of our lives. I will not mind. Maybe you will gain one million and we will live in a palace. Still, Samuel, I will not mind. But this Pak Suryono is a bad man. You should not go.'

'It is only a meeting,' Sam insisted. 'When I get back we can look through all the details and make a decision together. I won't agree to anything without talking to you first.'

'Sam, you talk about agreements, but you also break them,' Fon said.

'What do you mean, Fonny?'

'I mean that we had agreed to go to Ratu Boko, Sam. We had agreed to have a picnic. And now you say you are going to Jakarta.'

'Fonny,' Sam said, 'look, I'm sorry. But Ratu Boko will still be standing next week.'

Fon reached out her hand to touch his with her fingertips. 'Samuel,' she said. 'I am going to be your wife. Your wife, Samuel. Do you know what that means?'

Sam smiled. 'Yes, I know,' he said. 'I know, Fon.'

'You must cancel your appointment,' Fon told him.

'I can't, Fon. Not now. I've tried to contact Pak Suryono to rearrange the meeting, but he doesn't answer the phone. Fonny, it will just be one day. That is all. I'm just going to talk. We have the rest of our lives for Ratu Boko.'

Fon pushed back her chair. 'Samuel Rivers,' she said, very quietly, 'you are right. We have the rest of our lives. I am happy that we have the rest of our lives. But do not break my heart, Sam. I am afraid that you will break my heart.'

Sam smiled at her, but the smile was strained. Fonny got to her feet, leaving half her coffee undrunk. 'Call me after you have returned, Sam,' she sighed. 'Let's speak afterwards.' Then Sam's future wife turned and walked out of the Kafe Kopi into the street.

On the Saturday, Sam Rivers flew to Jakarta. Pak Suryono was waiting for him at the airport.

# 6

The Mandala flight from Jogja arrived at Jakarta at fourteen hundred hours exactly on the afternoon of 12 October. Pak Suryono met Samuel Rivers in the arrivals lounge, greeting him with a neat handshake. The businessman led him outside to where his car was parked, a grey estate with tinted windows and clean lines, smelling of fresh leather.

On the way from the airport, Sam tried to press the businessman on why he had been invited to the capital, but Pak Suryono refused to discuss it. 'You will see soon,' he said. 'You will see very soon.' Then he changed the subject, asking after Fon, talking about the *wayang*, and subjecting his guest to innumerable courteous questions about his time in Indonesia, without appearing to pay any attention to the answers.

Pak Suryono drove to the docks at Tanjung Priok. He parked the car at a place where thousands of tiny wooden vessels were tied up. He climbed out, walked round to the passenger side, and opened the door for Sam. Leading the Englishman along the harbour, he stopped by a small, sleek, unobtrusive wooden boat, well constructed, with an outboard motor at the back. 'This,' he said, 'is my boat. I call it the *Ratu Mela*. Welcome.' He climbed aboard.

Refusing Pak Suryono's offered hand, Sam stepped onto the deck. There was a strange smell he could not place.

'The cargo is below, Mr Sam. You will need to see it before you make a decision. I want to reassure you that there is no pressure on you to agree. If you do not want to invest, you can simply say no, catch the flight back to Jogja this evening and I will not contact you again. It is your own decision.'

Sam smiled nervously. Pak Suryono lifted the hatch on deck. The stench hit Sam immediately: an organic, animal smell. 'It is very important, Mr Samuel, that you remain calm,' Pak Suryono said. 'And, please, whatever you decide, do not say anything about what you have seen here. Not to anyone. It is a delicate matter. Please, follow me.'

Sam climbed after him down the ladder into the dark below decks.

'The smell will not kill you, Mr Sam,' Pak Suryono said as he descended. 'Come.'

At the bottom Pak Suryono stood to one side, eyes lowered, as Sam felt his way down the last couple of rungs. He turned and blinked into the darkness. In the corner was a kind of packing crate, or perhaps a cage, made of slatted wood. Something inside the cage stirred and let out a soft grunt. Sam waited for his eyes to adjust to the light. Then he gasped.

Pak Suryono smiled. 'I will be above,' he said. 'Do not approach too closely; but please take a good look.' He scuttled up the ladder, out of the fetid air below.

Sam stood in the pool of light under the hatch, his eyes riveted on the darkness. Squatting behind the bars of the cage was a shadow; and from out of the darkness of the shadow gleamed two eyes, peering with disconcerting intelligence through the wooden slats. Sam stepped out of the light, the hairs lifting on the back of his neck. His legs started to shake. 'Hello,' he whispered in English.

The creature did not reply. Unsteady on his feet, Sam lowered himself to his knees. He crawled forward two or three paces to get a closer look, resisting the prickling fear that was rippling down his back. The eyes inside the cage were fixed on his own. Occasionally they blinked, but they did not turn away. He edged further into the dark. 'What are you?' he asked.

As if in reply, the creature in the box thumped a limb against the floor and let out a gurgling whimper, a faint cry close to human speech. Sam bit his lip. The creature continued to stare him down.

'Hello,' Sam said again, but this time in Indonesian.

The creature did not reply. Sam's eyes were beginning to become accustomed to the dark. The thing in the cage was an ape of sorts. Its fur had a reddish tinge and the face was pale and intelligent. Sam told himself it was an orang utan – that at least would make sense; but when he looked again, he saw that it wasn't. The proportions were all wrong. It was something else.

'Hello,' Sam repeated.

Then he noticed something disconcerting: in the creature's eyes, tears were forming. Its shoulders started to heave with something like sobs and a hand reached forward through the bars. Sam caught a glimpse of fingernails, an opposable thumb, no more than two feet away. All he had to do was to reach out and his fingers could touch those extended towards him. But he didn't. The hand remained for a few seconds, shaking just a little, before the creature slowly withdrew it back into the cage. Then the thing turned its face away and shifted its weight so that its back was turned. It started to whine.

Now that the creature had broken off the gaze that had held Sam's attention, he became more aware of his surroundings. He could smell urine. He lifted a hand and sniffed it. The smell made him retch.

He crawled back to the pool of light. The thing in the cage continued whimpering. Sam grabbed the twin supports of the ladder, vomiting a thin stream of liquid, and hauled himself up into the sunlight. Slamming the hatch behind him, he lay gasping on the deck of the boat looking up at the overcast Jakarta sky.

Pak Suryono was sitting on a small crate, quietly smoking a cigarette, smiling.

'What is it?' Sam asked at last. 'Pak Suryono, what the hell is it?'

Pak Suryono passed Sam a rag. 'Please,' he said. 'Clean your hands. They are filthy.'

Sam wiped his hands with the rag and threw it to one side. Then he propped himself up against the side of the boat and looked up into the sky where the seabirds turned.

Pak Suryono waited until Sam turned to him again. 'Mr Samuel, I thought you should see for yourself. You will understand, I hope. Now, let me explain how I came to acquire this strange cargo.'

Pak Suryono talked for almost an hour. Sam sat and listened. When he had finished, they were silent for a long time.

Eventually Sam spoke. 'So, now you have this thing, what do you plan to do with it?'

Pak Suryono smiled. 'I knew you were a man I could do business with,' he said. 'It is very simple. I have two potential buyers. The first is in Australia and requires delivery. We will take the creature by boat. It is better if we do not stay long here in Jakarta. We should avoid major cities. One of my associates, Ibrahim, will travel with the cargo to Kenukecil in the Moluccas, via Lombok, Flores, Nusa Tenggara, East Timor. Then you and I will meet Ibrahim in Kenukecil and from there you will take the creature to Australia.'

Sam nodded cautiously to indicate that he had understood.

46

The businessman continued. 'The passage to Australia from Kenukecil is very short: it can be done in a single night. Look, I have a map. Please, Mr Samuel, look.' He took a map from his pocket, unfolded it carefully and passed it to Sam, who flattened it on the deck before him. It was upside down. He turned it the right way up and took a second look. A line had been drawn in blue from Jakarta heading eastwards all the way along the arc of islands to Kenukecil in the Moluccas, a tiny dot where it reached its terminus. From here another line, this time in green, plunged south towards Australia.

Sam studied the map for a few moments and then, folding it inexpertly, passed it back to Pak Suryono. 'Why should I do any of this?' he asked. 'Even if I agreed, why do you need *me* to take this thing to Australia. I am not a seafarer, I'm a teacher. On the telephone, you talked about investment. You did not mention seafaring.'

'We need somebody unobtrusive,' Pak Suryono said. 'If anybody sees you piloting a boat in Australian waters, they will just think that you are on a pleasure cruise from Darwin and they will not trouble you. However, if anybody sees Ibrahim, they will conclude that he is an illegal immigrant and they will board the boat to arrest him. That, of course, would be the end. For the same reason, I myself cannot make the trip. We need an *orang bule*, a Westerner.'

'But I'm not a sailor,' Sam protested.

'You do not need to be. All you need to be is a little brave and able to follow instructions with a map and a compass. It is an easy passage.'

Sam thought for a few moments. 'And when I get to Australia?' he asked.

'Once in Australia, you are to go ashore at a place called Turnbull Bay, to the west of Darwin. It is a very quiet place where you should be undisturbed. There you will meet Mr Geoffrey Sainyakit. He is an intermediary on behalf of Dr Plover, a zoologist from Adelaide. It is Dr Plover who is our buyer. Perhaps you have heard of him?'

Sam shook his head. 'No,' he said.

'He is very famous,' Pak Suryono said. 'He had a television show several years ago. Geoffrey Sainyakit will only pay if the cargo is delivered intact and alive. Dr Plover is a man of science and he wants a live specimen. He has assured me that the creature will be well treated. He does not intend to harm it in any way. He will pay two million, cash. We will split the money in half.'

Pak Suryono glanced at the Englishman, who was anxiously biting his thumbnail. 'Mr Samuel, come, don't look so worried: it is just a short trip, that is all. Of course, if you agree to our working together, then you will need to pay the thirty thousand into my account up front, to cover any past and future expenses. However, with a possible return of one million pounds, any sensible man would take hold of this opportunity with both hands.'

Sam said nothing.

Pak Suryono continued 'If you are agreed, I suggest that we meet in Ambon on the twenty-third of the month, where we can arrange any last-minute matters of business. The monthly flight from Ambon to Bantuk in Kenukecil leaves on the twenty-fifth. Ibrahim will meet us on Kenukecil at the end of October. Mr Geoff is expecting delivery by the end of the first week of November.'

Sam thought for a moment about the eyes that had held his gaze below deck, then he thought about Fonny. He shook his head. 'I'm sorry, Pak Suryono,' he said. 'Fon and I are to be married. We are to announce our engagement at the beginning of November. At her birthday party, on the fifth. I have promised her.'

'Congratulations, Mr Sam.' Pak Suryono beamed, looking genuinely pleased by the news. He took a cigarette packet out of his jacket pocket and offered one to the Englishman. 'Maybe you would like a cigarette to celebrate?'

Sam shook his head. 'No, thank you. I don't smoke.'

Pak Suryono lit one for himself and pulled on it deeply. He blew the smoke through pursed lips. 'If you do not want to take the risk, then that is not a problem. I will sell to my other buyer. It would be a shame, but I understand your reasons: you are a romantic, while I, on the other hand, am a businessman.' He took another drag on his cigarette, watching two seabirds squabbling on the docks for a scrap of fish.

Sam glanced at his watch. 'Well,' he said, 'perhaps we should be leaving.'

Pak Suryono looked thoughtful. 'Please, Mr Samuel. Please wait a little while. I must tell you about my other contact.'

'Your other contact?'

'He works at the National Museum in Jakarta. This man is offering me one hundred thousand dollars for the cargo. It is a poor profit, but it is better than nothing. The only thing is –' here Pak Suryono paused to pull on his cigarette '– a museum can do nothing with a living creature.'

Sam leaned forward a fraction. 'And so?'

'Have you seen the wildlife gallery in Jakarta?' Pak Suryono asked. 'It's very beautiful. The animals are all most lifelike. The men who work for the museum are clever, Mr Sam. They take out the insides and fill them with sawdust, they remove the eyes and replace them with glass and when they have finished it looks as if the animals are alive. Two or three years ago I saw a story in the newspaper about a woman who was so frightened by the Sumatran tiger in the museum that she had a heart attack and died.' Pak Suryono chuckled.

Sam trembled. 'You are going to stuff it?'

'Oh no,' Pak Suryono said. 'Not me. If you get back on the flight to Jogja today saying that you cannot help me, they will come tonight and kill the creature. Then they will take it to the museum. By next month, they will have a new exhibit. Imagine the news stories! Not as exciting as a live specimen, of course, but still it will be quite a sensation.'

Sam got to his feet. 'You are a monster, Pak Suryono,' he said. 'I'm going to the police.'

Pak Suryono gave a dismissive shrug. 'The police? And what will they say when an Englishman starts telling them such ridiculous stories? They will think this *orang bule* is mad.'

'Pak Suryono,' Sam said, 'can you give me a little more time? Can you give me until Monday to decide?'

'Of course.' Pak Suryono smiled. 'I knew that you would help. You can telephone me on Monday.' He looked at his watch. 'Now, your flight back to Jogja will soon be due, but first we must get you some new trousers. The ones you are wearing are in a terrible mess.' He got to his feet and looked out over the harbour. 'Come, Mr Samuel,' he said, 'we must go shopping.' He patted Sam on the arm. 'Let us go and purchase trousers,' he said.

# 7

The shopping trip with Pak Suryono was brief. Sam found a pair of passable trousers and caught the evening flight back to Jogja. He arrived home late, showered and sat naked on his bed. Three times he picked up the telephone: the first time to call the police, and the second and third to call Fonny. Each time he thought better of it and placed the receiver back on its cradle. He needed some time to think. He went over to his cupboard, took out a bottle of whisky, drank a large glassful and sat looking out of the window at the lights of the city street until he fell asleep in his chair.

On Sunday, he phoned Fon. There was no response. He called her again on Monday at work, at eleven in the morning, but she was not there. Then he called Pak Suryono's office.

'Pak Suryono,' he said. 'It is Sam Rivers.'

There was a pause.

'I will help you,' Sam said. 'If you give me your bank account details, I will transfer the money this afternoon.'

'Mr Samuel, we need a contract.'

Sam hesitated. 'Pak Suryono, I will trust you. If you aim to cheat me, then I do not think a contract will help. And I would rather not sign anything, if you do not mind.'

Pak Suryono giggled. 'You are a clever man, Mr Samuel. As you wish, we will do without contracts. I will not cheat you. I have my reputation as an honest man. I

51

am glad you have said yes, because I have already booked your flight from Jogja to Ambon for next Monday. That is the latest available before we meet on Wednesday.'

'You've booked me a flight?'

'I knew that you would agree. You are a man of good sense.'

Sam held the phone a little away from his ear. Christ, he thought. What the hell am I getting into?

'I will arrive the following night,' Pak Suryono continued. 'I suggest we meet in the Hotel Asmat in Ambon at two in the afternoon on the Wednesday.'

When the phone call was finished, Sam went to the director of the college and asked for four weeks' leave, with effect from the beginning of the following week. From the other side of an enormous desk, flanked by the *merah-putih* and the college's heraldic flag, the director looked at him sharply. 'Leave?' he asked. 'In the middle of the term?'

Sam nodded.

'Impossible,' the director told him. 'What is your reason?'

'I have some business in Maluku. It is important that I am there,' Sam said.

'Is it more important than your teaching?' the director asked.

Sam bit his lip.

The director spread his palms. 'You must understand my perspective,' he said. 'When you say that this business is more important than your work, then I come to the conclusion that your work as a teacher is not important enough to you. So either you should make a decision to stay and teach, or you should resign to do whatever it is that you find more important than your work here at Francis Xavier College.'

'In that case,' Sam said, 'I have no option but to resign.'

The director waved a hand in the air. 'Mr Samuel,' he

said, 'your resignation is accepted. There is no need to return to your classroom.'

Outside the office, Sam leaned against the wall and took a deep breath. 'Right,' he said to himself. 'That's it.' He made his way to the bank and there he transferred the equivalent of thirty thousand dollars into the account of a man he barely knew.

On the Tuesday morning, he confirmed his flight to Ambon. Late that afternoon he met with Fon at the Kafe Kopi. She greeted him with a muted warmth, flinching just a fraction as he kissed her on the cheek. They stared into their cappuccinos, watching them grow cold. At last, Sam lifted his cup and drank a swig. He wiped the foam away from his top lip with his sleeve.

'I have decided. I am going to Kenukecil with Pak Suryono. It's in Maluku.'

Fon stiffened. 'You said you would not make any decision until we spoke.'

'Fon, I tried to call you to discuss things first, but you weren't there. I called on Sunday and yesterday.'

He looked across the table. Fon was stirring her coffee, her eyes lowered.

'There's something else as well. I've resigned from my job.'

The spoon clattered against the side of the cup. 'Why are you doing this?' she asked.

'They wouldn't let me take the time off.'

'No,' Fon said, 'not the job. The job doesn't matter. You can always find a job. Why must you go?'

Sam's mind flickered back to what he had seen below deck on the *Ratu Mela*. 'I can't tell you, Fon. It's not about the money. It's more than that. I had no choice.'

'And my birthday?' Fon asked.

Sam shifted awkwardly. 'I am sorry, Fonny,' he said.

She started to cry. 'I told you when we first met that man, I told you he was a bad man.'

'I know, Fon. I know. I'm sorry.'

Fon looked across at Sam, her eyes red. 'Sam,' she said. 'Let us go. Let us go to your apartment. This is too public. I do not want to talk any more, Sam. I don't want to hear your apologies. I don't want to hear your reasons. I don't want to speak about Pak Suryono. I just want to know that you love me. I need to know that you love me before you leave. Sam – can we go?'

'OK,' said Sam, reaching a hand across the table. 'OK, Fon.'

The evening was a melancholy one. The slanting light poured through the window of Sam's apartment. As he closed the apartment door, Sam was in tears. Fonny led him to the bed, put her arms around him and, without tangling them up any further in words, without asking why, or whether things could be different, gently licked away his tears with the tip of her tongue. Then she undressed him. They lay together naked in the evening sunshine, Sam's white skin, sprinkled with freckles and moles, against Fon's brown. For a long time they just lay listening to the sound of each other's breath. Then Fonny reached her hand down to touch his stirring cock at the base, fluttering her fingers as she moved her hand along the shaft.

'Fon,' Sam groaned. 'Fon. *Fon!*'

They lay side by side, their fingers curled together. Eventually, Sam sat up and kissed Fon on the forehead. He went to look out of the window at the sunset.

Fon watched him. 'Put on your clothes, Sam,' she whispered. 'It is not good to stand in the window naked.'

Ignoring her, he leaned against the wall and, putting his forehead to the glass, gazed down at the street: a line of little *warung* with glowing lights, coils of smoke from their fires; some cycle rickshaws; a knot of young men, surly, bored and unemployed.

'Sam,' Fon murmured. 'You do not have to go.'

'I do, Fon. I have to.'

She sat up on the side of the bed and wrapped a sarong around her nakedness, tucking it in at the side by her breasts, raking her hair back with her hands. 'Don't go. *Jangan pergi!* I am afraid. I am afraid you will not return. Sam, Pak Suryono is a bad man. I am afraid you will die.'

Sam crouched down and bit his lip. Squatting naked on his haunches, he glanced up at her warily. 'I could explain, Fon,' he said.

Fon looked away. She got up from the bed and dropped the sarong to the ground, her back turned. Then she pulled on her knickers and bra before slipping on her shirt, smoothing her rumpled hair. 'I cannot stop you going, so why does the reason matter?'

She pulled on her trousers, did up the buttons from bottom to top; and as he watched her dressing he felt more exposed than he had ever felt before.

Fon looked at her fiancé. Then she held her palms open at her side in a gesture of resignation and turned, stepping over the used condom on the floor, and left the room, closing the door behind her.

When she was gone, Sam took a shower. Beneath the streams of hot water, he sobbed and sobbed.

# 8

Just under a week later, Sam stepped off the Mandala Airlines flight to Ambon and entered the small arrivals lounge. While his baggage was unloaded, he stood by the upright fan, enjoying the coolness. A man dressed in a short-sleeved batik shirt and a blue cap approached him with careful steps. The man was not exactly elderly, but he was marked by the passage of time more severely than most. He stopped in front of Sam, a little to the side, took off his cap and put out his hand. 'Hello, mister,' he said, rolling the 'r'.

Sam smiled weakly, but did not respond to the offered hand.

'My name is Pak Wim,' said the man. 'You are American?'

Sam shook his head. 'No,' he said. 'English.'

'Welcome to Ambon,' said Pak Wim. 'I will be your guide.'

'No,' said Sam, somewhat distractedly. 'No, thank you. I can manage by myself.'

'Mister speaks good Indonesian,' Pak Wim said with enthusiasm. 'Perhaps he thinks that because he speaks good Indonesian, he will have no trouble here in Ambon. But Maluku is not Jakarta, tuan. You will need a guide. In Jakarta they say *saya tidak mau pergi*, but in Ambon they say *beta seng mau pi*. Even the words are different, mister. You will have many troubles without a guide.' He smiled obsequiously. 'Where is your bag?'

57

An airline worker was heaving the bags from the flight on to a nearby counter. Sam pointed to his case and Pak Wim went to fetch it. Sam watched this frail man struggle with his bag back to where he was standing. On any other occasion, Sam would have refused such assistance. Today, however, he had neither the energy nor the heart to argue. Pak Wim had no doubt lived a difficult life. What did it matter if he took advantage a little? What loss would it really be? Sam asked himself. Why not just go along with things, for once?

'Come,' said Pak Wim.

Sam followed Pak Wim outside. Pak Wim spoke to a taxi driver. He opened the front passenger door for Sam and climbed in the back himself. 'Kota Ambon,' he said to the taxi driver. '*Terus!*'

Once they were moving, Sam turned to his guide. 'Where are you from?' he asked.

Pak Wim smiled. 'I am from Kenukecil,' he said. 'My village is Amasi Dol, although I once lived in Jakarta. Today, I live in Ambon.'

Small fishing boats were out on the bay and the ferry that carried the students from Pattimura University back to the city was churning from one side to the other.

'Kenukecil?' Sam asked. 'I am travelling there in a few days' time. I have some business on the island. What is it like?'

Pak Wim laughed. 'Kenukecil is a very ancient place,' he said. 'There are many strange things. There are many *barang aneh*. Tuan must be careful. He does not want to become sick. He must be careful. There is powerful *adat*. There are many dangers.'

'Oh,' said Sam. 'I see.'

When they arrived at the Hotel Asmat, where Sam and Pak Suryono had agreed to meet on the twenty-third, Sam paid the driver. Pak Wim climbed out of the taxi and stretched. The taxi pulled away, leaving Sam and Pak Wim standing together by the tinted doors of the Asmat. Sam reached into his pocket and took out a few banknotes. He handed them to Pak Wim as a tip. 'For you,' he said.

Pak Wim gave a submissive bow. 'Thank you, tuan.'

Sam was about to leave him on the pavement and go in to the hotel, but a passing thought stopped him. 'One moment, Pak,' he said to Pak Wim. 'Before you go – would you be willing to do some work for me?'

'Work, tuan?'

'Guiding work.'

'Of course, tuan. I would be very happy. I know all of Ambon island. I know the sacred eels in Waai. I know the beach at Natsepa. I know the village of Soya Atas, where white men should not go alone –'

'No, not Ambon, Pak. I may need a guide in Kenukecil.'

Pak Wim looked down at his shoes, silently. 'I cannot,' he said.

'I will pay you, Pak Wim,' Sam pressed.

'I do not know. It is a long, long way. Very expensive. Maybe it is better I stay here.'

Sam held up his hand. 'Do not worry about money, Pak Wim. I will pay you enough.'

'How much, tuan?' Hope entered Pak Wim's eyes.

'One thousand,' Sam said.

'One thousand rupiah?' Pak Wim spat at the ground and laughed.

'No, one thousand dollars,' Sam corrected him.

Pak Wim seemed to sway, as if struck by an unexpected blow. 'One thousand *dollars*, tuan?'

'One thousand dollars. One thousand United States dollars. That's right.'

'It is a long way,' Pak Wim repeated. 'Perhaps it is too far. I do not know.' He shuffled uncomfortably.

'But it is your home,' Sam said. 'It is not a long way if you are going home.'

Pak Wim's voice became very quiet, so that Sam had to lean towards him to be able to hear. 'It is a very long way, tuan. You do not know how long. But if tuan wishes it then I will be happy to act as his guide in Kenukecil.' Then he gave an uneasy smile. 'For one thousand dollars, no less,' he added.

'Meet me here at the Hotel Asmat in two days' time at two in the afternoon. We can talk about it then, along with my business partner. We will discuss terms then. Our journey to Kenukecil will only be a few days, perhaps a week. You can trust me, Pak. I am an honest man.'

'Yes, tuan,' said Pak Wim. 'Thank you, tuan.' Sam shook his hand and noticed that the man was trembling. He picked up his case and went through the tinted glass doors of the Hotel Asmat.

# 9

Pak Suryono appeared at the Hotel Asmat at the appointed time on Wednesday, 23 October. He entered the lobby to see Sam Rivers seated on the comfortable chairs along with another man, the two of them engaged in animated conversation. The presence of this other man unsettled Pak Suryono. He disliked two things above all else: trouble and riff-raff. This stranger seemed to him to be both.

Pak Wim and Sam looked up as Pak Suryono approached, somewhat stiffly. The businessman shook hands with Sam. Sam introduced Pak Wim. 'This is Pak Wim. I have hired him to be our guide. I tried to telephone you at your office to tell you about him, but there was no reply.'

Pak Suryono looked surprised and switched from Bahasa into English, assuming that the other man would not understand. 'Do you know this man?'

'I met him in the taxi to the hotel when I arrived in Ambon,' Sam explained. 'He is from Kenukecil. He knows a great deal about the island. It makes sense to take a guide.'

'You should not waste time with such men, tuan. Look at him: he is scum.'

Although he had a fair grasp of English and understood almost every word, Pak Wim did not protest.

'You should have told me, Sam.' Pak Suryono's voice was that of a disappointed parent reprimanding a child.

'I invited Pak Wim because he comes from Kenukecil,' Sam reiterated. 'We need a local guide. I will pay him myself in addition to the money I have already given you.'

Pak Suryono was not placated. 'We will only be two or three days in Kenukecil. Why should we need a guide?'

'Pak Suryono, neither of us speaks the language in Kenukecil. Neither of us knows the customs. I am sure that this man will help us.'

Pak Suryono sat back and steepled his fingers. He turned to Pak Wim and raised his eyebrows questioningly.

Pak Wim smiled. 'I can help you,' he said in English.

'*Kalau begitu* . . .' said Pak Suryono. If that is so . . . His voice trailed off.

Pak Wim leaned forward in his chair. 'I am a very good guide,' he reassured Pak Suryono in Indonesian. 'I know *everything* about Kenukecil. Do not worry, Pak. If I am helping you, you are sure to have success.'

'OK,' said Pak Suryono. 'How much have you offered him?'

'One thousand dollars,' Sam said.

'Mr Samuel, send this man away,' Pak Suryono snapped. 'Send him away now.'

Sam patted his pockets ruefully. 'Unfortunately, Pak Suryono, it is too late. I have already paid him half the money. Earlier today I went to the bank. I will pay the other half when the project is completed.'

At that moment, the waitress arrived. 'Would you gentleman like coffee?' she asked.

Sam glanced up, smiled at her – she was pretty, he thought distractedly – and ordered three coffees.

Pak Suryono looked from Sam to Pak Wim and then back again. 'All right,' he said with resignation, 'so it is. Let's get down to business. How much have you told Pak Wim about our project?'

Sam smiled. 'So far, only that we are going to Kenukecil.'

Pak Suryono looked relieved. 'Good,' he said. 'Pak Wim, we will give you more information about the nature of our business when necessary. Until then, it is your job to do exactly as you are asked. If you do not co-operate, you will not receive the second half of your payment. Do you understand?'

'Yes, tuan,' Pak Wim replied.

'Good. And if you try to cheat us, then there will be trouble, understood?'

'Understood.'

'Now, please leave us. I need to speak to the English-man in private.'

The coffee arrived. Pak Wim hesitated.

'You can take your coffee with you. Come back in one hour,' Pak Suryono said.

Pak Wim bobbed submissively. 'Thank you, tuan,' he said. 'Thank you.' He picked up his coffee and retired to a corner of the hotel lobby out of earshot. There he sipped his drink and thought about the prospect of returning home.

It had been a long time since he had seen his home island: how long, he was not sure. Looking back, he could only see a winding trail on which the sufferings had far outweighed the joys, a life of vain hopes and repeated failures. The thought of returning to Kenukecil made him shake with fear; but at the same time, the thought of the one thousand dollars, half of which was already in his pocket, gave him hope that perhaps now, at long last, his fortunes might be on the turn.

Pak Wim was born in the clifftop village of Amasi Dol, where the palm trees were blown by breezes from the sea, where there was good fishing off the reef and good hunting in the forest, where a flight of stone steps cut into the cliff led down to a sheltered bay in which many caves and coves could be found, hiding places haunted by lovers and ghosts. He was the fourth of five children, his family of no particular rank. Of these children only two, he and his elder sister, survived beyond the age of five. He was still a young man when he left Amasi Dol in disgrace, driven, now here now there, by the gadfly of shame throughout the archipelago.

The cause of his shame was a girl called Anna, the daughter of a high-ranking village official. Wim had loved her since childhood. One morning in his twenty-first year he descended the steps towards the sea, where the girl was spearing fish on the reef at low tide, and as he watched her, he found within himself the courage to call out. 'Ay! *Nona* Anna! Tell me, what have you caught?'

She glanced round, smiled and went on spearing fish. He was a handsome youth, and the girl Anna was impressed by his slender good looks. She started to sing:

> *Lover, I sing of wonderful things,*
> *Lover, I sing of such lovely things,*
> *Turn aside, my love:*
> *My breasts are plump like ripe papayas;*
> *My fingers cool as the moon;*
> *My mouth is as sweet as a jambu fruit;*
> *My skin smooth as a shell*
> *That is washed by the waves.*
>
> *The waves break before the village, my love.*
> *The waves break before the reef.*

When she had caught enough fish to feed her family, she came up the beach, the sand sticking to her wet feet; and she took the young man by the hand, drawing him into a cave by the shore. There they kissed, watched by the spirits of generations of their ancestors who had kissed in that same place, with the same fervour. Wim put his hands on Anna's body and she did not resist. As she embraced him, he cried out. Anna placed her mouth over his to keep him silent, afraid someone might hear their voices over the swell and surge of the sea.

Then, when it was done, she picked up her fish and, carrying them over her shoulder with her hips swaying, a woman now, she climbed the steps back to the village.

They met in that cave every day for several cycles of the moon before Wim asked Anna to marry him. She agreed without hesitation. Yet Wim's family had little in the way of rank, nothing in the way of wealth and, according to the cruel gossip of the village, even less in the way of sense and thus a proper marriage between the son of such an ignoble family and the high-ranking Anna was unthinkable. The conventional path being impossible, Wim and Anna resolved instead to make *m'houna*, the last recourse for hot-headed lovers.

The *m'houna* is described in considerable detail in Kruywers's ethnography and celebrated in countless love-songs from the island of Kenukecil. Kruywers first describes it, somewhat misleadingly, as a 'marriage without rite' in which those who seek a forbidden union sneak away into the forest and have their way. Yet while seeming to be without rite, in truth – as Kruywers's account makes clear – the *m'houna* is the most ritualized of unions.

When, two months after his proposal, Wim came on a full-moon night to the long grasses behind Anna's house with the intention of making *m'houna* and called to her like a strange bird before slipping away into the forest, he was merely doing that which had been decreed long ago by the ancestors. When he lay down by the side of a clear forest pool underneath the mango tree and gazed up at the heavens, waiting patiently until dawn for his lover, it was because that was what was required by tradition. The following morning, when Anna had not arrived at the pre-arranged spot and he returned alone to the village square to be beaten soundly by his family for his incompetence, this was because countless generations that had gone before had beaten their sons when they returned from the already shameful *m'houna* marriage without a bride. And, finally, when at such a young age Wim was faced with the terrible humiliation of having made bad *m'houna* – which is to say, when he was faced with the indignity of going to the trouble of making *m'houna* only to be stood up by the girl in question – the possibilities that remained open to him were similarly circumscribed by convention. He could take his own life; he could live the remainder of his days mocked and reviled as a bachelor (for who would be foolish enough to marry a man who had made bad *m'houna*?); or he could flee into exile. Pak Wim chose the latter course. His family put him on a boat to Ambon and told him that he should never, under any circumstances, return to his natal village.

By the age of thirty, after a number of jobs in various parts of the Indonesian archipelago, Pak Wim settled in Jakarta, where he established a successful small business providing girls for tourists. He did not call them prostitutes, a term that sounds harsh on the tongue. Instead he thought of them as *kupu-kupu malam*, butterflies of the night. Neither did he think of himself as a pimp. Instead he saw himself as a kind of butterfly-dealer. Had he possessed the vocabulary, he might have referred to himself as a lepidopterist of the twilight hours, a man who dealt not in the prosaic realities of bodies grinding on bodies, but rather in the ethereal trade of beauty, the fluttering of wings. He was charming to his customers; and he learned to speak English. 'Yes, sir, our service is very discreet . . . Very good girls, mister. You see first? After you see, then you say you like or no? Clean girls, mister. Nice. From the *kampung*, not the city. Maybe they also look for husband, no?' A smile, half-leer. 'Indonesian wife very good.

American woman fuck everyone. Best friend, neighbour. No good. Indonesian girl good. Only fuck you, sir. Every day. Every night. You like?'

This line of work was lucrative for a while. Pak Wim bought himself a car and a driver's licence, and he dreamed of ever greater success. As he lay in bed at night, he was visited by a recurrent fantasy. He would open a drinking establishment. It would be called Wim's Bar. Neon palm trees would glow gently outside, enticing customers in. There would be private rooms at the back for customers to enjoy themselves with the girls. Wim himself, in a batik shirt and chinos, would work behind the bar. His customers would include many important people: politicians, businessmen, artists, writers, foreigners.

After several years in the butterfly trade, Wim had saved sufficient funds to be able to think about investing in such a venture; and when the ideal property came up for sale, not far from the Jalan Jaksa, he used his savings for a down payment, approaching Sonny, one of his business associates, for a loan to cover the costs of redeveloping the property. With Sonny's help, Wim's Bar took shape. Finding that he had no money to purchase the neon palm trees – neon palm trees, he discovered, do not come cheap – he extended his loan a little further. Sonny obliged. When the palms arrived, Pak Wim realized that he had forgotten to budget for the alcohol to stock the bar. Sonny, once more, helped him out.

In this fashion, stage by stage, Pak Wim made over almost all he owned to Sonny, including his car, his home, his business and his liberty, in an attempt to pay back his ill-considered succession of loans. Within a year, he found himself working as debt collector for his erstwhile friend and sponsor, while Sonny himself took ownership of the lucrative little butterfly business and bar that Pak Wim had built from scratch.

Sonny's Bar, as it became known, was indeed a magnificent place, enough to bring tears to the eyes. The neon palm trees shone beautifully in the warm night: orange and green and red. The sound of laughter radiated from the back rooms. The bar itself stocked seven varieties of Scottish single malt. Meanwhile, Pak Wim lay in the miserable hut that Sonny now rented him and wondered how it had all gone wrong. Occasionally Sonny brought him a sheaf of documents demonstrating, contrary to all reason, that Pak Wim's debt had grown still further. At forty-five years of age, unable to face the humiliation of his position any longer, Pak Wim fled Jakarta, the equivalent of four hundred dollars in his pocket, back-payments reclaimed earlier that night from the clutches of an overweight New Zealander. He caught a boat to Lombok and from there he made his way to Flores, following the outer arc of the islands eastwards. Sonny, seeing that his indebted debt collector had absconded, contracted a killer to pursue Pak Wim as far as Flores. But business is business: one must weigh up costs against benefits, profits against losses. Thanks to the generosity of a family of Buginese seafarers, the fugitive slipped the net. Sonny called the killer off and Pak Wim returned to Ambon, fully intending to live out the remainder of his days engaged in acts of altruism, working for the service of the community.

In Ambon he contacted his sister, who by now had become a thoroughly modern woman, with two grown-up children and a degree from Pattimura University, a woman who set little store by the customs of the *kampung*, the intricacies of *adat*, the shame that came from making bad *m'houna*. On returning to Ambon, Wim discovered that his parents were now deceased. His sister helped him find a property to live in and gave him the funds to open a typing school, which he ran successfully for six happy years. On Sundays he attended the Catholic church with his sister, her husband and his niece and nephew, Selly and Nathanial. On occasion he shared their table, and his new-found family would ask him, over and over again, 'Why do you not marry, Wim?' He would giggle and shake his head. Or they would ask, 'What did you do for work in Jakarta for all those years?' and he would say, 'I worked in the tourist trade.'

One day, attending to the pastoral care of a student in his typing school, he suggested to her – a girl from a family of good standing, well known for their simple piety – that she should enter the butterfly trade as a way of helping her to pay her way through college. 'It is nice work,' he said, beaming. 'Very nice work. You will see.'

Although Pak Wim's motives were altruistic, the girl went home that evening to inform her family of this slight on her honour and, by extension, theirs. Her brothers took several cans of petrol and a box of matches and set fire to the typing school. By dawn Pak Wim's business was in ruins. He had no insurance. When he came knocking on his sister's door, his brother-in-law, having heard of his scandalous suggestion, merely commended the arsonists and told Wim to never bother them again. It was then that Pak Wim reinvented himself as a tour guide, a miserable occupation that paid only a little. He hung around the airport waiting for foreign tourists and latched on to them, telling them desultory facts about anything at all that entered his mind, until they paid him to go away.

Pak Wim finished his coffee and reflected on this sorry history. Looking across the lobby of the Hotel Asmat, he could see Pak Suryono and the Englishman had come to the end of their meeting. They were standing, exchanging courtesies, smiling fixed smiles. Pak Wim caught Sam's eye. The Englishman beckoned him over.

'It is all set,' Sam said. 'I will be travelling to Kenukecil by plane. Pak Suryono has already booked a flight for me this coming Friday. Pak Suryono himself will remain here in Ambon for another two days, as he has some business meetings to attend to. Unfortunately there will not be another flight until the end of November, so Pak Suryono will be chartering a fast boat to Kenukecil and has suggested that you and he travel together. I will leave Pak Suryono to arrange the details of the journey with you. Now, do you have any questions?'

Pak Wim smiled. 'Thank you, mister,' he said. 'Thank you.'

'Good,' Sam replied. He shook hands with both Pak Wim and Pak Suryono. 'In that case, I will see you in Kenukecil,' he said. 'Goodbye.'

'Have a safe flight,' Pak Suryono replied. 'We will see you after the weekend.' He glanced at his watch. 'Ah! It is already late. Excuse me, I have another meeting. I must go. Pak Wim, I will meet you here tomorrow and give you all the details you need.'

Pak Suryono hurried out of the Hotel Asmat and Sam climbed the stairs to his room, leaving Pak Wim alone in the lobby. The errant son of Amasi Dol thought of the prospect of a return home, where he would face the fact of his shame. He thought of the place where, one moon-addled night many years before, he had made bad *m'houna* out of love for a girl named Anna. Then he thought of the five hundred dollars that Sam had given him and concluded that perhaps, just perhaps, things were looking up.

# 10

Departing from Natsepa beach on the Sunday, the *Siwalima*, a charter vessel, arrived in Bantuk on the evening of Tuesday the twenty-ninth. Fast and sleek, the *Siwalima* was also spacious and comfortable. Pak Wim, Pak Suryono and the captain each had a cabin to themselves and they enjoyed a trouble-free passage, heading out of Ambon first to the Banda islands, then via Kei and Tanimbar to Bantuk. Pak Wim was seasick twice on the way, despite the fact that the sea had been a flat calm. They arrived in Bantuk after dark, tied up at the end of the pier and the three of them retired to their cabins for the night.

The *Ratu Mela* arrived on its long journey from Jakarta the following morning. Pak Suryono was standing on the deck of the *Siwalima*, brushing his teeth and squinting into the rising sun, when he saw the boat heading towards him across the bay. He smiled to see her clean lines and spat the foam of minty toothpaste into the water. When the boat was close enough, he shouted in greeting at Ibrahim. Ibrahim brought the *Ratu Mela* alongside and threw a rope to Pak Suryono, who tethered it, both fore and aft. Hearing the commotion, Pak Wim emerged from below, followed by the *Siwalima*'s captain. They watched as Ibrahim and Pak Suryono embraced.

'Success?' asked Pak Suryono.

'Success,' Ibrahim replied, giving a rare smile. 'The cargo is here.'

Pak Suryono introduced Ibrahim to Pak Wim and the captain. Then he turned to Pak Wim. 'Now, Pak,' he said. 'Would you like to see our cargo?'

Pak Wim nodded.

'Ibrahim will take you,' Pak Suryono said, nodding at his associate. 'After you have seen, then you must go and visit the Englishman to tell him everything is ready. He is staying in a hotel called the *Pandangan Indah*. It is on the main street.'

'Come with me,' said Ibrahim.

Pak Wim was so horrified by what he saw below decks that he fainted. Ibrahim and Pak Suryono had a hard job hauling him back up the ladder into the sunlight, Ibrahim pushing from below and Pak Suryono pulling from above. A splash of sea-water in the face brought him round, gasping and spluttering.

'Pak Suryono, it's not right,' he said when he had regained the faculty of speech. 'What are we to do with it?'

'Mr Sam is going to take it to Australia.'

Pak Wim shuddered. 'It is not right,' he repeated.

'Pak Wim, do not worry. Let us have breakfast. After breakfast you can go to find Mr Sam.'

Pak Suryono led his colleague back onto the *Siwalima* where the captain was cooking breakfast on a primus stove. He handed his passengers enamel cups of sweet tea, followed a few moments later by plates of *nasi goreng*. Pak Wim picked at his food without enthusiasm.

After breakfast, Wim went down the pier and cut through the Hope Market, an open square surrounded by shops. In the centre of the market were concrete slabs where women from the villages had laid out their goods: tomatoes, peppers, chillies, courgettes and carrots; deep sea fish, *trepang*, squid and reef fish. The market was bustling with housewives shopping for vegetables, ragamuffin children playing tag through the crowd leaving staccato trails of curses in their wake, young men loitering in the shade to watch girls, who in their turn giggled and watched the men. Several buses parked by the shops, blowing their horns as they touted for customers to ferry northwards.

Leaving the claustrophobia of the market, Wim walked out of town towards where he could see the spire of the Catholic church on the hill. At the top of the hill, he said a brief prayer by the statue of Christ the Sacred Heart, before entering the church. A figure of the Virgin stood in a niche in the wall. Pak Wim knelt before her and prayed. When his prayers and devotions were complete, for good measure he went down to the smaller Protestant church in the centre of town. There he recited a further barrage of prayers, slightly modified on the grounds that the God of the Catholics is not exactly the same as the God of the Protestants. Finally, he made his way to the *Pandangan Indah* in search of the Englishman. The owner, Thomas, was on the front desk, crouched over the glowing screen of a computer.

'Excuse me, Pak. Is there an *orang bule* in this hotel?' Pak Wim asked.

Thomas looked up. 'Mr Samuel?'

'Yes, Mr Samuel.'

'He is sick,' Thomas said. 'Are you a friend?'

'I am,' Pak Wim replied. 'I am a friend from Ambon.'

'He is on the first floor. Go on up.' Thomas turned back to his computer screen and Pak Wim climbed to the first floor.

Samuel Rivers' hotel room door was half open. Through the crack, Pak Wim could see the Englishman lying on the bed. He entered without knocking. Inside, the air was sweet with stale sweat. He could hear Sam's breathing. 'Mr Sam,' Pak Wim whispered. 'You must come to the harbour.'

The Englishman did not move. Pak Wim stepped tentatively towards him. Sam's eyes were closed. His breathing was both erratic and deep. Pak Wim reached out a hand and took hold of the sleeping man's arm. It felt cold and was damp with sweat. 'Mr Sam?' he said. 'Please, Mr Sam?'

The Englishman was taking no notice. Shaking his head, Pak Wim let go of his arm and left the room. He headed back to the boat.

On the deck of the *Siwalima*, Pak Suryono was cheerfully sipping a beer. He had his shoes off and was flexing his toes, which were remarkably long and agile.

'Where is Mr Samuel?' Pak Suryono asked.

Pak Wim crouched down on the side of the pier. 'Mr Sam is sick,' he said. 'He does not move. He does not speak.'

Pak Suryono pressed his lips together, causing his moustache to twitch. 'Have you spoken with him?'

'I have spoken, but he does not reply.'

Pak Suryono put his beer down. 'I will come to see him myself,' he said.

Back at the Lovely Vista, Pak Suryono got no more response out of Sam than Pak Wim had. He stood by Sam's bedside shaking his head. 'This is not good, Pak Wim,' he said. 'This delay is very inconvenient. I want you to visit the Englishman every day, and as soon as he is well, I want you to bring him to the boat. Do you understand?'

'Of course,' Pak Wim replied.

The businessman left the room, descended the stairs and returned to the boat. Pak Wim stood watching Sam for a while longer; then he too left the hotel. He was unsettled by what he had seen on the boat and further troubled by the Englishman's unexpected illness. He needed something to calm his nerves, something to soothe him. He wandered out into the main street, drank some tea at a street stall, and then – after making a few discreet enquiries in the market – he found his way to the door of the local butterfly house. He knocked three times. A smiling Chinese man answered. 'I have come for ladies,' Pak Wim explained.

'You have come to the right place,' the other man replied. 'Welcome. My name is Mr Gu. Do you have cash?'

Pak Wim patted his pockets in a gesture of genial resignation. It was astonishing how quickly he had spent Sam's initial five hundred dollars in Ambon – mainly gambled away – but this did not worry him unduly: he would be receiving another five hundred in a few days' time. 'Today, I have none. But soon I will be paid and then I will be rich. Can you give me credit?'

'When are you are going to be paid?'

'Maybe tomorrow,' Pak Wim replied. 'Or the day afterwards.'

Mr Gu studied Pak Wim carefully. 'One hour on credit with the girl of your choice,' he said. 'But you must pay me by Friday. Twenty thousand rupiah would normally suffice for an hour but because of the delay I think we should settle for forty thousand. If, of course, you cannot pay, or you try to cheat me, then I will slice off your balls and toss them into the sea. Do you understand?'

Pak Wim gave a shy, grateful smile. 'Thank you, Pak. You are very kind.'

The Chinese man held the door open for his customer. 'Come in, then, friend.'

Pak Wim stepped inside. Mr Gu looked critically at him. 'You have arrived on the *Siwalima*, yes?'

This surprised Pak Wim. 'How do you know?'

'I have a shop in the Hope Market. As a shopkeeper, I know many things. My contacts told me about your arrival. Please, we have many good girls. The choice is yours. One hour only. No more.'

*

Pak Wim made good use of the hour. When he left the butterfly house and returned to the *Siwalima*, his heart felt lighter. He spent the rest of his day in idleness, trying not to think about what he had seen below decks on the *Ratu Mela*, which was berthed alongside. In the evening, Pak Suryono invited him for a meal at one of the *warung* close by the market. They ate largely in silence, but Pak Wim appreciated the gesture of friendliness. That night he slept well and, the following morning, he returned to the Lovely Vista, expecting to find the Englishman had made a full recovery. Unfortunately Samuel Rivers was no more responsive than the day before. Pak Wim headed back to the boat.

On the way, while walking through the Hope Market, he was spotted by Mr Gu, who was sitting on the steps outside one of the shops. 'Hello, Pak Wim!' he shouted, waving cheerfully. 'Tomorrow we must settle our account. Do not forget.'

Pak Wim hurried past with a deferential nod.

The next day was Friday. Pak Wim was woken early by the call to prayer from Bantuk's single mosque. Unable to get back to sleep, he left his cabin and went to sit on deck and watch the sun rise.

He made his daily pilgrimage to the Lovely Vista, scuttling through the marketplace without Mr Gu spotting him. There was no change in Sam's condition. On his way back to the boat he was not so lucky. Mr Gu saw him slipping through the crowd and called out from the shopfront. 'Pak Wim, what is the hurry?'

Pak Wim stopped. 'I am heading to the harbour,' he said. 'I have to meet someone.'

'Stay for a while and drink tea,' insisted Mr Gu. 'It is from China. I even have some Dutch butter biscuits that arrived on the Perintis ship yesterday. Special order. They are quite delicious. The Queen of the Netherlands eats them. Come, we need to talk.'

*

Mr Gu was not a tall man. His hair was thinning prematurely and he wore a long, thread-like beard on his chin. His sarong was loosely tied, his feet bare and he wore a string vest through which it was possible to see his almost hairless chest. This was his uniform for the marketplace, studied in its carelessness. Mr Gu claimed for himself that most fragile of all virtues, humility. He had several Armani suits, but rarely wore them. He had a big, fat Rolex watch, although it did not often grace his wrist. In the garage that lay behind his not insubstantial house, stood not one but two new 4 x 4 vehicles. For all this, Mr Gu preferred to affect the air of a simple trades- man even if his little shop, selling envelopes, pens, malaria pills, out-of-date aspirin, notebooks, sweets for the school- children, mouldering deodorant for the few Western tour- ists who passed through, scissors, nail-clippers and other items of occasional necessity, accounted for only one tenth of a per cent of his income.

Mr Gu had started out as a shopkeeper and maintained his shop from a kind of nostalgia. He regarded himself as a tender-hearted man and was not incapable of shedding tears when he read the poems of Li Po and Tu Fu; but his tenderness was matched by his shrewdness: Mr Gu's investments, both legitimate and illegitimate, his good connections in government and the auspicious marriage of his son to the daughter of the boss of the ailing Kakatau airlines – a move which had been doubly fortunate, ridding him of that unbearable lout who passed for a son while opening up a free-of-charge means of freighting goods to and from Ambon – permitted him slowly to extend his power throughout the islands and beyond. Yet he liked to ask, pointing into his shop, the ceiling propped up by beams of wood, 'Do I look like a rich man?'

There was no line of business in the islands – the fishing industry, the logging of the forests, the trade in *trepang*, the tearing open of the land for minerals and several other businesses of questionable legitimacy – in which Mr Gu did not have a hand. While often protesting that he was nothing other than a shopkeeper trying to make an honest living, amongst his associates (a man such as this does not have friends, only associates) he was also fond of holding out a hand, palm upwards, and claiming, 'I have Kenukecil by the balls. One little squeeze, the island squeals.'

Pak Wim stepped into the shop. Mr Gu was all smiles and apologies: 'I am very sorry it is so simple here. I am, as you know, just a shopkeeper trying to make a living. Please make yourself as comfortable as is possible.' He indicated a chair. Ignoring it, Pak Wim squatted down on his haunches. Mr Gu boiled the kettle. He reached into a small wooden box and took out a handful of tea leaves that he threw into a pot. The kettle began to steam.

'There is a legend,' Mr Gu said conversationally, 'that tea sprang from the eyelids of the saint Bodhidharma, who tore them off and flung them to the ground because sleep interrupted his contemplation.' The kettle clicked and Mr Gu poured the water over the top of the leaves. 'From this legend I draw the following lesson: if a man wishes to succeed, then he must remain vigilant.' He looked up at Pak Wim and smiled. 'Come, let us drink.'

The merchant took two cups from the low shelf by the kettle. He took out a china plate and, opening the tin of Dutch biscuits, fanned them out with exaggerated care. He poured some tea and handed a mug to Pak Wim, who blew on it to cool it, so that he might absent himself all the sooner. Mr Gu watched him. 'Pak Wim?' he asked. 'That is short for Wilhelm. A good Dutch name.'

'Yes,' whispered Pak Wim.

Mr Gu thought for a while. 'The Dutch,' he said, 'are a barbaric race, but they are honourable in their barbarism. Whereas *orang Maluku* are so difficult to do business with.'

Pak Wim attempted a smile. He wanted sugar in his tea – sugar and condensed milk; but Mr Gu had not offered it and he did not dare ask. Without these things, the tea tasted terrible.

Mr Gu continued: 'Now, I may be mistaken, Pak Wim, but do we not have an account to settle?'

Pak Wim gave a deferential smile. 'Mr Gu,' he said, 'I have a problem.'

'A problem, Pak Wim?' The merchant looked sad.

Pak Wim looked at the floor. 'I am sorry, tuan,' he said. 'I am still waiting to be paid. It is not my fault. There is an Englishman who is paying me, but he is sick.'

Mr Gu sighed. He got to his feet and ambled towards the back of the shop, returning with a ledger, which he placed before Pak Wim. 'A simple tradesman such as myself,' he said, 'must keep accurate records.' He flipped the pages theatrically until he came to the appropriate page. 'Ah, here it is. Forty thousand rupiah, exclusive of service charges and tax. That makes sixty thousand.'

'*Sixty* thousand?' Pak Wim protested. Mr Gu's gaze was uncompromising. Pak Wim looked miserably into his tea. 'Tuan, I have no money.'

Mr Gu pulled on his beard thoughtfully. 'Perhaps we could agree on a revised date for receipt of the cash?' he suggested.

'Maybe,' Pak Wim replied, watching the leaves floating about at the bottom of his cup. Having himself been both pimp and debt collector, he could admire the Chinese shopkeeper's delicate menace. A true professional.

'Pak Wim,' Mr Gu said, 'I will give you five more days. That makes a week in all. After that, if you have not paid –'

here Mr Gu hesitated '– we can resolve this problem by another means. If you pay me one hundred thousand rupiah by next Wednesday, 6 November, then I will be satisfied.' Mr Gu snapped the ledger closed and passed Pak Wim another biscuit. 'Please,' he beamed, 'be my guest.'

Pak Wim put down his tea. 'I have to go,' he said.

'Of course,' Mr Gu replied soothingly. 'Thank you for your time. It is always a pleasure to have visitors. *Selamat jalan, Pak.*'

'*Selamat tinggal, tuan*,' Pak Wim muttered. He stumbled out of the shop to join the crowds milling through the Hope Market.

# 11

As the days passed and Sam showed no sign of recovery, Pak Suryono became increasingly irascible. Down below decks on the *Ratu Mela* the cargo was becoming restless too. Every morning Pak Suryono went to the bazaar to buy bunches of bananas and bags of sago biscuits to keep it fed but the creature was surly and bad-tempered and hurled the offerings out of its cage before falling into a fearsome sulk.

By Saturday evening, Pak Suryono was more depressed than he could ever remember. He bought a bottle of palm-wine to lift his spirits. That night he, Pak Wim and the captain of the *Siwalima* got drunk. Ibrahim – religiously opposed to alcohol and preferring the company of the cargo to a party of drunks – remained on board the *Ratu Mela*. It was one o'clock in the morning before the three men on the *Siwalima* slumped into their respective cabins and fell unconscious. Ibrahim, glancing around the bay and spellbound by the still loveliness of the night, crossed from the *Ratu Mela* to the *Siwalima* and from there stepped onto the pier. He breathed the night air deeply, relishing the happiness of solitude. Then he strolled down towards the town, to stretch his legs and to enjoy the beautiful night.

On Sunday morning, as the church bells were chiming up on the hill, calling the faithful to prayer, Ibrahim emerged from below decks on the *Ratu Mela*, a look of panic on his face. He crossed over to the *Siwalima* and burst into Pak Suryono's cabin.

'Pak Suryono,' he blurted, 'the cargo has gone.'

Pak Suryono opened his eyes. A headache stabbed him like a blunt piece of wood poked into his eye. 'Ibrahim,' he said. 'Go away. I'm ill.'

Ibrahim did not go. 'It's gone, Pak Suryono,' he said. 'The cargo is gone.'

Pak Suryono sat up. 'Gone?' he asked.

The expression on Ibrahim's face did not change.

Pak Suryono struggled to his feet. He was dressed only in a sarong, which he tightened around his waist.

'Come with me,' Ibrahim said.

Pak Suryono stumbled after him onto the adjacent boat. The hatch of the *Ratu Mela* had been lifted.

Ibrahim pointed down below deck. 'Take a look,' he said.

Pak Suryono climbed down the ladder. Inside, he sensed the disarray before he saw it. His eyes adjusted slowly to the light. The cage was shattered, a broken frame of splintered wood. The food cupboards had been forced open, their contents strewn everywhere. The seats had been torn up and shredded. Splintered planks lay about here and there on the floor. The cargo was not there.

Pak Suryono clambered back onto the deck and sat down, his head hanging, studying the grain of the wood. His head pulsed with a throbbing hangover. 'What happened?' he mumbled miserably 'Where has it gone?'

'I do not know,' Ibrahim confessed. 'It must have become bored with waiting. It is already four days since I arrived. Still the Englishman is sick.'

Pak Suryono massaged his temples in an attempt to ease his headache into submission. 'Where were you last night, Ibrahim? Were you not asleep on the boat?'

'I am sorry,' Ibrahim said. 'It was a beautiful night. I went for a walk. When I returned, I went to sleep on the deck. I only realized this morning that the cargo had gone.' Ibrahim paused. 'Pak Suryono, you have been drinking. You know that drink is a bad thing for a man. Many terrible things happen when a man is drunk.'

Pak Suryono glared at him. 'Ibrahim, save your moral philosophy,' he snapped.

Ibrahim shrugged. 'What do we do now?' he asked.

'Go and wake Pak Wim,' said the businessman. 'And make us some breakfast. Then we will decide.'

The three men – Pak Wim, Pak Suryono and Ibrahim – breakfasted together in silence. The captain of the *Siwalima* was still sleeping off the excesses of the night before. There was no reason to wake him.

When they had cleaned their plates, Pak Suryono cleared his throat. 'We must recapture our cargo,' he said.

'How?' Ibrahim asked.

'First the Englishman must recover, then we must hunt down the cargo. When we have found it, we can proceed as before. It is simple. These islands are not so large.' Pak Suryono gestured in the general direction of the north. 'We should be able to find the shipment without any problems.'

'But the Englishman? He is still sick,' said Ibrahim.

Pak Wim coughed. The others glanced over at him. 'There was a woman,' he said. 'She lived in Bantuk. Now she must be very old, but she was a healer. She had *adat* powers. Perhaps she can help.'

'Pak Wim, why did you not say this before?' Pak Suryono's voice was sharp.

'I have had many troubles,' Pak Wim said apologetically. 'Is this woman still alive?'

'Perhaps she is dead,' Pak Wim said. 'She cured me when I was a boy. She knows many things.'

Pak Suryono looked out to sea. 'Can you remember her name?' he asked.

Pak Wim dropped one shoulder a little, a gesture of respect. 'I am old, Pak. And my memory is poor. But if she is still alive, then I can find her.'

# 12

Suster Elena, convinced that the diagnosis offered by Pastor Niemann was wrong – one could not blame him for his ignorance, he was a Dutchman, after all – crossed town on Monday morning to confer with Ibu Lana, hoping that the renowned healer might be able to offer an alternative cure. Pastor Niemann would be angry when he found out; but it was necessary all the same, for the sake of the patient who was still raving and sweating and gibbering in her sick bed. In medical matters, Suster Elena was a pragmatist. She did not subscribe to any particular school of medicine: her sole criterion was that of effectiveness. She left the sick woman in the care of a novice called Maria and made her way to the healer's house.

Ibu Lana Lerekosu had a quiet life. Occasionally she was called upon to deal with some malady or other; but for the remainder of the time she was accustomed to spending her days sitting in her porch while the chickens pecked away at the dust, paring away at her betel nut, calling out greetings to everyone who came down the street and, when they were out of earshot, commenting that this person was guilty of the sin of copulation, that another had a weakness for *sopi*, or that a third had not been to church, not even a Catholic church, for three whole weeks. On the morning of Suster Elena's visit, she was sitting with a bowl in her lap containing three betel nuts. She was paring the nuts with a blunt knife and chewing on the parings. From time to time she spurted a stream of red saliva from her mouth and it splattered along the ground, sinking into the dust.

She saw the nun approach and raised a hand in greeting. 'Suster Elena! What are you doing?'

Suster Elena stepped up onto Ibu Lana's porch. 'I have come to ask for your help, Ibu Lana.' She smiled.

Ibu Lana pointed to the chair. 'Sit,' she said. 'Tell me how I can help you.'

Suster Elena did as she was asked. Having thoroughly described Ibu Nilasera's symptoms, she folded her hands in her lap. 'It is not malaria,' she said. 'With malaria, sickness comes slowly. This sickness was quick. I saw Ibu Nilasera yesterday at mass and she was well. In the afternoon, Benny came to find me, saying she was ill. The pastor is wrong.'

Ibu Lana sucked her gums and pushed her white hair back behind her ears. Her jowls wobbled ferociously. 'Has Ibu Nilasera wronged anyone?' she barked.

'Ibu Nilasera? Wronged anyone? Surely not.'

'Perhaps you are ignorant of her sins,' Ibu Lana suggested, with more than a touch of salaciousness.

'Good gracious, no, Ibu Lana!' the nun cried out, shocked.

'Perhaps she has an evil heart. Perhaps that is why she smiles so much, to hide the poison in her heart.'

Suster Elena shook her head. 'Ibu Lana, my friend Ibu Nilasera is a good woman. I know her better than anyone. This is not witchcraft. She has not been entered by a *swangi*. She has not angered anyone. This is something worse than witchcraft. She saw something in the church.'

'Ha! You Catholics and your visions!' Ibu Lana slapped a fat hand down on the arm of the chair. 'I suppose your Virgin spoke to her! That woman never stops speaking to you Catholics.' Being a Protestant, she had little patience with the Virgin.

'No, not the Virgin,' Suster Elena said quietly. 'Ibu Lana: it was a devil.'

This was more interesting. 'A devil? In the church?' Ibu Lana leaned forwards and her lower jaw dropped, as it did when she concentrated. She shook her head. 'Such sinful times, Suster Elena, such sinful times,' she said, with relish. 'I sit here in my porch, Suster Elena, and do you know what I see? I see sin, every single day.' She paused again, for effect. 'I see fornicators and I see drinkers and I see thieves and I see murderers. There is nothing I do not see from my porch. This world is rotten with sin.' Ibu Lana's eyes became misted with tears. 'Once, when we were young, Suster Elena, the world was good. But now . . .'

Ibu Lana had earned the right to speak like this by having lived for at least seventy-five years. Perhaps it was eighty-five. Nobody really knew. Like many of the old folk, she was closer to the *tetek-nenek-moyang* – the ancestors she would soon be joining – than to the rest of the living. It was as if she had already, long ago, been given permission to pass over into their shadowy kingdom, her exit visa stamped, her permit to travel approved, but she had decided to remain on this side of the border, either out of lethargy or out of nostalgia. 'What kind of devil?' the old healer asked.

'It does not matter,' Suster Elena said practically. 'A devil is a devil, and Ibu Nilasera did not describe it. She only said that it was seated in the front pew and it was praying.'

'A *Catholic* devil!' Ibu Lana wheezed with laughter, clutching at the arms of her chair, her great chest heaving.

Suster Elena ignored the comment. 'I do not know much about devils, Ibu Lana,' she said. 'I am merely telling you what happened. Ibu Nilasera saw the devil, and – being a good woman who fears for her soul – she fled for her life. She is not the kind of woman who would have any business with devils. She went straight to the pastoran, but by the time she got there, she was already on fire with fever. This really does not sound like malaria. She speaks with the voice of the devil as she lies on her bed. She sweats. She trembles with fear. Her skin is almost grey. Pastor Niemann has given her chloroquine, but it does not help.'

Ibu Lana nodded in agreement. 'No,' she said, 'this does not sound like malaria.' Then she stretched herself and smiled. It was a truly prodigious smile. Her jaw dropped. She drew back her lips to reveal receding gums, rotted by years of compulsive betel chewing, displaying her few remaining jagged, red-stained teeth. Her eyes rolled in their sockets. The overall effect was both terrifying and peculiarly charming, the balance between charm and terror being one that Ibu Lana had perfected over many years. 'If it was indeed a devil that Ibu Nilasera saw in the church,' she said, 'then I can help her.'

Throughout her long career as a healer, Ibu Lana Lerekosu had treated a wide range of maladies: madness suffered on account of the wrathful retribution of the ancestors; sores and pustules on account of the same; the expulsion of witches from the body (they gnawed out the insides, beginning with the spleen and moving on to the liver, leaving the heart till last); the subjugation of the *sawang* – the octopus not of the rockpools but of the body, un- known to Western science; dizziness because of the chang- ing winds; growths upon the toe caused by disrespectfully kicking sacred trees; inability to urinate because of a neighbour's malicious curse; inability to copulate for the same reason; blindness caused by the heat of an ancestral *walut* sculpture; barrenness arising from exposure of one's genitals to one's brother while climbing a palm tree; and one hundred thousand others besides. All of this learning had come not from books nor from long years of study, but rather it had been bestowed by the ancestors. It was what they called a *kekuatan mata rumah*, a power associated with her household conferred upon her by the ancestors themselves.

Some of Ibu Lana's enemies suggested that her cures had more in the way of vigour than they did in the way of effectiveness; but they never dared suggest it to the Ibu directly and these dissenting voices did not especially diminish Ibu Lana's enormous following. Her belief that, in matters medicinal, there could be no harm in a little extra vigour to help the cure along its way was widely shared.

Ibu Lana thought for a few more moments about the illness as Suster Elena had described it. Then she jutted her chin forward. 'I will cure her!' she snapped. 'I will cure her where that pastor of yours has failed, with his pills and his medicines and his virgins and saints. Mamma knows about these things.' As long ago as anyone could remember, Ibu Lana had adopted the curious habit of referring to herself in the third person as *Mamma*. She sat back and popped another bit of betel nut into her mouth, chewing thoughtfully. 'Mamma will cure Ibu Nilasera, even though she is a Catholic, because Mamma is a good woman.'

Suster Elena smiled politely. 'Thank you, Ibu Lana. But, please, do not let Pastor Niemann know.'

'*Pah!*' Ibu Lana spat the betel right out of her mouth. 'He is white and ignorant and his penis is shrivelled through lack of use. Even my husband is more of a man than him.'

Suster Elena smiled. 'Thank you,' she said.

At that moment, something caught Ibu Lana's eye. 'Look,' she said. 'Somebody is coming.' She pointed down the street with a pudgy finger. There was a figure in the distance coming towards them, shimmering in the haze.

Ibu Lana, who knew almost everyone in Bantuk by their gait, did not recognize the figure. When it drew closer, she saw it was a man, thin and somewhat frail, the frailty that comes not from age so much as from the difficulty of the passing years.

He stopped before Ibu Lana's porch and looked respectfully down at the ground. 'Ibu Lana,' he said in Kenukecilese.

Ibu Lana felt a tremor of recognition, but it ran so deep that she could not place it. She turned to Suster Elena. 'Who is this man?' she snapped.

Suster Elena held up a hand, a gesture of gentleness. 'Please, Pak, be seated,' she said. 'Do you wish to speak to the Ibu?'

The man remained where he was, looking at the chickens, nervous as a schoolboy. 'Ibu Lana, maybe you do not remember me. My name is Pak Wim.'

'Pak Wim? Where are you from?'

'I have lived in Jakarta and Ambon for many years. But once I lived in Amasi Dol.'

The name seemed familiar, but Ibu Lana was unsure why. It had about it a whiff of scandal. She remembered the scent of the scandal, but not the details. 'Pak Wim,' she said, 'Mamma is a busy woman. She is talking with the Suster. Leave us.'

Pak Wim didn't leave. 'There is a man who is sick,' he mumbled. 'I have been looking for you since yesterday.'

Ibu Lana folded her arms. Suster Elena looked anxiously at Pak Wim. 'Tell us about the man,' she said.

'He is in the Lovely Vista Hotel. I think that the Ibu will be able to cure him. I came to ask. I know that she has much skill.'

'Is he Protestant or Catholic?' Ibu Lana demanded.

'Ibu Lana,' Suster Elena gently interjected. 'Do not ask such things. A man is sick. That is all that matters.'

'He is an Englishman,' Pak Wim explained, resolving the question of the sick man's religious affiliation, it being well known that Westerners are entirely without religion.

'An Englishman? In Kenukecil?' Ibu Lana laughed. 'What is his sickness?'

'He cannot move from his bed. He just lies there. Sometimes he sweats, but mostly he just sleeps. He is very weak.'

Suster Elena smiled at Pak Wim. 'We will come,' she said firmly, before Ibu Lana had a chance to refuse. Despite the appearance of gentleness, Suster Elena was perhaps the only living person who could stand up to Ibu Lana. 'First we must go and treat another patient, but then we will come to the hotel.'

'Thank you, Suster,' Pak Wim said and then, turning to Ibu Lana, 'Thank you, Ibu.'

Ibu Lana shrugged her massive shoulders. '*Ayo*,' she said to Suster Elena, 'let us go and attend to the sick woman. We can see the Englishman later, if he is still alive.'

They left Pak Wim standing just outside her porch. He watched as the two formidable women headed down towards the sea, in the direction of Ibu Nilasera's house. Ibu Lana kept her eyes lowered, trying to sniff out the scent of the hidden disgrace she had intuited.

# 13

An hour or so after Ibu Lana had finished attending to the sick woman's devils, Mr Liao the Taiwanese fisherman appeared on the jetty at the back of the Lovely Vista Hotel. He performed a few stretches, facing into the sun, then sat down on a low stool and crossed his legs. He closed his eyes, feeling the cool breeze on his face. A fly buzzed past his ear. The lap of the waves against the jetty soothed his heart. Ah, he thought, the sufferings of cyclical existence! His head was thumping just a little and the pain in his side that he had first noticed a month or two ago had returned that morning. Mr Tan, his assistant, was dozing like an ox upstairs. Fugitive images flitted across his mind: fragments of conversation, memories, hopes, desires. He made another subtle adjustment to his posture, trying to settle his body so that his mind might follow suit.

It had been a long time since Mr Liao had experienced the delicious fruits of meditation. How hard it was, he thought, to be a man both of the world and also of the spiritual realm. He should have become a monk: it was the good fortune of monks that they lived off the fortunes of others and had no work of their own, other than that of treading the noble path with its eight incomparable limbs. Like an octopus, he thought. As a fisherman, the imagery came naturally to him and did not seem strange. Like an incomparable octopus.

Once, Mr Liao had seriously considered taking monastic vows, but the itching of the flesh had been too hard to resist. He had dreams, sometimes, of himself in saffron, in a cloud of incense, serene and untroubled. The most persistent of his dreams was this: he was dressed as a monk and walking in quiet meditation when he was set upon by women, who cavorted around him naked. In this dream, Mr Liao walked through their midst like a bull elephant in the Himalayan forest walking through a herd of elephant cows, for these mere women were incapable of disturbing the meditative equipoise of his mind. The dream ended with him sitting before a shrine and the women abruptly disappearing, leaving him alone with a ribbon of incense smoke snaking up to the ceiling.

Outside his dreams, however, the fleshly itching was too strong and Mr Liao had taken a wife, having read in a primer on religion that the life of a virtuous householder was better than that of a bad monk. Not long after his marriage, he realized that even this life was beyond his moral grasp. Although it pained him to confess it, he had often partaken of the pleasures offered by Mr Gu's establishment in Kenukecil. Thus, Mr Liao was a man of contradictions: capable of subjugating the itching of his flesh in his dreams, but not in his waking hours; a model husband and a perfect father to his son while at home in Taipei, who drank deep of the pleasures of the whorehouse when he was away.

Mr Liao had worked for two years for the Matsya Corporation, the Sanskrit name indicating that this was a fishing company based on strict Buddhist principles. Every day before work, the employees at Matsya sat in silent meditation for half an hour before rising with renewed vigour to continue their mission of bringing fish from the most obscure reaches of the world's oceans to the tables of the rich. Mr Liao had spent most of his time with the firm negotiating a lucrative fishing concession in the waters around Kenukecil. He saw his departure to Kenukecil, leaving behind his wife and young son in Taipei, as a kind of Going Forth, as the Lord Buddha himself had departed his homeland, his wife and son – although not, of course, at the behest of a large corporation and without the extended visits to houses of pleasure. *The household life is full of dust*, Mr Liao thought as he sat in meditation. Then another thought came unbidden to his mind: *the whorehouse is swept clean each morning*. Only the first of these lines can be found in scripture.

As he continued to sit, the Taiwanese fisherman's mind eased. The gross defilements were overcome; and then, quite unexpectedly – for the mind is a curious organ, unpredictable and fickle – he found himself settling into a condition of equipoise, body and mind as one, consciousness of breath blending with breath so that one could not be distinguished from the other. His mind was a clear blue sky, untroubled by the passing clouds of thought; his body was at ease. He was free from distractions and perturbations.

He continued sitting in this blissful state until a pain jabbed sharply into his shoulder. Mr Liao gasped and opened his eyes. His meditation dissolved, as must all things, like a flash of lightning in the dark of night, like the morning dew touched by the sun, like a bubble in a stream. Ibu Lana was standing by his side, preparing to poke him a second time. Mr Liao knew the healer, who had cured him of an unpleasant rash the previous year, and he quite rightly feared her. Looking up, he could see that she was in fighting mood. She had returned from Ibu Nilasera's house, where she had cast out the devils – there had been more than one – taking refuge in the vessel of the woman's body. Now she was in the Lovely Vista to attend to the Englishman.

'Mr Liao! Wake up!' she barked.

In his mind there burst a brief fluorescence of hot anger but his face remained calm. '*Ibu Lana, bagaimana?*'

The healer had a nun at her side. 'Oh, *baik-baik aja*,' she said. 'I am looking for the sick man from England.'

'He is on the first floor,' Mr Liao replied. 'Please, do not disturb my meditation.'

Ibu Lana pulled a face. 'Come on, Suster, let us leave this man to his sleeping,' she said. She marched off towards the stairs, Suster Elena following behind.

Mr Liao closed his eyes again, but he could no longer concentrate. Angry, tangled thoughts filled his mind. He was uncomfortable. His right buttock itched. His shoulder still hurt where she had poked at him. 'Damned woman,' he muttered. He opened his eyes, stretched and got to his feet. He wanted a beer. He set off to wake Mr Tan.

In his room on the first floor, Sam Rivers was in a chair, dressed in a sarong and T-shirt, staring into the middle distance. It had been triumph enough that he had managed to move himself from the horizontal to something approaching uprightness. For the first time in his life, Sam had a beard, not having shaved for ten whole days since his arrival in Kenukecil. It was patchy and did not suit him.

Ibu Lana's pounding on the door with her fist stirred him from his stupor. 'Come in!' he called.

The door opened. Sam looked up at the astonishing mountain that was Ibu Lana, her thin white hair unkempt, her huge arms bulging. He smiled weakly, attempted to get up to greet his guest and, realizing that this was beyond his powers, slumped back into the chair.

Ibu Lana barged into the room, grinning her terrible grin, her eyes rolling. '*Tuan sakit?*' she bellowed. Suster Elena followed, smiling sweetly at Sam.

Yes, he nodded. He was *sakit*. 'Malaria,' he said.

'Pah!' Ibu Lana spat on the floor. She strode over to the sick man, pulled back his eyelids, peered into his ears, prised open his mouth – Sam's weakness prevented any effective resistance – and then, unexpectedly, pulled up his shirt to reveal his pallid and slightly rounded belly. Sam closed his eyes, as if this might drive away the hallucination. Ibu Lana poked at his stomach with fat fingers, harrumphing as she did so; apparently satisfied, she sharply tugged his shirt back down again. '*Bangun!*' she snapped.

Sam tried to get to his feet. Suster Elena helped him, lifting him from the chair and leading him to the bed.

'Lie down,' Ibu Lana commanded. The Englishman did as he was told. She rolled up her sleeves. For a second time, she pulled up his shirt and prodded thoughtfully at his stomach. '*Tuan ada sawang,*' she proclaimed authoritatively. You have a *sawang*.

'*Itu apa?*'

Ibu Lana explained. Then, to demonstrate the existence of this creature, this stomach-octopus unknown to Western science, she plunged her hands without warning into Sam's side, digging around with her fingers until she found a tender spot, which pulsed desperately beneath her fingers. Sam let out a breathless cry of pain as she jabbed at the throbbing place beneath her fingers. 'See!' she cried. 'It breathes!' And then she made a sound rather like this: *Doumm! Doumm! Doumm!*

Sam tried to lift an arm to wrestle her away, but he had no strength. Ibu Lana released the pressure and straightened her back. She cracked her fingers against each other. 'I will cure you,' she said with a smile. 'I will send the *sawang* back to sleep.'

So saying, she forced her fingers again into Sam's exposed belly, jabbing and poking as the thing beneath her fingers writhed and pulsed. Her face lit with an almost prophetic zeal, sibylline and ecstatic. The healing spirit of her ancestors entered her, took possession of her, directed her fingers as they poked and prodded. Sam writhed on the bed and cried out weakly but the Ibu's arms were strong, her enthusiasm for her healer's art unbounded.

It occurred to Sam that he might die there, on the bed in the Lovely Vista Hotel, far from his home soil, far from Fon, his internal organs ruptured by the onslaught of a madwoman. Then his body relaxed.

Ibu Lana sensed the change. 'Good,' she said. She gave a final jab and withdrew. She put a surprisingly gentle hand on the foreigner's brow. 'Sleep now,' she crooned. '*Tidurlah anakku!*'

Sam Rivers slept. He dreamed the sweetest and most untroubled of dreams and did not wake until the following day. He had only a faint recollection of Ibu Lana's incursion into his room. His body felt different. His limbs were light and at ease. His bed-sheet was not soaked with sweat as it had been for the days of his sickness. He got to his feet, waiting for the giddiness to catch up with him, but the nausea and heaviness did not return. He looked at his watch and saw that it was not long after noon. Very gingerly, he went down the corridor to the *kamar bak* and there he scooped cold water over his body, washing away the smell of sickness and the dried sweat of his fever. He towelled himself dry and put on a clean set of clothes: an open-necked shirt, a pair of loose cotton trousers and flip-flops. Then he shaved off the beard with slow, steady strokes of the razor, and examined himself in the mirror. He had lost weight. His eyes were sunken. But he looked better without the beard. He returned the towel to his room and made his way downstairs.

Thomas was seated at the reception desk with his laptop. The computer had been given him by a generous Australian woman who had visited some months ago. When Sam appeared at the front desk, Thomas was playing minesweeper, an activity that was beginning to occupy all of his waking hours. He was concentrating so hard that he did not look up when Sam entered, continuing to point and click.

'*Selamat siang*,' Sam said.

Thomas looked up. 'Mr Samuel!' he said warmly, in English. 'You are better?'

'It seems so.' Sam smiled.

'Ibu Lana came yesterday to make you well.'

'Ibu Lana?' asked Sam. His memory of the large woman who had come into his room – she had come with a nun and had done something painful to his stomach – was hazy; but he would not forget the pain. 'Yes,' he said, 'I think I remember. Thomas, tell me: what is the date?'

Thomas looked down at the bottom right of his screen, gave a couple of clicks and looked up. 'The fifth of November,' he said.

The cargo must already be in Bantuk, and today was Fonny's birthday. 'Shit.' Sam shook his head. 'Oh, shit.'

'You've been sick a long time. I will bring food. Would you like pancakes? I can bring them outside. It is a very nice day.'

'Yes, thanks, Thomas. First, however, I must make a phone call.'

'Please,' Thomas said, indicating the telephone.

Sam picked up the receiver. He looked at Thomas, hoping he might leave him a little privacy, but he was immersed in his game. Sam sighed and punched in Fonny's number.

He hadn't thought through what he might say, so he was unprepared when she answered. Hearing her voice, he hesitated. 'Hello,' she said, and as there was no response she repeated the word as a question: 'Hello?' The echo on the line seemed to amplify the distance.

'Fon,' Sam stammered. 'It's Sam. I wanted to wish you a happy birthday. I'm sorry.'

Silence.

'I've been ill,' he said. 'Very ill.'

'. . .'

'That's all, Fon. I just wanted to wish you a happy birthday.'

'. . .'

Sam turned his back on Thomas and lowered his voice. 'Fon, please. Say something. Speak to me.'

There was another pause, followed by a short gasp and a click. Then nothing but the sound of a dead line. Sam glanced at Thomas, who was pretending to concentrate hard on his game. 'Thank you,' he said quietly. 'I will be outside.'

He took a seat at a table on the jetty. Mr Liao was meditating again, motionless on his stool as he faced out to sea, attempting to recapture the deep concentration of the day before. By his side, drinking beer, sat Mr Tan, short and stocky with an angry look on his face and a mass of alarming tattoos swirling down each of his arms.

A line of boats – shark fishermen returning from a pre-dawn poaching expedition in Australian waters – straggled back into the harbour. A single thread of smoke trailed upwards from the forest into the clear sky. Sam thought of Fonny and a sob rose in him, like an air bubble rising from the sea-bed. He put his hand up to his face, waiting for the tears that he expected to follow, but to his frustration his eyes remained dry. Had anybody noticed him as he made these few short, broken gasps, they might have thought that he had something stuck in his throat, or a mild cough. He put his hand down again and looked up at the frigate birds. 'Oh, Fonny,' he murmured. 'Fonny.'

Thomas brought tea, sweetened with several large spoonfuls of sugar. Sam drank it in short sips, allowing the images of the previous days – part recollection, part dream, part hallucination – to reform themselves into something like a single story. He remembered Ibu Lana more clearly now, her white hair and hanging jowls, the pain of her fingers jabbing into his belly. He remembered Pak Wim's visits. More than one, he thought. And he remembered long hours where he had looked up at the ceiling and wondered if he was going to die there, in an upstairs room in the Lovely Vista Hotel, never to see Fon again.

He tipped his head back and watched the frigate birds gliding effortlessly overhead. He raised his cup of tea in a toast. 'Happy birthday, Fon,' he whispered. Remember, remember, the fifth of November. *Fuck*, he thought.

Thomas reappeared with pancakes and laid them on the table. 'I am happy you are no longer sick,' he said. 'May I join you?'

'Sure,' Sam said. He could do with some company.

Thomas sat down. 'Your friend Pak Wim came for you this morning,' he said. 'You were asleep, so he left you a message.'

Sam nodded, his mouth full of pancake. 'Was it good news?'

With a grin, Thomas shrugged. 'I do not know,' he said. 'There was a note. I will fetch it.'

Over the other side of the jetty, Mr Liao continued to sit without moving. Mr Tan, who did not share his boss's spiritual aspirations, signalled to Thomas by holding up a finger, his personal sign-language for 'another beer'. Mr Tan did not drink water. Only beer. 'Beer,' he liked to say, flexing his tattooed muscles, 'makes you strong.'

'Excuse me,' Thomas said, and went inside to fetch the drink and the note.

Sam watched as a sea eagle took off from the side of a building just along the shore. It climbed up into the brilliant sky and arced over the bay for a few moments before plunging for a fish. The fish bucked and writhed in the eagle's grip and then, with a violent spasm, shook itself free and dropped back into the water. The eagle flapped back to its perch, its talons empty, and hunched on the ledge, ruffling its feathers in disappointment.

Thomas returned with Mr Tan's beer. Then he passed Sam a scrap of paper. 'This is the message.'

Sam unfolded it, smoothing out its creases on the table. The note read:

*I hope you are better, Mr Sam. Ibu Lana is a very good doctor.*
  *We have a big problem.*
  *Come as soon as you are well.*
                                      *Pak Wim.*

# 14

As Sam re-read the note, Thomas frowned and scanned the skies overhead. 'Mr Samuel,' he said, 'listen.'

Sam looked up and listened. For a few moments he heard nothing, just the sound of water against the wooden piles of the jetty and the slurp of Mr Tan getting to work on his bottle of beer.

'Can you hear?' asked Thomas.

Sam shook his head.

Thomas turned his head to one side. 'Listen!' he urged again.

This time, Sam heard it: the distant sound of an engine.

'A plane?' Sam asked.

'Yes, a plane. But I do not know which plane. The next Kakatau flight is on the twenty-fifth.'

Sam saw it first: a gleaming splinter of silver that appeared to the south-east and began to describe a broad curve, as if the pilot was unsure where exactly to find the airstrip. Mr Liao broke his meditation and looked up. Mr Tan pointed. Sam put the last piece of pancake in his mouth.

'Come,' Thomas said. 'Let's go to the airport. If there is a plane, it may mean customers. I'll give you a ride. Since you arrived here in Bantuk, you have only seen the inside of my hotel. There is more to Kenukecil than the Lovely Vista, Mr Samuel.'

Sam hesitated. 'I have an important meeting,' he said. But as soon as he said it, he realized that the thought of facing Pak Wim and Pak Suryono – not to mention the preposterous sea-crossing to Turnbull Bay – was too much. What difference would a day make? It didn't matter. First, he needed to recover. To eat, to build up his strength.

'Mr Samuel?' Thomas pressed him. 'We must leave now.'

'Sure,' Sam said. 'I'm coming.'

They headed out into the street and climbed into the little Suzuki van. Thomas started the engine. They careered along the high street and headed north out of Bantuk, towards the airport. It was only three miles to where the track to the airport diverged from the main road. The verges were lush and green. Cows grazed idly by the roadside, looking up with languorous eyes as the Suzuki sped past. Sam gazed out of the window. The plane was lower now, flying a tighter circle as it got into position for landing. It was smaller than the Kakatau planes: a little single-prop, a two-seater at the most.

Thomas swerved around a pothole. 'Look' – he pointed out of the window – 'the plane is going to land.'

They turned off the main road and headed up the track towards the airport. Very low in the sky now, the plane's fuselage was glinting.

'Who is it?' Sam asked.

'I do not know,' Thomas replied. 'Government official, maybe? Bishop? ABRI officer? Prime minister? President? Pope?' He giggled.

'Pope?' Sam smiled.

'Who knows?' Thomas spun the wheel to avoid another pothole. The low concrete arrivals and departures building came into view. By the side of the road was a sign written in English: WELCOME TO BANTUK AIRPORT: PRIDE OF KENUKECIL.

At the end of the track, the bamboo barrier was lowered. Sam recognized Pak Amukwasi, the moustachioed chief of police who had checked his passport when he first arrived. He was standing by the barrier, one hand on his hip, the other sheltering his eyes from the glare of the sun as he looked up into the sky. A small crowd had already gathered. Several *petani*, having rushed from their plantations with machetes in hand, stood around restlessly. Thomas braked sharply before the barrier, leaned out of the window and called to Pak Amukwasi. '*Selamat siang, Pak Polisi*. What is happening?'

The police chief grinned, a crescent of magnificent white teeth appearing below his moustache. 'Who knows, Thomas?' he said.

'We're hoping for the pope!' joked Thomas.

'The pope?' Pak Amukwasi laughed. 'Maybe so. Come and see.' He eased up the barrier and Thomas drove through, pulled over onto the verge and cut the engine. Thomas and Sam jumped out of the van. Sam listened. Beneath the sound of the plane's engine, there was something else: the sound of singing, a choir of sorts; and it was approaching.

'I can hear singing.'

Thomas laughed. 'That will be the nuns.'

A few moments later, in a cloud of dust, the minibus arrived. Suster Elena was in the driving seat, steering the vehicle with the gusto of one convinced that she was under the protection of the Lord. Pastor Niemann sat beside her. In the rear seat were three other nuns dressed in white – each of whom had found a pretext to accompany the Suster to satisfy their curiosity about this unexpected apparition – and the earnest Benny, his guitar in his lap. Finally, Ibu Nilasera was crammed in amongst them, smiling, enjoying her return to good health after Ibu Lana's timely intervention. All the nuns were singing, accompanied by Benny's strumming, Ibu Nilasera improvising intricate harmonies over the top: *Puji Dia, puji Dia, puuu-jiii Diii-aaa* – Praise him, praise Him, praiiise Hiiim – they sang, the end of their song coinciding perfectly with their arrival. Suster Elena stopped the minibus and the nuns tumbled out. Suster Elena pinched Pastor Niemann, who had been sitting silent and stoical, on the arm. 'Why don't you sing, Pastor?' she asked, laughing. 'We need a bass voice.'

The pastor did not reply.

Giggling and chattering, Ibu Nilasera and the nuns flocked to the side of the airstrip. The pastor followed, a tired, strained smile on his face. Benny walked alongside him. As the priest passed Sam, he nodded in greeting, as one *orang bule* to another: a reserved greeting, not overly friendly.

The plane lined up for its final descent. The chief of police assumed his most genial smile of welcome. The wheels touched the tarmac. The aircraft bounced twice on the runway before its nose sank, then it disappeared behind the rows of palm trees. The spectators burst into spontaneous applause. The nuns cheered and waved.

Soon it reappeared, having turned at the end of the runway, and came taxiing to a halt. The propeller – a blur of metal and air – slowed until it was still.

Pak Amukwasi rushed onto the tarmac, his hand extended in welcome. Pastor Niemann stepped from the crowd, a second line of welcome. The nuns clustered together, chattering excitedly. Thomas stood to attention, ready to welcome this latest arrival to his hotel.

The cockpit of the plane opened and the pilot clambered out: tall, dressed in a hat and scarf, a small backpack on his back. He jumped down onto the runway and pulled off his hat. A flood of luxuriously curly blond hair, tinged with red, cascaded around his shoulders. The islanders stepped back in horror. Two of the nuns crossed themselves.

Truly the Last Days were nigh if a woman could fly a plane unaided, without even a husband by her side.

*

Dr Aletheia Groeber, PhD, MPhil, FRAS, FAAA, surveyed the crowd that had gathered to welcome her to Bantuk Airport. Then she strode across the tarmac and shook hands with Pak Amukwasi. 'Hello, Pak Polisi. Good afternoon. I am Dr Groeber.'

'Pak Amukwasi.' The police chief beamed.

Six foot three, in her late thirties, with her spectacular hair, utterly at ease with the fact of her own well-seasoned desirability, Dr Groeber was the most astonishing thing to have appeared out of the skies over Bantuk for a very long time. Pak Amukwasi – not ignorant of how handsome this woman was – switched to English. 'Welcome, Madam. Welcome to Kenukecil. How may we help you?'

'Well,' she said, 'what I'm really looking for is a husband.'

Pak Amukwasi could find no fitting response to this. He gulped. His smile wavered on his lips. Then he chuckled nervously.

Dr Groeber switched back to Indonesian. 'But before that, Pak Polisi,' she said, 'I'll need somewhere to stay, and I could do with a drink. Flying is thirsty work. Can I leave my plane here?'

'Of course,' Pak Amukwasi replied. 'We are not expecting another flight until the twenty-fifth, so it is no problem until then. Let me introduce you to Thomas. He owns the hotel. You must also meet Pastor Niemann, the priest. He is from Holland and is a good man. He knows a lot of things about Kenukecil. Come with me.'

The chief of police led Aletheia across the tarmac towards the pastor. 'Pastor Niemann,' Pak Amukwasi said.

Pastor Niemann spoke in English. 'Miss . . .'

'Groeber,' Aletheia said. '*Doctor* Groeber. Anthropologist. But you can call me Aletheia. Or Ally, if you like. And you are Pastor *who*?'

'Pastor Niemann. Welcome.'

She beamed. 'A missionary? Fan-*tas*-tic. Talk about lost tribes.'

Pastor Niemann gave a wan smile.

Aletheia looked around the crowd and saw Sam a few yards away, next to Thomas. 'Another missionary?' she asked him.

'No. Not at all. Really, no,' Sam replied.

'English?'

Sam laughed. 'Yeah. How did you guess?'

Pak Amukwasi took the anthropologist's arm. 'And this,' he said, indicating the man at Sam's side, 'is Thomas. He owns the hotel.'

There was a great deal of discussion and handshaking before they were ready to leave the airport. The pastor was the first to depart, nodding towards Benny with a curt 'We go.' They started to walk back to the minibus. The nuns followed, whispering and glancing back over their shoulders at Aletheia. Once back in the minibus, even before Suster Elena had started the engine, they had resumed their rendition of *Puji Dia*. Benny hauled the guitar back onto his lap and started to strum. Pastor Niemann sat in the passenger seat, frowning. Suster Elena turned the key in the ignition and put the minibus into reverse to execute a tight turn, before setting off back to Bantuk. The farmers trickled back to their fields, discussing the new arrival in animated Kenukecilese.

Aletheia turned to Pak Amukwasi. 'Thanks for the welcome party,' she said.

'OK. Good luck, Dr Groeber,' Pak Amukwasi replied, giving her a warm handshake. 'If you have any trouble, then please contact me at the police station. I will be able to help.'

'Thanks. See you again.'

'*Ayo!*' said Thomas. 'Let's go.'

Thomas, Sam and Aletheia Groeber walked towards the van. Thomas opened the door for the American, inviting her to sit in the front. As they pulled away from the airport, Thomas sounded the horn in farewell and Pak Amukwasi gave a good-humoured salute. They started down the track to rejoin the main road.

'Is that your plane?' Sam asked, leaning forward so that his head was between the two front seats.

'Sure is. Learned to fly in Montana. Dated a flying instructor, so got my lessons free. It's a great plane: Indonesian made, Italian design – but I try not to think about that when I'm in the air.' She turned round and gave Sam a brilliant smile. 'And what are *you* doing here, Englishman?'

Sam hesitated. 'It's a long story,' he said. 'How about you?'

'Me?' Aletheia replied. 'As I told the policeman, I'm looking for a husband.'

Aletheia Groeber was the offspring of not one, but two philosophers. Her mother, Dr Frances Groeber, was a Wittgensteinian working in the analytical tradition while her father, Professor Andreas Groeber, was a scholar of Heideggerian, which is to say continental, which is to say decadent, propensities. The Groebers' marriage was marked by perpetual cerebral warfare. Andreas had given their first child the name Aletheia, out of the desire to irritate his wife, and after the birth of their second child his wife had had her revenge: she had insisted on the name Ludwig.

Both children were a disappointment to their parents. Ludwig left school at sixteen, despite every sign of early promise, and found work in a sawmill. Meanwhile Aletheia won a scholarship to study anthropology at the University of Pennsylvania. Her parents were united for once in their disapproval, regarding her chosen discipline as intellectually bankrupt. She studied first for a BA and then an MA and was widely recognized as a student whose intelligence was only matched by her daring. Her PhD thesis, based on fieldwork in Peru, was provocatively entitled *Participant Penetration: Sex, Savagery and the Collapse of Epistemological Boundaries*. At the age of twenty-three, doctorate in hand, she became assistant professor of anthropology at the University of Montana, where she learned to fly and rewrote her thesis as a popular work. *Fuck the Savages* entered the *New York Times* bestseller list, leading to a flurry of envious sniping in anthropological journals. The first and second editions sold out almost overnight.

After ten years in Montana, Aletheia applied for a grant to carry out a research project in Indonesia. Her application was successful. She flew to Jakarta, bought a plane and took to the skies. When Aletheia manifested herself in the forest clearing of Bantuk Airport and announced to Pak Amukwasi that she was in search of a husband, this was neither a joke – as he had imagined – nor was it a sign of desperation in a woman who had experienced bad luck in love. She had enjoyed many lovers in the course of her life and had no trouble in finding new ones to fit her protean sexual appetites. Her desire for a husband was motivated only by the most elevated intellectual aspirations. With commendable fearlessness, Aletheia Groeber aimed to get to the bottom, once and for all, of the question that stalked the borders of anthropology. The question was this: was there not after all some truth in what the soft-hearted liberals liked to refer to as the 'myth of primitive sexuality'? Or, to put it more simply, do savages do it better? In pursuit of an answer to this question, Dr Groeber was looking for a savage to marry. She was looking for a savage to fuck.

Thomas parked outside the hotel. Aletheia climbed out, glancing up and down the high street. Most of the shops had their shutters down as the shopkeepers dozed through the heat of the afternoon. A few knots of bored youths lurked in what shade there was. Other than this, the street was deserted. 'Phew!' she said. 'One-horse town. Looks pretty Wild West around here.'

'Yeah,' Sam agreed as he stepped out into the street. 'Isn't it?'

Aletheia grinned at him. 'Hey, Englishman, I need to have a wash and take a break,' she said. 'Is there anywhere to have dinner in this island?'

'The hotel's fine,' Sam said.

'See you at dinner, then? It's a date. What time do you eat?'

'Um,' Sam hesitated. 'Seven? I don't know. I've not eaten for days. I've been under the weather.'

'Not the food, I hope?'

'No.' Sam laughed. 'Malaria. Or something.'

'OK,' Aletheia said. 'See you at seven.'

# 15

From the point of view of the local population, Dr Groeber's arrival in Kenukecil was both astonishing and at the same time somehow predictable, being only the latest in a long line of clear manifestations of the madness of *orang bule*. If the people of Kenukecil believed that Westerners were not entirely sane – predictably unpredictable, occasionally amusing, sometimes alarming, often arrogant and stupid, sometimes friendly, but never sane – this was not an arbitrarily formed opinion, but based on years of close observation and much perplexed thought.

Legend had it that the first Western visitors to Kenukecil were a few unfortunate Dutch sailors, marooned on the west coast of the island in 1789. The Dutchmen, it was said, intermarried with the local population; and it was their genes that accounted for the fact that one in every fifty or so children in Kenukecil was born with blue eyes. Leaving these perhaps mythical sailors on one side, it was not until 1912 that the Dutch government first took an interest in Kenukecil, a year in which the inhabitants of the island came to understand that Westerners were a race of people who believed, above all, in the importance of making an entrance.

Pastor Kruywers, the ethnologist-priest, armed with higher degrees in both anthropology and theology, was the first to arrive, coming to claim the island for God and the Dutch Crown. He was the beginning of the lineage of Dutch priests of whom Pastor Niemann would be the last.

In contrast to Pastor Niemann, Kruywers was given by nature not so much to contemplation as to action. Backed up by a contingent of fierce Dutch troops, the priest's innovative methods – of which his superiors disapproved while at the same time commending their expediency – ensured that little blood was shed in his conversion of the heathen Kenukecilese.

In addition to being a priest, a theologian and an anthropologist, the polymathic Kruywers was also a trumpeter. His trumpet, supported by his impressive beard and enormous girth, was his chief instrument of conversion. His arrival in Kenukecil was, quite literally, with a fanfare.

Kruywers and the small platoon appeared one Thursday afternoon in March 1912 when the tulips were blooming back home, in a vessel carrying a month's supplies. A nervous white horse stood in the bows, the priest, resplendent in a white surplice, mounted on its back. The soldiers crouched down with their guns pointed shoreward as the boat sailed into the bay. The Kenukecilese, armed with spears, bows and arrows, launched a small fleet of canoes and paddled to meet the visitors, thirty dugouts in all, heading towards the boat where Kruywers sat motionless and erect on horseback, beard quivering, gaze straight ahead, a trumpet and a cross hanging from a strap around his neck. When the canoes were within range, the priest raised the cross to the heavens. At this pre-agreed sign, the soldiers let fly a volley of bullets into the air. Then the priest put the trumpet to his lips and played a fanfare from Handel's *Water Music*.

He had not planned to play the *Water Music*, leaving the choice of welcoming tune to providence, the circumstances of the moment and whatever inspiration the Lord saw fit to provide. Removing the trumpet from his lips, Kruywers cried out, in Dutch: 'In the name of the Father and of the Son and of the Holy Ghost, I claim this island and all the souls therein for the Lord our God. Amen!' This, too, the pastor had not planned to say: when the occasion came, the words burst from him almost prophetically.

Naturally enough, the Kenukecilese were thoroughly bewildered by this display. Having the good sense to realize that there was no enemy more dangerous than an unpredictable one, while also being mindful of the fact that this lunatic was accompanied by a contingent of heavily armed Dutch soldiers, they responded in the appropriate fashion, letting out a loud cheer of welcome. It was then that one of the soldiers, younger than all the rest and with an itching trigger finger – he had not been in battle before – panicked, thinking that this cheer was a war cry. The muscles in his finger contracted, his finger twitched on the trigger and a small explosion within the gun chamber sent a bullet hurtling across the waters to lodge itself – the fear that compromised his restraint did not compromise his aim – in the chest of a young Kenukecilese man who had been, until his mouth gaped in the surprise of death, cheering in enthusiastic welcome.

What followed could have been a bloody fracas had the formidable Kruywers not been equal to the situation. Letting go of the reins, he flung his arms wide, his trumpet in one hand, the cross in the other, his white vestments shining in the sun, and bellowed, 'Lord, have mercy upon your servant, afflicted by fear.' Then he leapt from the horse, which tottered anxiously, snatched the gun from the recruit, held it above his head and tossed it into the salt waters. Turning to the other troops he commanded them with a glance to do the same. Nine more rifles went plunging into the sea, leaving the priest and his followers unarmed. Then, to make his point perfectly clear, Kruywers tore open his vestments, baring his naked breast tangled with dark hair. 'We come in peace!' he hollered, and for good measure he played another few bars of Handel.

The reception party, bewildered, nevertheless understood the symbolism of this gesture. They let up another cry, less enthusiastic than the first. The two largest canoes pulled up alongside the boat and escorted the visitors towards the beach.

As the boats came ashore, the soldiers – afraid now that their guns had gone – pictured cauldrons in which they would be boiled alive, sacrifices before strange gods. The half-naked Kenukecilese crowded round. The pastor did not blanch or blink, nor did he stare rudely at the women's breasts. Instead he went over to the man with the biggest head-dress of all and put out his hand in greeting. Shaking hands was not a habit of the Kenukecilese, so there was a brief pause. The pastor leaned forward and gave the man a bear hug. Then he leaned back and beamed.

The bear hug led to some intense discussion in Kenukecilese. Perhaps the poor recruits imagined that the locals were debating how best they might be cooked, whether boiled or baked or slowly steamed in a pit with hot stones, but their fears went unrealized. This brief conference was followed by further cheering and then the little party of Dutchmen was escorted up the beach and given *sopi* to drink.

By the middle of the afternoon, everyone except Pastor Kruywers was drunk. The Christian faith being one of the few in which the consumption of alcohol is ritually sanctioned, throughout his long and rigorous training for the priesthood Pastor Kruywers had necessarily undergone a slow process of inurement to the effects of ethanol. It is no accident that the saying, 'He holds his drink like a priest,' has been recorded in at least thirty-seven countries. Nevertheless, it was in a state of some high-spiritedness that the pastor led the first twelve Kenukecilese down to the river to be baptized. The baptism was somewhat improvised. The pastor stripped down to his underwear and wrapped a sarong borrowed from the local village headman around his waist. As he poured the redeeming waters over the heads of the new converts, twelve souls were saved from damnation – even though those souls, drunken and excitable, knew neither that hitherto they had been damned nor that henceforth they were saved. Such are the mysteries of faith.

Thus when Aletheia Groeber stepped out of the plane, the Kenukecilese did not think, 'What kind of creature is this?' but instead, with the benefit of more than eighty years of accumulated understanding, 'May both God and the ancestors protect us, for here comes another one.'

At seven o'clock on the evening of Dr Groeber's arrival, Sam waited on the jetty at the back of the hotel. That afternoon he had slept a little, taken a stroll around Bantuk, avoiding the area around the harbour, and done everything in his power to put off a meeting with Pak Wim and Pak Suryono. He had bought some paper, stamps and an envelope and attempted to write a letter to Fonny, but after eleven drafts – some a single sentence long, others running to two or three pages – he had given up in despair.

Aletheia arrived at seven thirty. 'Hey, Englishman,' she said. 'You been waiting long?'

'Not long,' lied Sam.

Aletheia pulled up a chair and sat down. 'What's there to eat?'

'I think whatever they've dragged out of the sea today,' Sam said. 'I haven't managed to eat much since I arrived here. Anyway, fancy a beer?'

Dr Groeber nodded. Sam went inside and ordered a couple of beers. He returned to the jetty, sat down and smiled across the table at Aletheia. She was pretty, he thought. No, pretty was not the word. Striking, perhaps. But she was not his type. He did not know what his type was – Vanessa had not been his type; and Fon, well, Fon wasn't exactly a *type* – but he was sure that, whatever his type was, Dr Groeber wasn't it. Anyway, he reminded himself, he was engaged to be married. Or he hoped as much, despite the difficult, silent phone call earlier that day.

For the first few moments, Sam didn't know what to say. He made a few opening gambits, mentioning the weather. It was a warm evening, he said. Very nice. Aletheia Groeber seemed to find this funny. Having as yet no idea what other topic might be fruitful, with that curious awkwardness that characterizes the English he continued to discuss meteorological concerns that neither of them shared.

Thomas rescued the conversation, bringing more beer and two plates of food. 'So, what do you think this is?' Aletheia asked, looking at the plate – the usual combination of exotic sea-creatures, rice and limp dark-green vegetables, served with the cook's superb *sambal* – and lifting something unidentifiable up with her knife.

'Your guess is as good as mine,' Sam said. He put a forkful in his mouth. 'Tastes OK though. It's best not to think too hard what it might be.'

By the time they finished their meal, the conversation was flowing. When they ran out of beer, Thomas appeared with more. Had Sam known the expression, he would perhaps have noted that Aletheia held her drink like a priest. Not only this, but she was an enthusiastic conversationalist. She talked with passion about her research, making frequent, breathtaking diversions – discourses on the initiation rites of the Sambia; diatribes against the philosophers, the clergy, the relativists, the liberals, the conservatives, the Americans, the English and the Indonesians; long, rambling accounts of the effects of the publication of

Malinowski's scandalous fieldwork diaries; paeans of praise to the virtues of home baking and the work of Irma S. Rombauer. Sam managed to keep up for four beers, but by nine o'clock exhaustion was getting the better of him.

'You tired?' Aletheia asked him.

'A bit,' he said. 'I've been ill.'

'Yeah.' She yawned. 'You said. One thing you haven't told me,' she said, 'is what you are doing in Kenukecil. Why are you here?'

Sam's eyes slid towards the horizon. He sighed. 'As I said, it's complicated.'

'You're not a smuggler, are you?' Aletheia asked.

'No. Well . . . No,' he said. 'I'm buying and selling.'

'Contraband?'

Sam attempted a laugh. 'No,' he said. 'Handicrafts.'

'Handicrafts,' she said thoughtfully. 'Right. By the way, you haven't seen any savages out there for me?'

'I haven't seen anyone.' Sam smiled. 'Except Thomas here in the hotel and some old woman who . . . Christ, I don't know. She did something to me to cure me of my fever. I've lost track of things since I arrived here.'

Dr Groeber looked at her watch. 'Hey,' she said, 'it's been a long day for me too and I'm going to start work tomorrow. I think I'll head north up the island. Or perhaps I'll go into the forest to the west. Either way, I should turn in. Nice speaking to you.'

'And you,' Sam replied.

Aletheia got to her feet. She paused, a thought flickering through her mind, a whim. 'Hey, Mr Englishman, you wanna sleep with me?'

Sam looked at this astonishing woman with few traces of desire. 'Um,' he said.

'*Um?*' She laughed without mockery. 'That's what you English guys say, right? *Um!*' She shook her head. 'I'll take that as a no.'

'It probably was,' Sam agreed. Then he added, 'You wouldn't like me anyway.'

'I wouldn't?'

'Not savage enough,' said Sam, taking a sip of beer.

Aletheia Groeber paused for another second or two. Sam shrugged.

'Goodnight, Englishman,' she said.

Sam smiled as he watched Aletheia walk back into the hotel. When she had gone, Sam went in to order another beer. Only when he got to his feet did he realize how drunk he was. He ordered the beer regardless and worked through it systematically. The evening was warm and he had a light sweat on his forehead. He pressed the cold beer bottle to his skin.

When he closed his eyes, the memory returned: the gloom of the *Ratu Mela*, the thing that gazed back at him from the crate, like a glimpse in a dark mirror, the outstretched hand that he had not taken. He removed the bottle from his forehead and took another swig. Then he heard a voice, not much more than a whisper: 'Tuan.' He looked round. It was Pak Wim.

'Pak Wim! *Selamat malam,*' Sam slurred, his voice dragging with tiredness, drink and the fever's lingering undertow. '*Bagaimana?*'

Pak Wim drew closer to the table, his face crumpled with awkwardness. 'Tuan,' he said again. 'How is tuan's health?'

'*Baik*, Pak Wim.' It is good.

Pak Wim sat down, tentatively, his knees pressed together and his hands clutched in his lap, like a petitioner at the office of a minor official. 'I called for Ibu Lana. She cured you,' he said.

Sam thought about this. 'Thank you, Pak Wim,' he said quietly. 'I appreciate that.'

'She is very good doctor. Traditional doctor. She knows many things.' Pak Wim smiled, looking down at his feet.

'Is everything in order?' Sam asked. 'You left a note. It said there was a problem.'

'Yes, everything is in order,' Pak Wim replied, a little too hastily.

'The cargo is safe?'

Pak Wim paused. 'It is safe,' he said, his eyes not meeting Sam's.

Sam studied Pak Wim's face. The man looked across the bay at the lights of the boats out night-fishing. 'Are you sure?' he asked.

'Maybe, tuan. We thought you would come this afternoon, but you did not come. You must come to speak with Pak Suryono tomorrow. We must talk.'

'OK,' Sam said. Pak Wim looked tense and worried. He was making Sam nervous. 'You want a beer?' Sam asked, hoping that this might put him at ease.

Pak Wim shook his head. 'I must go, Mr Sam,' he said, fidgeting. 'I have things to prepare. You come tomorrow morning at eleven. We will meet on the pier, on the *Ratu Mela*.'

'OK,' Sam repeated.

Pak Wim got to his feet. 'Good night,' he said.

'Good night, Pak Wim.'

Pak Wim disappeared through the hotel out into the main street. Sam finished his beer and meandered back up to his room. He looked out of the window. He watched Pak Wim heading back through the market and then along the pier.

'I'm a fucking idiot,' he said to himself. 'What have I got myself into?'

# 16

At about the time that Sam Rivers was eating his pancakes and mulling over his silent conversation with Fonny, a little way up the coast from Bantuk the headman Pak Masela was standing at the gateway to the village of Desa Baru, fretting over a different birthday celebration. He was looking up at the ceremonial concrete arch that spanned the road, pulling nervously at the edge of his moustache. Another man stood by his side with several pots of paint, a clutch of brushes and a long bamboo ladder. They were gazing at the signboard above the arch. Painted on the board was a young couple, all idealistic dewy eyes and smiling mouths, a chubby, laughing baby nestling in the woman's arms and, behind them, a pretty village of white houses on an impossibly flower-strewn hill. Above this bucolic scene was the legend: WELCOME TO DESA BARU: KENUKECIL'S NEW MODERN VILLAGE.

'One year,' Pak Masela was murmuring, his eyes moist from recent tears. 'It has been only one year, and look!'

The arch was already beginning to crumble, the paintwork peeling. Nothing lasts in the heat and the damp. Only in the northern hemisphere would anyone have bothered to invent history. But it was not the signs of everyday decay that worried Pak Masela. More disturbing was the deliberate care with which somebody had scratched out the eyes of the baby, transforming that happy scene into something monstrous. And – just in case anyone from the village might believe that the baby's sudden blindness had been accidental – an anonymous hand had added a single word, scrawling it across the family group in red paint: '*Death!*'

'I will paint over it, Pak,' said the man with the brushes. 'The people from Amasi Dol did this. They are bad people.'

Pak Masela continued to fiddle with his moustache. 'We must have it repainted by sunset,' he said. 'We cannot welcome people to the party like this.'

He took a couple of steps back towards the village, but something stopped him. It would be bad luck to pass under a sign that said 'Death'. He skirted the arch and then resumed his passage along the road.

As he headed back to the village, he heard the distant purr of an engine. He looked up into the sky and saw a sliver of light, a plane. He watched it for a few moments, puzzled. Then Pak Masela shrugged and continued on his way back to the village. He had other things on his mind.

Of all the villages in Kenukecil, Desa Baru – the island's New Modern Village – was the most exceptional. In contrast with the orderliness of other villages, arranged with rows of houses running parallel to the sea, the most noble houses situated in the centre by the ceremonial square with its flagpole and church, Desa Baru looked as if some god had dropped a handful of houses on the hillside while hurrying to attend to urgent business elsewhere. Desa Baru was conceived in the minds of a progressive cabal of bureaucrats and architects in Jakarta who burned with missionary zeal at the thought of bringing the light of modernity to the benighted people of the outer islands. Despite every appearance of disorder, Desa Baru was built on impeccably rational principles. Each of the one hundred and fifty identical houses was surrounded by a small plot of land sufficient to grow food for a single family. Every plot was of an equal area, the individual plots tessellated together across the hillside to the south of the main road. In the centre, there was a village meeting hall, dubbed the Pancasila Hall, which doubled up as a venue for religious gatherings. By the roadside, three or four buildings were set aside as shops and general stores. As a finishing touch, two ceremonial arches spanned the main road at either entrance to the village. They were decorated with uplifting slogans and images of progress.

The one thing the developers, enlightened though they were, had not accounted for was the Byzantine complexity of Kenukecilese land disputes, a system of rights and entitlements and ritually sanctioned methods of retribution for those who infringed them. Thus when construction started in 1995, the people of the nearby village of Amasi Dol, affronted by this violation of their ancestral claim to the land on which the village was to be built, launched a series of guerrilla raids on the builders. One construction worker was impaled on an arrow and died in the hospital in Bantuk. Several more suffered injuries before they abandoned their work and fled the island. A few weeks later the builders returned, this time protected by a contingent of troops. The people of Amasi Dol, knowing that they had nothing to gain and everything to lose by prolonging their resistance, immediately ceased their assault.

The first families moved in at the beginning of November of that year, and the village was officially born on November the fifth. Government officials had selected these new villagers from across Kenukecil and surrounding islands. One hundred and fifty couples, all as yet childless, chosen for their youth, vigour and moral uprightness, moved in to Desa Baru to begin their new, progressive life. The opening ceremony was beautiful. The architect, arriving in Kenukecil for the first time, cut the ribbons on the arches at either end of the village. The inhabitants cheered with all the vigour of youth. A procession of old men from

Bantuk, in full *adat* dress and playing traditional songs on their flutes, marched down the street while women danced like noble frigate birds alongside, their head-dresses and ancestral gold resplendent. As the procession passed, schoolchildren, bussed in from Bantuk and dressed in red and white, lined the roads and tossed fresh flowers. Then, in a solemn ceremony held in the Pancasila Hall, attended by Pastor Niemann, Pak Amukwasi, the *adat* chiefs in ceremonial dress and countless government officials crowded on to rows of chairs, Pak Masela was anointed *kepala desa*, village headman, having been elected to this post according to the principles of guided democracy.

The new headman was a mild man with the watery eyes of an idealist and the moustache of one who feared that his claim on his own manhood was less than it should have been. Despite the air of dampness that hung about him, he was both young and ideologically sound: the ideal head-man. His wife did not attend the opening, for she was at that moment back at home, going through the labour pains.

On the night that he was sworn into office, Pak Masela's first child was born. It was a boy.

Two days after the ceremony, the army withdrew, handing over control of the village to Pak Masela. As a gesture of goodwill and to ensure the safety of the village they left behind a fierce individual with leathery skin from the island Flores who soon became known as 'the Colonel'. The Colonel had been a *peon* in charge of catering. His official title was 'Village Warden', but once the troops were out of the way he promoted himself to a higher rank. He had been given a rifle to help him carry out his duties, a house on the outskirts of the village, a stipend of small monthly payments and two sets of combat fatigues to lend him an air of legitimacy.

The night after the troops left, a raiding party from Amasi Dol, assisted by their northern neighbours in Amasi

Da, descended on the village to reclaim their lost territory. Fourteen of the one hundred and fifty houses in Desa Baru were burned to the ground. The ceremonial arches were defaced. The windows of the Pancasila Hall were broken. Thirty-five gardens were trampled. Twenty-five families fled into the night. At one point it looked as if the village might be razed entirely. Disaster was only averted when one of the raiders from Amasi Da accidentally speared a man from Amasi Dol, causing the two raiding parties to fall on each other, forgetting their mutual hatred of Desa Baru as they were reminded of the ancestral enmity between their two villages. The two parties battled each other in the streets until dawn while the New Modern Villagers trembled in their homes.

With the rising of the sun, the Colonel crept back from the beach where he had been hiding. He spent the first part of the morning marching through the stricken streets, waving his rifle in the air, proclaiming victory.

After the punitive raid, an uneasy truce settled between Amasi Dol and Desa Baru, and Pak Masela was able to turn his attention to other problems. Foremost amongst these was the question of the village's spiritual welfare: although the Pancasila Hall could serve adequately as a venue for religious gatherings, the village was without a priest. Pak Masela was not so idealistic that he was blind to the moral dangers of a village composed only of the young and fertile.

Two weeks after the foundation of the village, Pak Masela travelled to Bantuk for a meeting with Pastor Niemann. Over tea and some delicious Dutch fruit cake, he asked if the priest would be willing to conduct a weekly service in the Pancasila Hall.

The Dutchman refused. 'The building is not consecrated,' he said, 'and I already have several Sunday services to conduct. If the people of Desa Baru wish to worship on a Sunday, they can do so in the church at Amasi Dol, or else make the journey to Bantuk.'

Hanging his head in disappointment, Pak Masela left the pastoran. How could he ask his people to worship in Amasi Dol, the home of their enemies, the people who had burned down their homes and trampled their gardens? How could he ask them to travel seven miles to Bantuk just to pray? The spectre of a morally rudderless village, adrift on the seas of ignorance and desire, rose before him. Then, as he walked towards the Hope Market to catch the bus home, he remembered his cousin, Pastor Freddy. He changed course, heading up to the telephone exchange.

Pastor Freddy was born in the village of Sapratian, although he had lived most of his adult life in Ambon, where he had become a Pentecostal minister. Pak Masela had not seen Pastor Freddy for several years, but he knew that his cousin was famous for his piety and for the depth of his religious conviction. Desa Baru was nominally Catholic but – here the headman thought along impeccably modern lines – didn't *pancasila* morality insist that there was only one God, worshipped by Protestants, Catholics, Muslims, Hindus and Buddhists alike?

At the telephone exchange he called his brother in Ambon, who found Pastor Freddy's number. Pak Masela wrote it down. Then he called the priest. 'Pastor Freddy?'

'Yes?' The voice at the other end was curt, almost angry.

'It is your cousin, Pak Masela. I would like to make you an offer.'

Drawn by the promise of one hundred dollars, his own church complete with congregation, a regular stipend to be funded by subscription, and free housing, Pastor Freddy arrived in Kenukecil on Christmas Day, 1995. He came on the Perintis ship from Ambon, a journey which had taken five nights, and was met on the docks at Bantuk by the headman and the Colonel. Pak Masela had not seen Freddy since they were children, but despite the passage of years he recognized the cousin he had known as he came storming down the gangplank. Pastor Freddy was a stocky man. His hair was wild and stood out almost horizontally from either side of his head in bold defiance of the law of gravity. His forehead was cut with deep furrows, the marks of a lifetime of scowling. Hanging from around his neck was an ostentatious silver crucifix, and his shirt buttons were undone to mid-chest. Luxurious dark hairs curled on his breast.

Pak Masela and the Colonel greeted the priest with a handshake and then an embrace. They hurried him back to Desa Baru where, in the Pancasila Hall, a communal meal had been arranged to welcome him. Trestle tables were laid out along the length of the hall and a kind of throne – a chair raised on a dais, swathed in *ikat* cloths – had been prepared for the new priest. When Pastor Freddy entered the hall, the villagers all cheered and, garlanding him with flowers, led him to the seat.

First they ate. Pastor Freddy broke bread with the people of Desa Baru, and they celebrated the feast of Christ's birth with rice, fish and *sambal*. When the meal was over, Pak Masela made a short speech, wishing everybody a happy Christmas and welcoming the pastor, who lifted the crucifix from around his neck and clasped it between his hands.

Then Pastor Freddy rose to his feet. 'Thank you for your welcome,' he said. He gave a smile that swept across the audience like a beam of light cutting through a fog of darkness. 'When I look at this village,' he said, 'I see only hope. I see only faith. I see only youth. I see only joy.' He smiled. 'Let us sing together, in hope and faith and youth and joy.'

Freddy's new parishioners stood to sing a hymn. The priest sat down, closing his eyes. It was one of those songs which leaps maniacally around the stave in an attempt to emulate the delirium of the soul that has found its joy in the love of Jesus. When the hymn was finished, the congregation sat down, gazing at Pastor Freddy adoringly: their own priest!

Pastor Freddy opened his eyes and gave a great sigh. Now he scowled at his audience. 'Christ,' he said softly, 'is Batjameni.'

And then, so that there could be no doubt about the matter, he added, 'Batjameni is Christ.'

Several members of the audience exchanged puzzled looks.

'Amen,' Pastor Freddy concluded.

'Amen,' the people of Desa Baru replied.

Pastor Freddy's first sermon was finished. 'Go in peace!' he said. And with dignity, the pastor rose to his feet and left the hall.

# 17

So began the curious rule of Pastor Freddy in Desa Baru. Pak Masela and his wife were the first converts to the syncretic faith that he had gnomically announced on the day of his arrival. Bunny Masela, the headman's younger sister, who was both sweet natured and willing – willing, that is to say, in those areas where willingness is commendable – and who was living with her brother, was the next convert. The Colonel joined up soon after. By the first Sunday after Christmas, which also happened to be New Year's Eve, Pastor Freddy had a small committed flock; and such was the stir his early sermon had caused that the Pancasila Hall was full for the service. Unfortunately, Pastor Freddy, carried away by the size of the congregation the week before, misjudged his second sermon. He spoke without pause for one hour and thirty minutes all told, expanding on his cryptic claim of the week before that Christ was Batjameni and Batjameni was Christ. As he spoke, he began to lose the hearts and minds of many who had gathered to hear him. The following Sunday, the church was a little less full and again the Sunday after that the numbers had appreciably diminished. His congregation settled down at somewhere around eighty regular devotees, the remainder of the villagers preferring to spend their Sunday mornings otherwise and elsewhere engaged.

For those eighty, however, Pastor Freddy offered more than a morning's distraction and the chance to daydream along with one's neighbours. For those who could penetrate the complexity of his theology, he offered hope: the hope that, when the Millennium arrived, Christ-Batjameni would return to redeem the faithful. The sky would roll back like a scroll and He – Batjameni and Christ, blessed with both male and female parts, a warrior and a man of peace, a man and a God – would appear from the sea towards the land. The faithful would be rewarded with microwave ovens, air conditioning, video recorders, televisions and eternal life; all others would be sucked down into the belly of the earth to burn in hellfire.

Although initially an enthusiastic adherent, Bunny lost her faith quickly. One evening after he had been in the village only a few weeks, the pastor – left alone with the girl in the headman's house – suggested that an effective means by which she could prepare for the coming of Christ-Batjameni was by providing relief to His servant on earth, after which he opened his trousers and attempted to grab poor Bunny's hand and guide it towards his stubby, twitching organ. Bunny kicked him in the shin, hard, and then ran out into the street, spluttering with angry humiliation. After that the pastor left her alone, but Bunny refused to have anything more to do with his faith. Her church attendance ceased. Pak Masela's eyes clouded with sadness as every Sunday he contemplated how her lack of piety might lead her to hell.

The religious diversion offered by Pastor Freddy conveniently distracted Pak Masela from the fact that the village of Desa Baru was dwindling. The abandoned houses were already falling into ruin. The gardens around those that were still occupied were overgrown. And now – on the first anniversary of the village – the arch that stood over the road from Bantuk was defaced. Nevertheless, he speculated as he returned to the village, they had survived a whole year, they had purified themselves in anticipation of the coming of Christ-Batjameni, and this at least called for a *pesta*.

In the spirit of good-will, fraternal invitations had been issued to the people of Amasi Dol and Amasi Da for the celebration that evening. The women of Desa Baru were ordered to prepare food: rice, fish and *sambal*. A sound system was acquired from Bantuk so that there could be dancing. Mr Gu was contacted and asked to send his finest prostitutes, on the basis that even the most moral and upstanding of villagers might on occasion be inclined to err and that erring with a prostitute was – on balance – a lesser sin than erring with a neighbour's wife. The Colonel was appointed to guard duty, bribed by several packets of clove cigarettes. Pastor Freddy spent the forty-eight hours prior to the party shut away in his house, claiming that he wished to pray and reflect at this auspicious time.

The guests arrived at the Pancasila Hall soon before seven. The Colonel checked the credentials of all who entered, glaring furiously at the visitors from Amasi Dol and Amasi Da, although they were polite and courteous and not even the Colonel could find any reason to evict them. Pak Masela turned up at seven precisely, accompanied by Bunny and his wife, who carried their son in her arms. A little later, Pastor Freddy emerged from his confinement and also joined the party. A dais had been set up at the front of the hall in the place where Pastor Freddy was accustomed to delivering his sermons. As he did not dare sit in the place where the prophet customarily sat, Pak Masela stood to one side to give his short speech. He thanked all those who were present, praised the slight achievements of the previous year and expressed the hope that the coming year would be an even greater success.

Then he invited Pastor Freddy to speak. The audience response was mixed: those for whom Freddy was indeed a prophet held their breath in anticipation of a great and lengthy oration, while those for whom he was nothing more than an inconvenience began to shuffle with the expectation of boredom.

Freddy scowled at the audience and installed himself on his throne. 'In the name of the Father,' he began, 'in the name of Christ-Batjameni the Son, and in the Name of the Holy Spirit. Welcome to Desa Baru. Tonight we celebrate our first birthday, here in the sight of the Lord.' He paused, the tension in the air palpable. Then, to sighs of both disappointment and relief, he simply said, 'Enjoy the party. Thank you,' rose to his feet, smiled a saintly smile and left the hall.

The music started and the dancers took to the floor. The *kepala desa* relaxed, smiling across the room at his wife, who cradled their sleeping child in her arms. The Colonel marched in and out of the hall with his rifle. A group of women started to serve food to the gathered guests, a small scoop of rice, a little fish and some *sambal* each. Mr Gu's butterflies arrived punctually, after no more than three or four songs, their appearance signalled by the horn of a truck outside. Pak Masela left the hall to greet the women who had come as guardians of public morality, their exquisite yellow dresses gleaming in the light that flooded out of the hall into the warm evening: Mr Gu's best girls. Pak Masela smiled to see the women laughing and joking as they climbed down from the truck. What sacrifice is theirs, he thought. They might burn in hell themselves, but their clients, committing lesser sins in the place of greater, might thereby be saved.

The driver leaned out. He knew Pak Masela: they had been classmates at school. 'Are *all* these for you?' he asked, with a raucous laugh.

Pak Masela laughed. Turning to the women, he greeted them: 'Welcome. The dancing has begun. Please, first you must eat. The dancing and . . .' he paused, momentarily flustered, before continuing '. . . and all of that can come later.'

Fifteen women dressed in yellow burst into the Pancasila Hall and began to dance through the crowd. They were brilliant while all the other dancers were dull, fluid while the others were brittle. The village women turned their faces away at the shame of it, the men grinned in delight.

Pak Masela sat down beside his wife. 'The party is very good,' he said. 'Everyone is happy.'

The moon began to climb over the palms. Outside, huddles of drinkers clustered around bottles of palmwine. The Colonel chased them away with his rifle, but given that he was one and they were many, for every group he dispersed, another formed. It kept him busy.

At intervals one of the women in yellow would interrupt the dancing by dragging a man from the hall, out into the night. Somewhere, not far from the hall, Pastor Freddy had retired again to his house. If anyone had walked past, they might have wondered at the most unholy sounds that were emanating from inside.

It was close to the end of the evening, when the dance floor was beginning to empty, that Pak Masela asked himself, for the first time, 'Where's Bunny?'

The girl had disappeared. The headman had given his sister instructions not to step out of the hall, not even for a moment, out of fear of the immorality that might be taking place in the dark. But she was gone and he had no idea how long she had been missing. He went over to his wife. 'Where is my sister?' he asked.

She looked up at him. 'I don't know. Is she not here?'

He shook his head.

'Outside?'

'I will look.'

Pak Masela left the hall. There were knots of young men drinking *sopi*. From somewhere in the dark came the sounds of immorality, the squeals of women, the panting of men. Bunny? Pak Masela thought. No, not Bunny. He heard more squeals, followed by muffled giggles. Pak Masela felt sad at the sounds of sinfulness so close to hand. He went over to a group of young men, these from the village of Amasi Da. 'Have you seen my sister?'

'Is she the one with a mole on her tit?' one of them asked. The others all started to laugh. 'Or is she the one who is good with her tongue?' He made an obscene gesture.

Pak Masela looked confused.

'Perhaps she's the one who likes it at both ends at once?' a third man asked.

Pak Masela opened his mouth, a reprimand on his tongue, but then he blushed at the anger beginning to rise within him. 'Christ is Batjameni,' he whispered to himself, in the hope that this might calm his sinful heart. 'Batjameni is Christ.' As he walked stiffly away, he felt the pricking of tears that he interpreted as tears of compassion at the thought of these lost souls.

Pak Masela went to his house. Bunny was a simple girl. Perhaps she had retired to bed early. The little concrete house was empty. 'Bunny!' he called. There was no reply.

Pak Masela returned to the hall. 'She's gone,' he said to his wife.

'She will return,' his wife replied: a woman herself, she knew that women usually did. In their own time.

Ibu Masela was right. Bunny returned an hour later, dragged by the Colonel into the Pancasila Hall, his right hand clutching at her long, dark hair as he waved his rifle in the air with the other, shouting. Somebody turned off the music. Those who had been wheeling on the dance floor scurried towards the walls. The Colonel pulled

Bunny into the centre of the hall. Her clothes were in disarray so that while she was not exactly indecent her state suggested the aftermath of the most profound indecency.

It was at that moment that Pastor Freddy stumbled back inside, accompanied by three yellow butterflies. He straightened his back and puffed out his chest, brushing off the butterflies, who fluttered towards the wall, where they came to rest. Somewhere, in the sudden silence, a lizard could be heard calling: *tok-eh, tok-eh, tok-eh*. Just the lizard and Bunny's rasping breath, the Colonel's hand tight around her hair. Her eyes were lowered and her cheeks flushed. A smile flitted on her lips.

Pak Masela stood at the side of the hall. 'Bunny,' he asked quietly, 'where have you been?'

'She has been fucking, Pak,' the Colonel said. He showed considerable delight in unmasking Bunny Masela's misdemeanour.

Pak Masela walked slowly across the hall towards his sister. 'Bunny,' he asked gently, two hundred pairs of eyes on him, 'can this be true?'

Bunny's lip trembled, but she said nothing.

Pak Masela touched her arm and then lifted a strip of her torn clothing. 'Who was it that did this?'

He wanted to see distress, remorse, modesty on her face; but instead he could detect that same half-smile. It made him want to strike her, he who had never struck anyone in his life, not even his wife.

His fingers continued to feel the cloth. 'Tell me who it was, Bunny.'

Bunny's smile grew wider. It was not a smile for the benefit of those around her but purely private.

The headman let fall the torn fabric and turned to the Colonel. 'Did you see the man?'

'He escaped,' the Colonel said. 'I fired into the woods. I might have struck him.'

'Who was he, Bunny?' Pak Masela took her by the hand, imploringly.

She started to giggle.

'Why did you go with him? Did he force you? Was it one of the men from Amasi Dol or Amasi Da?' He began to tremble with that horrible violence peculiar to weaklings.

Bunny pulled her hand away and looked her brother in the eye. 'I fucked him,' she said softly. 'It was so good, brother. If only your wife was as lucky as I am.'

The headman struck his sister on the cheek. Bunny winced and staggered back a few paces.

One of the whores ran over, a flurry of yellow, and interposed herself between the headman and his sister. 'Tuan,' she said. 'No.'

Bunny wiped the blood from her mouth. The blow had not dented her smile. 'Brother,' she repeated, peering over the prostitute's shoulder, 'it was good. It was so good, I'm going to do it again. I'm going to do it every night. Every single night. I'd rather be a whore than live in this excuse for a village with that excuse for a priest who shows his taboo parts to the girls.'

Pak Masela took a step backwards. He could not allow this insult to pass. 'You would dare to slander our man of God? Bunny, what kind of devil has taken you? Tell me, Bunny: who was the man? What was his name? Your honour may be destroyed, but the honour of our family must be avenged.'

'His name?' she asked. 'I don't know his name. It is not his name that I was interested in. It was his cock.'

The Colonel leaned over to interrupt. 'Excuse me, Pak Masela. It was too dark to see clearly,' he explained, 'but I think that it was a short man.'

# 18

By the time Bunny departed the village of Desa Baru the following morning, 6 November, she had transmogrified into a butterfly of shimmering yellow. As she sat on the truck in the clear sunlight, toying with her hair, laughing freely, singing along with her sisters and fellow whores, Bunny Masela had every appearance of being, for the first time in her life, happy.

Riding in triumph to Bantuk, she passed not one but two *orang bule*. The first was a woman, astonishingly tall, with an arrogant bearing and a mass of reddish hair. She was striding along the road northwards, a pack on her back, sweating profusely. The second *bule* was a man with a troubled air who, as they drove along Bantuk high street, was walking from the Lovely Vista Hotel down towards the docks.

In Desa Baru, Pak Masela shut himself up in his house and refused to emerge. His wife, Ibu Masela, on the pretext of visiting her sick mother in Sapratian, left her husband's house in shame and never returned. Meanwhile Pastor Freddy took advantage of the events of the night before and of the rumours filtering up the coast from Bantuk that devils were abroad in the island, even daring to enter the Catholic churches, and told the Colonel to gather the village together for a meeting. The Colonel went from door to door, hammering on each one and dragging the hungover inhabitants out into the street, and herded them into the Pancasila Hall. Here the priest was enthroned, ready to address them on matters of the greatest importance. For the first time since his arrival, Freddy had an almost full house.

That same morning, a Wednesday, Pak Wim woke on board the *Siwalima*. After breakfast he made his way down the pier to the Hope Market to see Mr Gu. It was a fine morning and he was relieved that the Englishman had recovered. He only needed another day or two and then he would be paid his second five hundred dollars, easily sufficient to settle his debt. He was confident that Mr Gu would understand.

Mr Gu was sitting in front of his shop, sunning himself.

'Good morning,' Pak Wim said, raising a hand in greeting.

'Pak Wim, what news?' Mr Gu replied.

'I have come about the money,' Pak Wim said.

Mr Gu smiled. 'Good,' he said. 'Come in.'

He ushered Pak Wim into his shop. 'Tea?' he asked.

'No, thank you.'

'Just one cup,' Mr Gu insisted. 'Wait. I will boil the kettle.'

Once Mr Gu had attended to the kettle he settled down on a chair and smiled at Pak Wim. 'So, Pak, you have the money with you?'

Pak Wim nodded. 'Yes, everything is arranged. The Englishman who owed me is now better. He will pay me soon.'

Mr Gu narrowed his eyes. 'I asked if you have the money *with* you.'

'Not with me, tuan, no. But soon.'

'You will bring it later today?'

Pak Wim squirmed. 'Maybe today, maybe tomorrow, maybe the day after. The money is coming, Mr Gu.'

Mr Gu stood up. 'Two more days?' he asked. 'We agreed you would bring the money today. You owe me one hundred thousand rupiah, Pak Wim. Today is the deadline.'

'Two days is not long,' Pak Wim protested.

Mr Gu sighed. He turned away from Pak Wim and walked barefoot out onto the step in front of his shop. '*Ayo!*' he called. 'Karel!'

An enormous man who had been sitting chatting a little distance away got to his feet. He brushed down his trousers and then lumbered amiably over to the shop. On his face was a benign, almost sleepy expression.

Mr Gu nodded in greeting. 'Karel, we have a customer who cannot pay,' he said. 'I think that you will need to settle his debt.'

'He does not pay?' Karel's voice was unexpectedly high. An industrial accident several years before had stripped him of the attributes of manhood. Since then he had found employment as a guard in the butterfly house. 'Mr Gu,' Karel warbled, 'this is terrible.' The eunuch turned to Pak Wim and furrowed his forehead. 'You have no money, Pak?' he asked.

Pak Wim shook his head. 'Tomorrow,' he said. 'Or maybe the next day.'

Karel gave a sweet, sad smile. 'But tomorrow you might be dead,' he said. 'Then who will pay?'

Pak Wim carefully got to his feet. Karel was blocking the door. Mr Gu walked past the eunuch and pulled down the shutters, which screeched and rattled. He clipped on a padlock, locking the three of them inside. Pak Wim backed into a corner.

'Karel,' the Chinese merchant said, 'I will be upstairs, doing my accounts. Call me when you have finished.' He smiled at Pak Wim. 'Excuse me, Pak. Please, think of your debt as henceforth cancelled. But please do not return to my little business in future, or I will have you killed.'

Then he climbed the wooden flight of stairs up to the floor above and carefully closed the trapdoor behind him.

Karel grinned at the debtor.

Sam left the hotel just before eleven. In the Hope Market, Mr Gu, his shop-front open again now that Karel had finished his work, was sitting on the steps and enjoying a *kretek* clove cigarette. Seeing the Englishman, he called, in the fashion of local shopkeepers, 'Hello, mister,' rolling the final 'r'. 'Where are you going?'

'To the docks,' Sam replied without stopping.

Mr Gu waved him on his way. '*Selamat jalan*, mister,' he said.

'*Selamat tinggal, Pak.*'

Sam squeezed through the crowds and the buses that belched fumes into the air and hurried down the pier to where the boats were moored at the far end. He looked at his watch. It was eleven o'clock. He cast his eyes over the gathered boats – there must have been at least twenty, sometimes two and sometimes three abreast. He could not remember whether the *Ratu Mela* was painted red or blue, nor even whether it had a mast or not. All he could remember of that morning in Jakarta were the eyes that had stared out at him from the cage, holding his gaze.

'Pak Suryono! Pak Wim!' Sam called.

There was no reply.

'Pak Suryono! Pak Wim!' he repeated.

Again no reply.

'Shit,' Sam muttered. He sat down to wait on the low wall at the end of the pier. Fucking *jam karet*: fucking rubber time.

Sam looked out to sea. The day was becoming hot as the sun climbed to its highest point. He picked up a stick and doodled distractedly in the dust. The distant sounds of the marketplace and the suck of the sea on the pier calmed his jitteriness. He began to daydream, distractedly worrying at a small flap of skin hanging loose by the edge of his thumbnail.

*

Pak Wim appeared close to noon at the landward end of the pier. As he emerged out of the haze, calling out, 'Mr Sam! Mr Sam!', Sam returned to his senses and realized that his throat was parched. There was a burning sensation on his forehead where the sun had caught him. He rubbed his eyes with the thumb and forefinger of his left hand. Pak Wim was hobbling and one arm was lifted into a sling. Sam rose uneasily to his feet.

'Where the hell have you been?' Sam asked when Pak Wim was within earshot. Pak Wim took another few steps forward and then held out his one good hand palm upwards in a placatory gesture. '*Ma'af,*' he said. I am sorry.

Sam looked at Pak Wim's swollen face and his bandage. 'What news?' he asked.

'Accident,' said Pak Wim. 'I have been to the hospital. Nothing is broken, only bruises.'

Sam raised an eyebrow. The two men stood side by side, awkwardly. Sam looked about him. 'And Pak Suryono?'

'I do not know,' Pak Wim said. 'I have not seen him.' He winced with the pain of speaking. Sam studied his wounds and bruises. They were freshly minted. He decided not to ask. 'We must wait,' Pak Wim said.

Sam sat down and picked up the stick again. He scrawled spirals in the dust. Pak Wim walked over to the edge of the pier and watched the crabs crawl in and out of the cracked concrete.

Not long afterwards Pak Suryono appeared, ambling down the pier with some shopping bags. He smiled as he approached and put the bags down at Sam's feet. 'Good day, tuan. You are better?'

Sam put down his stick and, standing, shook hands. 'I think so.' He looked at his watch. 'Pak Suryono,' he said, 'our meeting was more than two hours ago.'

'I have been shopping,' Pak Suryono replied. 'I have bought food for our journey.' Sam was about to reply, but

Pak Suryono turned to Pak Wim, blinking at his wounds. 'Pak Wim? What has happened?'

'Accident,' mumbled Pak Wim.

Pak Suryono peered more closely at his broken face, the arm in the sling, the bruises. 'It looks bad,' he said. 'Were you in a fight?'

'I fell,' Pak Wim said. 'I have been to the *rumah sakit*. They have given me bandages and medicine. It is all right.'

'Pak Suryono,' Sam interjected, 'you said *our* journey? Are you now coming to Australia as well?' The relief brought about by the mere thought of having some company on his crossing to Turnbull Bay was so intense that he had to sit down.

'Yes, all three of us will be travelling,' Pak Suryono said, turning away from Pak Wim and becoming businesslike. 'First we must travel together. Later, you go alone to Australia.'

Puzzled, Sam frowned.

Pak Suryono's eyebrows arched. 'You see, Mr Samuel, we have a problem. Come and see for yourself.' The businessman held out a courteous hand, directing Sam along the pier towards the *Siwalima*. Pak Suryono climbed lightly onto it, crossed the deck, and stepped over the low guard rail to the vessel next door. 'The *Ratu Mela*,' he said. 'You remember? Come on.'

Sam followed. Glancing back over his shoulder, he saw Pak Wim lost in his own world, studying the commerce of crabs.

The Javanese businessman knocked once on the hatch. It lifted and Ibrahim emerged from the darkness below. Sam watched this unsmiling man, delicate in his gestures, as he lowered the hatch.

'Ibrahim. Good afternoon. The Englishman has come to see the damage.'

'Follow me,' said Ibrahim. 'Please.'

Sam followed Ibrahim below decks, leaving Pak Suryono outside in the sunshine. The first thing he saw was the shattered wooden cage, the bars forced back and splintered. The stink of animal was less strong than Sam remembered, more a memory than a presence. The creature had gone.

'And the cargo?' he asked Ibrahim.

The other man shrugged. 'Not here,' he said. 'The cargo is not here.'

Sam started to chew on the flap of skin by his thumbnail again. He tore it off with a sharp tug of the wrist. Wincing, he sucked the blood that was beading at the edge of his nail. 'What do you mean?'

'It has gone,' Ibrahim repeated.

'When?' Sam asked.

'Sunday morning, before light.'

'You didn't hear it?'

'Pak,' said Ibrahim, 'I was walking. It was a beautiful night –'

'What about Pak Wim and Pak Suryono?'

'Drunk,' Ibrahim replied. 'Pak, you were ill. We waited too long for you to recover. The cargo was . . .' Ibrahim trailed off while he searched for the right word. 'It was impatient,' he said. 'Please, Pak. You must speak with Pak Suryono. It is better you speak with Pak Suryono.'

Sam climbed back up the ladder, out into the open air. He glanced down at the fresh blood welling on the side of his thumb and lifted his hand to his mouth to suck it away.

Pak Suryono's face was all apology. Sam switched into English. 'Now what?' he asked.

Pak Suryono did not reply. He looked embarrassed. Then he smiled awkwardly. 'Gone, mister.'

'Where the fucking hell is it, Pak Suryono?' Sam snapped. 'You've dragged me all the way to Kenukecil, I've missed my girlfriend's birthday, I've probably ruined my chances of marrying her, I've invested the money left to me by my parents – and you just say "Gone, mister"?'

'Yes, Pak Samuel,' said the businessman evenly. 'Gone. So we must find it.'

Sam swore and sucked his thumb angrily.

Pak Suryono gave a tight smile and rubbed his hands together. 'I'm sorry, Mr Samuel. If you had not been sick, this would not have happened.'

Sam glared at him. 'What do we do?' he asked.

Pak Suryono's voice was soothing. 'Do not worry. There have been reports,' he said. 'I have been investigating.'

'What kind of reports?'

Pak Suryono reached into his jacket pocket and pulled out a notebook. He scanned a few pages. 'A woman saw something in the church at Bantuk, on the hillside over there. That was on Sunday afternoon. There were several sightings on Monday, although none of these can be confirmed. But last night – well, there was an *incident*.'

'What kind of incident?' Sam asked.

'It was in the village of Desa Baru. There was a party, a birthday party.'

'On the fifth?' Sam asked.

'Yes, Pak, yesterday.'

Sam smiled grimly. 'Shit,' he said. 'What happened?'

Pak Suryono gave Sam a curious look. 'It was,' he said, 'some kind of abduction.'

'Abduction?'

'A girl,' explained the businessman. 'A girl was abducted. But that's not all. This morning there have been more reports. I spoke to a woman who had come down to the market from Amasi Dol. She told me that she saw something in the forest. The cargo is heading north, Mr Samuel. We must take the boat, we must hunt it down and we must capture it.'

Sam looked back along the pier, his eyes skimming over

the low roofs of Bantuk. The spire of the church was visible a little way to the right and he could see the jetty at the back of the Lovely Vista. 'And when do you propose we leave?'

'Immediately,' Pak Suryono said. 'I will call Pak Wim and we will prepare ourselves.'

# 19

It was, however, late afternoon by the time they cast off from the end of the pier on board the *Ratu Mela*. Ibrahim set a course eastward first of all, towards Kenubesar, before they turned north, following the coastline of Kenukecil. Pak Suryono was at the stern next to Ibrahim, who held the tiller. Pak Wim sulked and nursed his wounds in the bows.

Sam, wrapped in a sarong, propped himself against the cabin amidships and gazed out towards the open sea on the starboard side, the land and the descending sun behind him. He could still feel the tug of lingering sickness, as if his mind might at any moment lose its buoyancy and pull him under into the waters of unconsciousness. Once they were out on the open sea, it was breezy. With every gust a shudder passed through the flesh of his body. He pulled the sarong closely about his shoulders, shifting his weight to be out of the wind. The background sound of the engines and the slap of the waves against the wood were soothing. On the port side, the tangled roots of mangrove swamps slid by silently. Down below in the clear waters jellyfish swarmed, the ghosts of fish. *Don't let the fever return*, Sam murmured, to no god in particular. *Please, don't let the fever return.*

His thoughts arced in a double orbit, describing tangled figures-of-eight between two centres of gravity: the first of these was Fon; the second was the memory of those eyes that had peered at him, a question, below the deck of the

*Ratu Mela* at Tanjung Priok. In his imagination, the hand still stretched out to him from between the bars, the hand that he had refused to take. He could still hear the noise the thing made, as if it was crying.

That afternoon in Jakarta seemed a long time ago. Back then, when he had emerged from below deck and regained his composure, he had asked Pak Suryono: 'What is it?'

'*Orang pendek*,' the businessman had replied. A short man.

In his first year in Indonesia, during a college holiday, Sam Rivers had visited Sumatra. There he had bought a book from a street stall with the title *Legends of the Forest-Men*. It was written in curious, broken English as if the author, knowing only a smattering of the language picked up from American films, had translated an Indonesian text word for word with the help of a dictionary. The subject of the book was Sumatran legends of the *orang pendek* or *Gugu*, an ancestor of sorts who lived in the depths of the forest and murmured in something strangely like human language. The tales were standard fare – the Gugu kidnaps a human child so that the child might teach it how to use fire, clever villagers trick the Gugu into giving up hordes of precious jewels from another world – but the book helped Sam pass what would otherwise have been a boring afternoon. Before he flew back to Jogja he left *Legends of the Forest-Men* behind in a café with a tourist book exchange to provide entertainment for some other bored Westerner and thought no more of it. Not, that is, until Tanjung Priok.

When Pak Suryono confirmed what Sam Rivers had suspected, the Englishman's initial instinct was to seek refuge in the comfort of old certainties. Surely, he told himself, these were only tales fit for children, for the elderly and insane, for those who had yet to be lifted out of the ignorance of superstition by the light of science and reason. The unicorns were no more – horses with tusks of narwhals created by idle taxidermists; no basilisks lurked in the crevices of the rocks breathing fire; the satyrs had long fled the hillsides so that not even the sound of their flutes remained. With a pride peculiar to *orang bule*, Sam believed himself beyond such phantoms and fantasies that belonged to the infancy of human thought. *But*, on the other hand, he asked himself, *was it not possible*? Was it not possible that in some hidden places – in isolated valleys in the forests of Sumatra where the rapaciousness of the logging companies had yet to penetrate, in the obscure reaches of some of the archipelago's remotest islands – creatures such as this might still flourish, no more or less monsters than we ourselves, creatures who went on two legs and who, were they to gaze into our eyes, might seem to be thinking thoughts not far different from our own as we, too, gazed back? Sam recalled those eyes that had looked into his below the deck, that outstretched hand. It seemed to him now, as he sat watching the sea's unchanging horizon and the languid drift of the jellyfish, that they had been groping towards a question; or if not a question, then a protest: *Am I not a man and a brother?*

At the helm of the boat, Pak Suryono's thoughts were not so metaphysically inclined. He was irritated by the disappearance of the cargo and resentful of the Englishman's illness and earlier rudeness. The procurement of the Gugu had been a long and complex process, and its loss at such a late stage was frustrating.

The Gugu had been discovered in the district of Kerinci in Sumatra, surprised by a pair of young lovers who, seeking a place to consummate their love far away from the prying eyes of their families, crept into a storehouse, trembling with desire, only to see what they first believed was a child rummaging through some sacks of dried fish. The creature turned to attack and the young man – being sharp-witted and seeing that here was no ordinary child – picked up a rock and, aiming it with considerable skill, rendered the intruder unconscious. He tied it up and had his way with the girl, reluctant to waste the opportunity. Then he dragged the stunned beast off into the jungle and left it in a forest hut. He went directly to the nearest town to speak with a Chinese merchant and together the two men returned to the forest to find the Gugu snarling with indignation and thirst. They gave it water, which it drank greedily. The merchant paid the young man two hundred thousand rupiah before administering another blow to the Gugu's head to silence it. The merchant took the creature back to his house, where he put it into a large wooden cage that he had bought along with a Sumatran tiger several years before. The tiger had died before he could sell it on and he had not managed to sell the empty cage, so kept it in storage. Once in the cage the Gugu promptly woke up and created a terrible hollering. The Chinese merchant gave it a bowl of food, which it knocked over, and another of palmwine, which it seemed to enjoy. It held the bowl in its hands like a man. He gave it four more bowls until it collapsed sideways and fell into a deep, contented sleep.

At first the merchant supposed that this creature was none other than one of his own ancestors, who had managed through the practice of various forms of Taoist magic to attain the longevity of the sages. He resolved to keep the creature in his household. The Gugu, however, was not a good guest. It masturbated frenetically whenever any female members of the family were present, pursing its lips into something like a kiss, and the merchant, scandalized by such behaviour, resolved to sell it, ancestor or no ancestor. The creature fetched one hundred thousand rupiah from a middle-man who received the creature comatose, smelling of palmwine, and kept it well topped up with drink while he took it by truck to Medan.

There Pak Suryono bought it for a very reasonable million rupiah. Pak Suryono locked the creature in a storage vault with food and water but no palmwine, and set about making arrangements for its sale overseas. He telephoned his associate Geoff Sainyakit in Australia, who found a buyer in Dr Plover. Next he rang Ibrahim, who worked for him in the capital, to arrange the passage to Kenukecil. The only difficulty was the short journey from Bantuk to Turnbull Bay, a journey that would take a single night, no more. It was then that he remembered Sam and, being a man of instinct as much as of reason, telephoned the Englishman to make him an offer.

Pak Suryono reflected that his instincts had not failed him; but Sam's illness had been unfortunate. The creature, Ibrahim had told him, had been seasick for most of the journey from Jakarta. A few days in port recovering from the swell of the sea must have done a great deal for its strength and courage. Pak Suryono had not imagined that it could have splintered the wood of the cage. And now? Now they were having to chase across Kenukecil in pursuit. Pak Suryono had little taste for this kind of enterprise. Were it not so extremely valuable, he would have instructed Ibrahim to take him back to Jakarta immediately. What held him there was the promise of unprecedented profit: although circumstances had turned against him, Pak Suryono had not yet given up on this particular deal.

It was dark when the shout went up from Pak Wim in the bows of the boat. They had rounded the cape and turned westwards again to the bay overlooked by Amasi Dol. The scattered lights of Desa Baru slid by on the hillsides towards the south. The stars in the lower part of the sky were blotted out by the hills in front of them. A little later the pale shore of the bay was visible and the steps leading up to the village, a grey shadow in the blackness of the cliffs. Ibrahim shut down the engine and tossed an anchor over the side of the boat to drag on the sea floor.

'Amasi Dol,' Pak Wim said, making his way down the boat to the stern and pointing upwards in the direction of the bluff. 'We will go ashore tomorrow. Tonight we will sleep on the boat.'

Sam stirred himself and rolled his shoulders, feeling the stiffness of his back. The tide of his sickness seemed to have drawn back a little. 'Why not go ashore now?' he asked.

Pak Suryono nodded vigorously. 'Yes, Mr Sam is right. We should go ashore this instant.'

Pak Wim held up a warning finger. 'We shall spend tonight on the boat,' he said. 'It is bad *adat* to arrive from the sea after sunset.'

Pak Suryono looked as if he was about to object, but then thought better of it. 'All right,' he said. 'Tomorrow morning. Tonight, we sleep on board.'

So they remained on the boat, around half a mile out from the shore. Ibrahim lit a small gas lamp and then set about cooking a meal on the battered primus: instant noodles, egg and a large fish that he had caught by dragging a line behind them as they had travelled up the coast. It was a meal eaten, for the main part, in silence. Then the passengers, finding what sheltered spots they could, settled down to sleep.

Sam lay looking up at the scattered stars. How strange, he thought before he fell asleep, that life has conspired to bring me precisely here, to the deck of this boat, underneath these stars, with these companions.

They woke just after dawn on the Thursday morning. Before them was a sandy bay overlooked by a steep cliff.

Steps, carved into the cliff, led up to a ridge. The foot of the cliff was pockmarked by caves where once a young man called Wim had kissed a girl called Anna. Pak Wim, sitting on the port side, was up already, staring towards the village in silence. Sam stirred and came to sit next to him.

'That is my home,' said Pak Wim. 'That is my village.'

Sam looked at his associate and saw tears in his eyes. The Englishman was surprised by a surge of fellow-feeling. 'How long?' asked Sam. 'How long has it been?'

Pak Wim frowned to himself and started counting, but then he stopped. He had not kept a tally of the years. 'Many years,' he said. 'Too many years.'

Ibrahim was already boiling water. They breakfasted on coffee, noodles, eggs and some dry, grainy sago biscuits bought in Bantuk. Only when they had finished their breakfast did Ibrahim lift the anchor and start the engine, nudging the boat towards the shore. As they approached the bay the sea floor and the glassy surface of the waters converged. Ibrahim cut the engine again and lowered the anchor: by daylight it was possible to see the sandbanks and the reefs more clearly.

'Someone's coming to meet us,' said Sam, pointing to the cliff.

A man was clambering down the steps to the beach. He pulled a dugout canoe into the water and began to paddle towards them. He was wiry and dark-skinned, dressed in a torn short-sleeved shirt and a pair of shorts. He had been sitting at the top of the steps, smoking a clove cigarette and turning over the worries of the night before when he had seen the boat, which had been anchored in the bay all night, begin to turn landwards. As the laws of hospitality demanded, he had descended onto the beach to collect his canoe so that he might be able to ferry the passengers ashore. He paddled in short, swift strokes until he drew alongside the boat. He looked up at the curious trio of characters waiting to disembark: one man with an arm in a sling, clearly Kenukecilese, who, although Pak Wuluruan could not place him, looked curiously familiar; a gentleman who looked as if he might be Javanese, possibly a government official; and an *orang bule* so pale and sickly that he might at any moment breathe his last, may God and the ancestors prevent such a thing happening in his village. A fourth man was sitting astern. The owner of the boat, he assumed.

The three men climbed down into the dugout, an operation that was particularly difficult for the now one-armed Pak Wim. When they were underway on their short journey towards the shore, their ferryman introduced himself. 'I am *kepala desa* of Amasi Dol,' he said. 'My name is Pak Wuluruan. It is my duty to welcome you to the village.'

Sam and Pak Suryono introduced themselves. Pak Wim, however, remained silent. 'This is Pak Wim,' explained Pak Suryono. Pak Wim flinched and turned his battered face away from the headman.

'Pak Wim?' The headman's face became thoughtful, as if chasing an idea or a memory just out of reach. He paddled a little more slowly, looking closely at Pak Wim. When the water was calf-deep they climbed out and pulled the canoe up the beach. Pak Wuluruan bent down and tethered it to a post with a skilful knot. Then the headman straightened his back and turned to Pak Wim. 'Now I remember,' he said. 'We were once friends.'

'No,' Pak Wim said distantly. He was looking across the sands to the place where he and Anna had kissed, day after day, long ago when he was young and when he thought that his bliss might continue for ever.

The headman lapsed from Indonesian into Kenukecilese, so that the others might not understand. 'But you are,' he said. 'You *are* Pak Wim. I know you. You are a son of Amasi Dol. You made bad *m'houna* with a girl called Anna, so you left the village in shame. They say you went to Ambon and then to Jakarta. There were many stories. And Anna – she married another man . . .'

Pak Wim kept his head turned away, his eyes half-closed. But the headman touched his arm with great gentleness. 'Your shame,' he said, 'is finished. Gone.'

With that touch and that blessing, it was as if the shame that had burdened Pak Wim for so long simply flowed out of him, draining away into the sand. For the first time, he looked at Pak Wuluruan.

'Welcome,' said the headman. 'Our village today is suffering from a greater shame than bad *m'houna*. Your shame will be forgotten in the greater shame that we all share. You are welcome.'

Pak Wim smiled. Yes, he knew the man now. 'Damianus,' he murmured. 'Your name is Damianus.'

Pak Wuluruan smiled. 'My name,' he said, 'is indeed Damianus; and it is a long time since I have heard it spoken by Wim, who was my friend.'

Hearing this, the tears that, earlier, had been inching from the corners of Pak Wim's eyes now broke in waves. Pak Wim went down on his knees, his shoulders arched, and he sobbed on the white sand of Amasi Dol, the tears stinging his black eye and his cut face, watering the land that had nurtured him. '*Terima kasih*,' he said. Thank you. '*Terima kasih, terima kasih, terima kasih . . .*'

Pak Suryono and Sam understood nothing of the conversation. They had no inkling of the terrible shame that had inscribed deep lines into Pak Wim's face and moulded his stooped and diffident posture. The two men stared at this unexpected display with bewilderment.

'*Adik* Wim,' Damianus Wuluruan said, switching back into Indonesian, 'we must go. There are terrible things happening in our village. We can talk of other things later.

Please, you and your friends will be my guests. I will do all I can, but I too have many troubles. We cannot waste time sobbing over things that are past. We are living in strange times, Pak Wim. Come.' He put out a hand and helped Pak Wim to his feet.

Damianus Wuluruan led them up the steps. He was followed by Pak Wim. Sam came next and Pak Suryono brought up the rear. Coming over the ridge, they emerged into the centre of the village, where the houses of those families of noble rank could be found. The village was curiously empty of human activity. At this time of day, one would have expected to see children carrying over their shoulders long poles hanging with fish – their mouths gaping, their scales breaking the sunlight into a thousand colours – hawking them from door to door. One would have expected gossips on the bamboo benches, men and women going to and from the plantations with machetes and baskets on their backs, young people casting flirtatious glances at each other. One would have expected old men seated on logs on their porches in the sun and chewing betel while they scratched their chins. But there were only a few hunting dogs skulking in the shadows as the day became hotter, twitching as they slipped in and out of dreams.

'Welcome to Amasi Dol,' said the headman sadly. 'Let us go in to the house quickly. I will ask my wife to bring tea, and then I shall tell you of our shame.'

The four men entered a house that stood on the south side of the square, leaving the dogs dozing in the sun.

# 20

Ibu Wuluruan brought sweet tea and stale, sugary biscuits while Pak Damianus Wuluruan made small-talk.
He asked Samuel where he was from and how it was that
he knew such good Indonesian. He asked his old friend
Pak Wim how he had passed that time, but as Pak Wim's
activities throughout the previous decades were hardly a
matter for small-talk, he responded in the vaguest terms.
Damianus had the sensitivity to change the subject and,
still keeping up the small-talk, asked his visitors what had
brought them to the village. They hesitated, awkwardly.

Pak Suryono was the one who broke the silence. 'We
are here on a matter of some importance,' he said, 'a
matter about which we shall no doubt have cause to speak
in the due course of time.'

The evasion worked. Pak Wuluruan, awed by his
Javanese guest's gravity of tone and his elevated language,
behaved as if this response had given him a full and complete answer to his question.

When they were sufficiently refreshed, Pak Wuluruan
gave a tired smile. 'I must tell you that these are bad times
for Amasi Dol,' he said. 'Last night a daughter of this very
village, Lucia Balakana, was dishonoured. The night
before that, the same happened to a girl called Bunny
Masela in the village of Desa Baru. The Masela girl has
gone to Bantuk. She has become an employee of Mr Gu.'

At the mention of the Chinese merchant's name, a jolt
passed through Pak Wim, subtle but still obvious enough

for the others to glance at him momentarily. He smiled queasily and they looked away.

'We are fearful of what will happen next,' said Pak Wuluruan.

'Lucia Balakana?' Pak Wim frowned. 'I know the name.'

'The grand-daughter of Ibu Balakana, my father's sister. You remember the Ibu?'

On hearing the old, familiar names, Pak Wim laughed. 'I remember. This Lucia is her grand-daughter?'

'Seventeen years of age, and beautiful. She was found this morning, as Bunny was found. She came from the forest with a smile on her face. Her clothes were torn.'

'She had been making *m'houna*?' Pak Wim asked.

'Not *m'houna*, Pak Wim,' said the headman. 'This was rape.'

'She smiled. You said that she smiled. A girl who is raped weeps, but a girl who makes *m'houna* smiles.'

Pak Wuluruan lifted his tea and took a swig. 'You are right, Pak Wim. She smiled, as they say Bunny Masela smiled. I do not know why. But it was not *m'houna*. This was not *adat*. She disappeared in the night, without saying a word, then reappeared after dawn, her clothes in a disgraceful state. Her parents beat her but they could not beat the smile from her face. They have now locked her in the house while they decide what to do with her. They say that they may send her to join Bunny Masela in Bantuk as a whore.'

Sam leaned forward. 'Did the girl say anything about who was responsible?'

Damianus looked up towards the rafters. 'Here in the village, they say many things. The night before last when Bunny was taken, the people of Desa Baru blamed us. Yesterday an old man from our village was going to the plantation in the early morning and a group from Desa Baru chased him with knives. They said that Bunny was taken by a short man and this grandfather was short. Can you imagine? A son of our village hiding in the forest? Now they say that some men in Desa Baru have put a price on his head.'

'Could an old man do such a thing?' Pak Wim asked.

'Of course not,' the headman replied. 'His stalk is as dry as an old bamboo tube, but not nearly as stiff. These are the times we live in. Our daughters are violated at night and the grandfathers hide in the forest out of fear.'

The headman paused and let out a long, low sigh. Sam winced at the sweetness of the tea as he drank and looked out into the empty village square.

'That is not all, my friends,' he continued. 'There are people in this village who believe that our Lucia was taken by a man from Amasi Da, the village to the north. They are asking me to declare war upon our neighbours.'

Pak Wim looked surprised. 'They ask you to *declare* war? What is this? Can we not just march on the village and torch some houses, like we used to do when we were young?'

The headman looked affectionately at his old friend. 'Times have changed, *adik*,' he said. 'Things are not as they used to be. Today there must be declarations. It is the modern way. But to declare war on our neighbours, we must be certain that they are responsible. We need evidence.'

'But they are the Amasi Da people!' Pak Wim protested. 'They are our enemies. Why do we need evidence?'

The headman chuckled. 'You have indeed been away a long time, Wim. No. Without evidence, there is nothing we can do. Lucia says that she does not know the man's name. She would only say that he was a short man. Our honour as a village has been slighted, but we cannot regain our honour or avenge the insult, because we do not know who has slighted us or who we should punish.'

Pak Suryono was beginning to fidget, his eyes casting

around the room anxiously. Sam glanced sideways at the businessman and then turned his attention to the headman. 'Surely,' he said, 'you must have some idea . . .'

'Of course,' the headman replied. 'There is a priest in Desa Baru. He is a great man, a holy man. He has been chosen by God. This priest – his name is Freddy – says that it is not a man who has taken these girls, but a devil. And there is another testimony to be added to this one, from an Ibu in Bantuk. She was going into the church to pray last Sunday and she saw a devil there. On a Sunday, I ask you! These are evil times, mister. This pastor in Desa Baru, he says that we are in the final days, that Christ is coming; but he calls Christ by a different name. He calls him by the name Christ-Batjameni.'

'Batjameni?' Sam looked puzzled.

The headman opened his eyes wide and leaned towards Sam. '*Bat-ja-men-i*,' he repeated, giving emphasis to every syllable. 'Christ is coming. He will take the form of Batjameni. He will come first to Kenukecil and then to the rest of the world. He will curse the evil-doers and he will make a paradise for all the rest. If our hearts are pure, we will be like you in the West. We will have big houses and many machines. But we must keep our hearts pure or we will burn.'

Sam thought about this. 'And do you believe this, Pak?'

The headman's eyes flickered restlessly. 'I do not know,' he said. 'Perhaps yes, perhaps no.'

Sam sat back and looked steadily at the headman. 'Pak,' he said at length, 'I believe we may be able to help you.'

Pak Suryono, who had been listening to this strange theological discourse with a combination of frustration and contempt, gestured sharply towards Sam, as if to tell him, 'Whatever you are about to say, do not say it.'

Sam hesitated for a moment.

'How can you possibly help us?' the headman asked.

'How can you keep our daughters safe? How can you help us prepare for the Last Days?'

'You must not worry,' Sam explained in the most soothingly authoritative tones that he could muster. 'We are experts. We know what to do.' Without looking at him, he could almost feel Pak Suryono begin to sweat with anxiety.

'You are experts?' The word *expert* held a kind of magic for Damianus Wuluruan. The headman's eyes lit with hope.

Sam nodded. 'My colleague and I' – at this he pointed to Pak Suryono – 'are experts. We are researchers.'

'Research?' Again, at the uttering of this magic word, the headman felt tremors of awe.

Sam nodded with the greatest seriousness. 'There is no need for you to panic,' he said. 'We will look into the situation and we will see what we can do. We do not promise that we will be able to sort out this matter today, but we can guarantee that we will be able to resolve it very soon.'

'And you?' Damianus asked, turning to Pak Wim. 'Are you now a researcher also?'

Mindful that Pak Wim's response might not be entirely helpful, Sam interjected swiftly. 'Pak Wim is our assistant. He is a very fine assistant.'

Pak Wim beamed.

Damianus fell silent, overawed by the fact that he had not one but two researchers in his house. He was impressed that his childhood friend had risen so far in the world to become an *assistant* to these researchers – this rise through the world of consequence was one that could easily eclipse the shame of *m'houna*. Convinced that before him were men of an intellectually superior order, Damianus did not dare ask them exactly what it might have been of which they were researchers, nor how precisely they might be of assistance. That they were researchers and that they were guests in his very own house was sufficient. Perhaps, Damianus told himself, they had been sent by Christ-Batjameni. 'Please,' he said, 'stay in my house as long as is necessary. We are very grateful.' He bowed his head in humility.

'Thank you,' Sam said. 'But first, we would like to meet this Lucia Balakana. She may be able to help us.'

So it was arranged. Towards noon, Pak Wim, Pak Suryono and Sam Rivers were admitted to the house of the Balakana family and shown into the room where the girl was incarcerated.

She was sitting on the floor with her legs spread out before her in a fashion that was far from modest, and she was still grinning widely. She had not changed her clothes since her ordeal and they were in such disarray that the prudish Pak Suryono gazed at a point above and to the left of her right shoulder while Pak Wim, being constitution-ally rather different, gazed with undisguised lasciviousness on the girl's not unenticing form.

Sam, attempting to push to the fringes of his awareness her state of undress, asked her a single question. 'Who was he?'

Lucia's smile faded. She nudged her bottom lip forward petulantly and refused to answer.

Sam crouched down onto his haunches. 'Lucia,' he said gently, 'we are researchers. We do not need to know his name. We do not need to know the village he came from. We do not need to know anything except what *kind* of man he was who did this to you.'

Lucia looked levelly at him. 'Who did *what* to me?'

Sam paused. 'What kind of man was it who gave you so much pleasure?'

At the mention of *pleasure*, Lucia let out a dreamy moan. 'Ah, tuan. There was so much pleasure. I did not know his name and I did not ask. We did not speak. He took me

into the forest and we lay together. He was a short man.'
Then she laughed. 'Who would have thought that a short
man could be so good?'

'Where did he go?'

Lucia opened her eyes wide. 'I don't know,' she said.

'Did he go back to Bantuk?'

'Maybe,' she said.

'To the forest?'

Lucia thought. 'Maybe,' she said. Then a shadow seemed
to pass over her face. 'Will you kill him if you find him?'

'We will not kill him,' Sam reassured her and put a
hand on her shoulder. He could feel the warmth of her
flesh through her thin shirt.

Lucia seemed to lose her self-assurance. 'What will happen to me? Will they kill me because of what I have done?'

Sam looked Lucia in the eye. 'What do you want to
happen to you?' he asked kindly.

Then the girl started to cry. 'I don't know,' she snivelled.
'I don't know.'

They could get no more sense out of her. 'Come on,'
Sam whispered to Pak Wim and Pak Suryono. The three
men filed out of the room, back to where Ibu and Bapak
Balakana were waiting. 'We have spoken with her and we
have some information,' said Sam. 'Please, do not punish
her. It is not her fault.'

Lucia's parents did not respond.

'Thank you,' Sam said. 'Thank you for allowing us to
see her.'


Sam, Pak Wim and Pak Suryono spent the remainder of
the day interviewing the villagers of Amasi Dol. The
information they gleaned was scant and often fanciful, but
by the early afternoon they were fairly certain that the
creature was heading north and would therefore be found
somewhere in the territory of Amasi Da. Given the record

of the previous two nights, this was not promising news for the people of the more northern village.

An hour or so before sunset, Damianus Wuluruan requisitioned a truck and travelled north with Sam, Pak Wim and Pak Suryono. The headman of Amasi Da, a man called Pak Talamosu, by nature mistrustful and taciturn, greeted them with every appearance of suspicion and invited them into his house only grudgingly.

Pak Wuluruan came straight to the point. 'Tonight,' he said, 'you must lock up your daughters.'

'You threaten us?' asked Pak Talamosu.

'No,' said Pak Wuluruan. 'We only warn you. These men here, they are researchers.'

'What do they research?' Pak Talamosu looked contemptuous.

This was a question that Pak Wuluruan had not thought to ask. A muscle in Pak Suryono's cheek twitched.

Sam stepped forward. 'We are here to help with your troubles,' he said. 'You have heard of the difficulties in Desa Baru and Amasi Dol. Tonight we recommend that you make sure that all of the daughters of Amasi Da remain indoors after sunset.'

Pak Talamosu hunched his shoulders a little. 'You talk about the devil?'

Sam bit his lip, wondering how to proceed.

'Pak Talamosu,' he said after a short pause, 'I know that many in Kenukecil are talking about devils, but this is not a devil.'

'Then what is it, mister?' The headman of Amasi Da looked belligerent and sceptical.

'It is only a monkey,' Sam said.

'A monkey?' Pak Wuluruan looked at him in disbelief. 'A monkey who violates our daughters? How can this be? There was an Ibu in the church at Bantuk who saw a devil. The priest in Desa Baru talks of the Last Days. This is not a monkey. You do not understand, mister. You have no devils in America.'

'England,' Sam said.

'You have no devils in England. But here, things are different.'

Sam maintained the grave demeanour of an expert. 'I have heard these stories,' he said, 'but I can guarantee that it is not a devil that you have here in Kenukecil. It is just a large monkey that we have been transporting to Java from Irian Jaya. The monkey is very rare and is protected by the government. Unfortunately, he has gone mad out of loneliness. That is why he attacked the girls from Desa Baru and from Amasi Dol. But now that we are here, there is nothing to worry about. We' – pointing to Pak Wim and Pak Suryono – 'have been sent to catch him.'

Pak Talamosu and Pak Wuluruan looked sceptical.

'Pak Suryono and I have studied monkeys in universities in Indonesia and America. We know a lot about monkeys. Pak Wim has worked for many years with us.'

'But what about our daughters?' Pak Talamosu asked, less belligerent than before.

'You must lock your doors. You must close your windows and make sure that they are secure. If you take precautions, then they will be safe.'

Pak Talamosu looked appraisingly at the Westerner, his scepticism now muted a little. 'And how do you, with your science, plan to catch the dangerous monkey who steals our daughters from us?' he asked.

'No problem,' Sam said with every appearance of confidence. 'Catching monkeys is our job.'

# 21

Pak Amukwasi, the chief of police, kept a tidy desk. When he arrived in Bantuk from Jakarta to take up his new post three years before, he had been appalled by the state of the offices at the police headquarters. Reports were stacked in every corner, desks were piled so high with papers that there was no room to work at them, and the single filing cabinet had one drawer that continually jammed.

The policeman's ancestral home was the next-door island of Tanimbar, but he had been born and brought up in Jakarta. He had returned to the south-eastern Moluccas three years before, after a dream in which he clearly saw his ancestors squatting in ranks above his head and chattering with the voices of lizards. His own interpretation of the dream was that the ancestors were calling him home. When, in the same week of his dream, a posting came up in Kenukecil, so close to his beloved islands of Tanimbar, he made clear his intention to transfer. Pak Amukwasi's wife, a Jakarta socialite, and his three thoroughly urban children remained in the capital city. They did not want to be consorting, they said, with ignorant farmers.

After his arrival, Pak Amukwasi – proclaiming the dictum, much to the annoyance of his new colleagues, that 'a tidy desk means a tidy mind' – demanded a paperwork audit. The old filing cabinet was discarded and several more were bought in its place. The piles of reports were dusted off and the spiders that had made comfortable homes for themselves behind them were chased out of the building. The piles of paper were tidied and stacked. Then began the task of working through, deciding what could be discarded – most of it, it turned out – and what could be filed. By the time a month had passed, the offices were immaculate. The new filing cabinets, with their drawers that opened and closed with barely a whisper, positively gleamed with virtuous orderliness. Pak Amukwasi took his place behind his huge desk with its green leather covering with justifiable satisfaction. Modern policing had come to Kenukecil.

Once order had been restored, Pak Amukwasi found that he loved being back in the east. He became a common sight in Bantuk, wearing his large stomach with pride, and styled himself as the genial face of public law and order: approachable, considerate, understanding and firm. Here, after all, was a man who truly, genuinely and authentically believed in the astonishing proposition that the task of the police force was to serve the people.

It was mid-morning when news of Lucia Balakana's abduction reached the police chief. One of his officers appeared with a breathless, hand-written report about the events of the night before. Pak Amukwasi read the report and then went over to the filing cabinet. Within no more than fifteen seconds, he had laid out a number of reports and memos on his desk: there was, he thought as he arranged them neatly, a deep pleasure to be had in a good filing system. He sat back and let his mind wander, his eyes coming to rest on the map of Kenukecil that hung on the wall.

Pak Amukwasi's approach to police-work was intuitive. He believed that the most obvious story was rarely the correct one and that, the world being such a tangled and complex place, the most disparate occurrences often turned out to be tied together in the most unexpected ways. In front of him on his desk he had a number of pieces of paper. First there was the report on the continuing problems in Desa Baru, an ill-conceived village if there ever was one and one that gave Pak Amukwasi endless headaches. Next there was the growing dossier on Desa Baru's priest, Pastor Freddy. Freddy, as far as he knew, had not yet committed any crime, but Pak Amukwasi had asked to be kept informed of the development of his church in the village. Then there was the report concerning Bunny Masela's abduction. This report was unfortunately incomplete as the officer who had been sent to Mr Gu's butterfly house to interview Bunny had come back without any information at all, his uniform crumpled, and was now subject to disciplinary procedures. The report just in, the one concerning Lucia, was alongside Bunny's. Finally there was a brief memo on Ibu Nilasera's experience in the church at Bantuk.

Pak Amukwasi rang the bell on his desk. When one of his junior officers appeared, he ordered him to bring a cup of tea. The officer departed, reappearing not long afterwards with the drink, which he placed on Pak Amukwasi's desk. The police chief thanked him and went back to studying the map. Something, he was sure, was going on. One abduction was regrettable, but two abductions on successive nights was wholly unacceptable. It was not only out of concern for the girls that Pak Amukwasi was worried. He had been in Kenukecil long enough to know that inter-village warfare broke out for the most trivial of reasons. The most recent clash had come about on account of a young man from Sapratian who had been sent into Bantuk by his parents to buy rice. In the pool hall, he had gambled away not only his money but also his jeans and had returned home in bare-legged shame. Unfortunately, his opponent at pool had been a man from Amasi Da and the people of Sapratian, their honour infringed, had launched a punitive raid. If a lost pair of trousers could cause such an attack, then the abduction of village girls was potentially a serious matter indeed.

Pak Amukwasi looked over the papers. Ibu Lana's report. Accounts of Pastor Freddy's increasingly apocalyptic ravings. A few snippets in the reports concerning Bunny and Lucia, interviews with villagers. 'Devils,' he said to himself, sitting upright for a moment in his chair. 'What is all this superstitious stuff about devils?' He resolved to go and speak to Pastor Niemann. He returned the documents to their correct places in the filing cabinet and left the police station.

The priest greeted the police chief cordially and invited him to drink tea. The two men enjoyed good relations and they were, broadly speaking, of one mind. They saw each other as allies, united in bringing progress and reason to the people of Kenukecil. Over tea, Pak Amukwasi asked the pastor, somewhat casually, about Ibu Nilasera's experience in the church.

'She has malaria,' the priest said.

'Perhaps. But my own investigations are taking me down curious paths. I came here to talk to you about devils, Pastor.'

The police chief was met with the sheer, blank wall of Pastor Niemann's scepticism. 'There are no devils, Pak Polisi,' the Dutchman said. 'Perhaps you should be investigating more important matters, the abduction of the girls from the villages of Desa Baru and Amasi Dol, for example. You have heard the news, I suppose?'

Pak Amukwasi smiled. 'That is precisely my concern, Pastor. I am not a student of theology and were it not for these abductions I would not be taking an interest in the Ibu's vision. But I feel that they are connected.'

Pastor Niemann looked unimpressed. 'There *are* no devils,' he said. 'What is the point in further discussion?'

'Pastor, you misunderstand me. I do not ask you whether there are devils or whether there are no devils. I am sure, Pastor, that we both are agreed on that point. I only ask you to explain the circumstances of the Ibu's purported encounter in the church last Sunday.'

'There was nothing in the church. I went to check myself.'

'Perhaps. But also maybe whatever or whoever it was that the Ibu saw had already left. You know churches, Pastor: people come and people go, and generally speaking they seem to go more than they come.'

'Pak Polisi,' the pastor protested, 'let us not trade in superstition. Ibu Nilasera is sick with malaria. That is all.'

'Although I hear that she has now been cured by Ibu Lana Lerekosu.'

'More likely by the chloroquine I gave her. Yes, she is a little better. I saw her last night and encouraged her to take another dose.'

'Do you think that she will be well enough to answer some questions?'

'She will be well, but please, Pak Polisi, do not feed her superstitions.'

'I will ask her what it is necessary to ask her, Pastor Niemann. I am a policeman and not a priest. All I would like to know is what it was that the Ibu believed she saw. Did she describe it to you in detail?'

'Pak Polisi,' the pastor protested, 'the hallucinations of a sick woman have nothing to do with police work.'

'They may have everything to do with police work. I am, I believe, the better judge of these matters. Questions of religion I leave up to you and I would ask that you leave matters of police work to me.'

The pastor sighed. 'As you will,' he muttered.

The two men fell silent for a few moments before the policeman spoke again. 'There is one more thing, Pastor. What do you know about the situation in Desa Baru?'

'The priest, you mean?'

The policeman nodded.

'Not much. He is a Protestant. Pentecostal, I think. He was born in Sapratian, but lived in Ambon for a long time. He was invited back to Desa Baru last Christmas.'

Pak Amukwasi looked thoughtfully at the pastor. 'Pastor, is it *true* that you refused to take services in Desa Baru?'

The priest gave the policeman a weary glance. 'Yes, it is true,' he said. 'The headman, Pak Masela, came to ask me, but I refused. There is no consecrated building, only – what do they call it?'

'The Pancasila Hall?'

'Quite,' said the priest with distaste. 'I have a very busy schedule on Sunday. Unlike the Lord, I cannot be omnipresent.'

Pak Amukwasi paused, as if uncertain of what he was about to say next. 'Do you know that Pak Masela brought Pastor Freddy to the island because – how can I put this – because of your refusal?'

The priest sighed. 'Maybe,' he said. 'But I am not responsible for foolish superstition. Why are you asking about all of this?'

'Let me tell you plainly. I believe that this Freddy is somehow connected to these abductions. I don't think that he is responsible. But there is a connection, I am sure of it. So there is something I wanted to ask you. There is a name in the report from Desa Baru that I do not recognize. Christ-Batjameni.'

'Christ-Batjameni?'

'Yes, Pastor.'

Pastor Niemann shook his head sadly. 'Pak Polisi, why are you worrying about devils and old legends? Why are you concerning yourself with the madness of Pastor Freddy? Girls are going missing from their homes. That should be your concern, not all this nonsense.'

'When the imagination of the people becomes fevered, many crimes take place,' Pak Amukwasi said.

The pastor regarded him steadily. 'Batjameni was a folk hero in the old times. I have a book which I can lend you, if you think it will help. Have you heard of Kruywers?'

'Of course, but I have never read his book.'

'It is only in Dutch, I am afraid. Wait.' He went to the bookcase and pulled down the large yellow hardback. Flicking through the pages, he found the picture of the wooden sculpture. 'This is Batjameni,' he said.

The policeman looked at the image.

'Half-man, half-woman,' the priest pointed out, indicating the double genitals. 'This sculpture stood in Sapratian until twenty, maybe thirty years ago.'

'On the cape? Where the sculpture of the Virgin now stands?'

The pastor nodded. 'Yes, where the sculpture of the Virgin now stands.'

'And what did this Batjameni do?'

'According to legend, he shattered the sun with a spear and set time in motion.'

The policeman smiled. 'We have a similar legend at home in Tanimbar,' he said. 'Tufa, he is called, or Atuf. Do you mind if I take this book? My Dutch is not so good, but I have a dictionary. I think that it may help in my investigations.'

'No, not at all. If you really think it will help, please do.'

'Thank you, Pastor,' the policeman said. He tucked the book under his arm and rose to his feet.

The Dutchman showed his guest to the door. Just before the policeman crossed the threshold, he turned to look the priest in the eye. 'Pastor,' he said, 'have you ever thought about taking a wife?'

'I am a priest,' said Pastor Niemann wryly.

The chief of police smiled. 'Of course,' he said. He walked out into the morning sunshine and the priest closed the door behind him.

# 22

Pak Amukwasi headed straight to Ibu Nilasera's house. By this time, thanks to the curative powers of Ibu Lana's root, she was fully recovered and in excellent health. Three days ago, when Suster Elena had led the healer to see the sick Ibu Nilasera, Ibu Lana found the patient lying on her sick bed, groaning and muttering incomprehensible syllables. She pulled back Ibu Nilasera's eyelids, felt her pulse, poked her in the stomach to check for *sawang* – there were none, God and the ancestors be thanked – tweaked her ears, peered up her nostrils, felt the heat of her legs, arms, forehead, side and buttocks, examined her mouth, listened to the rasping of her breath, whispered strange words into her ear, struck her hard on the leg with the flat of her hand and tugged at her toes. Whether these actions were diagnostic or curative in intent was known only to Ibu Lana, who at the end of the entire process straightened up and pronounced that Ibu Nilasera was possessed.

'Possessed?' Suster Elena asked. 'Are you certain? She saw a devil in the church and now she is possessed?'

'The devil has entered her. Many devils have entered her,' Ibu Lana replied. She leaned towards the nun, opening her eyes wide, and whispered, '*Tomorrow.*'

'Tomorrow?' Suster Elena looked puzzled.

'She will die tomorrow,' Ibu Lana said.

Suster Elena gasped. 'Ibu Nilasera will die?'

Then Ibu Lana gave an enormous smile, displaying her betel-stained gums and jagged teeth. 'No, no, no, Suster

Elena!' she laughed, clapping the nun on the back with a large hand. '*Without my cure*, she will die. But because I am here, and I am a good woman who even helps Catholics, she will not die. I have my root. My root can drive out devils. I can trap them in the joints of the body. Ibu Nilasera will not die.'

'I have heard that your root can drive out witches. Is it effective also against devils?' Suster Elena asked.

'Witches are not different from devils. Devils are not different from witches. They all have light souls. They all fly about here and there and enter the bodies of those who do not guard themselves. They all feed upon our living souls. But Mamma's root is powerful. She will drive them out of Ibu Nilasera's body and they will be like clouds torn by the wind. Do not fear, Suster Elena. By tomorrow, perhaps by tonight, Ibu Nilasera will be well.'

Having finished her brief discourse, Ibu Lana ordered Suster Elena to fetch a glass of water, a bottle of palmwine and five men from nearby noble households, for if there is nothing more light and flighty than a devil, then there is nothing of greater weight than a nobleman who calls upon his ancestors.

Suster Elena bought a bottle of palmwine from the shop a hundred yards down the road. Then she set about tracking down the five noblemen, which took a little more time, but after half an hour she returned with five individuals not entirely without nobility. She placed a row of chairs before the sick bed and the noblemen took their seats for the ceremony. Ibu Lana shaved the root into the glass of water with the knife she used for paring her betel nut while the men of modest nobility prayed to the ancestors for their assistance. 'Palmwine,' she snapped. Suster Elena passed her the bottle. Carrying both palmwine and glass of water, the healer went over to the patient, placed the glass on the table, sprinkled a baptism of the alcohol over

Ibu Nilasera's head, with her fingers flicked a few droplets up into the air and then down to the ground, sucked her fingers to remove the remnants, placed the palmwine down on the table, took up the glass of water, yanked her patient upright and forced the entire contents of the glass, wood-shavings and all, down the woman's throat.

Ibu Nilasera took the final gulp and then her spine straightened and she sat up with bulging eyes. 'Oh!' she cried, the meaning of which utterance was open to several interpretations.

At this point, Ibu Lana grasped the seated patient from behind in a firm embrace, taking hold of her with her strong right arm, and jabbed the inside of the Ibu's elbow-joint with the thumb of her left hand. Immediately the patient cried out in pain. 'The devil speaks!' Ibu Lana gasped, letting go of her patient and flinging her arms towards the heavens with a shout: '*Ha!*'

On cue, with the most astonishing and wholly unexpected agility, Ibu Nilasera leapt to her feet, scuttled five paces across the room, put her head outside her front door and puked copiously. Ibu Lana beamed to see her vomit.

Since then, Ibu Nilasera had been feeling much better.

When Pak Amukwasi arrived at her house to interview her about the devil, he found the Ibu positively cheerful. As he knocked on the front door, he heard the sound of laughter. A few moments later, Suster Elena answered the door. She was still giggling and wiping the tears from her eyes. 'Ah! Pak Amukwasi,' she said. 'Come in. I was just telling a funny story.' She ushered him into the house.

The Ibu was sitting up at the table and drinking tea, a plateful of sugar sandwiches in front of her. This Pak Amukwasi took to be a good sign, a sign of robust health.

Sugar sandwiches were one of Ibu Nilasera's favourite foods, although she considered them something of a luxury.

She would buy bread from the market, proper sliced bread in plastic wraps, and smear it with margarine before sprinkling it liberally with sugar crystals. She preferred the sugar that was just a little off-white and came in big, translucent granules. Along with hot, sweet tea, she ate this breakfast on those mornings when she felt that life was truly worth celebrating, this life of freedom without a husband, when the sun filtered through the papaya tree outside her door making the leaves glow yellow and green.

'Pak Amukwasi,' Suster Elena said to the policeman, 'do you want to hear a funny story?'

The policeman smiled at the nun. 'Perhaps,' he suggested, 'I could hear it at a later date. I have come on important business. I need to speak with Ibu Nilasera.'

With discretion, Suster Elena made her apologies and left. Pak Amukwasi placed the book the pastor had given him down on the table and turned to the woman, giving her a big smile. 'Ibu Nilasera,' he said, 'I trust you are better?'

'I am, thank you, Pak Polisi.'

'I have to ask you some questions. I hope that they will not be too distressing.' He took out his policeman's notebook and the enormous fountain pen that he carried as a sign of his importance.

'Would you like tea?' Ibu Nilasera asked him.

'I have just had some, thank you.'

'A sugar sandwich?' She pushed the plate towards her visitor.

The policeman's hand twitched. 'No,' he said, with considerable willpower. 'No thank you. I want to ask you about last Sunday, if you do not mind.'

Ibu Nilasera's smile was not without coyness. She gazed at the police chief's magnificent, shiny pen, at his fine moustache beaded with drops of sweat and at his deep-set eyes. She suppressed a giggle by forcing another sandwich into her mouth.

Ibu Nilasera was pleased that the chief of police had come to see her. She had been upset that the priest had not believed her testimony and that he seemed to consider the presence of a devil in the church over which he presided to be no more than a passing inconvenience; so this visit from the police chief, dressed in his splendid uniform, acted as some compensation.

'Tell me what happened,' the police chief said gently, resting his notebook on his lap, his pen poised.

Ibu Nilasera started to narrate her tale. Swept up in the excitement of her testimony at last being officially recorded, however, it may be that the Ibu deviated slightly from the strictest accuracy in submitting her report. She extemporized on her terrible experience with minute care and considerable enthusiasm, describing the colour of the devil's skin, the horns on his head and how he spoke to her in the most terrible bass voice. All these elements of the story were quite novel, having just arisen in her mind, but such is the pliancy of memory that the moment she related these embellishments, they were woven into the fabric of her recollections and became to her as vivid as truth. By the end of the interview, Ibu Nilasera's experience in the church had become not just a glimpse of something in the gloom of a dusty building on a Sunday afternoon, but rather a happening of cosmological significance. She concluded her testimony with the words: 'There. It is finished. There is no more to say.' Then she sat back and her eyes shone with pride.

The police chief signed off his written account with a flourish of his pen. Pak Amukwasi did not necessarily believe the Ibu's story in its entirety. He was accustomed to the unreliability of witnesses. Nevertheless, he knew that even half-truths and inventions could lead inchwise – if one sifted through them with sufficient patience, and by many winding and treacherous pathways – to a final truth. 'Ibu,' he said, 'your testimony will be very valuable to me. Thank you.'

The interview finished, the chief of police put the lid back on his pen. It made a satisfying click. He shook hands with Ibu Nilasera, told her that everything would now be fine because it was in the hands of the police, and reminded her that the task of the police was to protect the public and that, whatever it was in the church, she could be sure that the police would track down the culprit and bring him to justice. It would be the first time, Ibu Nilasera thought, that a devil had been put on trial. Nevertheless, she was reassured by the policeman's confidence.

The police chief picked up the copy of Kruywers's book which he had put on the table while interviewing the Ibu and said, 'Ibu, I must go.'

Ibu Nilasera stood shyly and the policeman strode out into the morning sunshine. Ibu Nilasera followed him, chirruping and fussing.

As he reached the gate, the police chief paused to inspect the papaya tree. 'Your papaya,' he remarked, 'looks wonderful.'

'Wait!' Ibu Nilasera said.

She scuttled back into her kitchen and a few moments later reappeared carrying a large machete. Then she trotted over to the gate and chopped the ripest, juiciest papaya off the tree. 'For you, Pak Polisi,' she said. 'It is good to give to those who help us.'

The policeman placed the papaya in the crook of his spare arm. He gave her a jocular salute – as best he could, thus hampered by a large papaya and a heavy book – and marched off up the road.

That afternoon, he read Kruywers closely with his Dutch–Indonesian dictionary to hand. As he read, he became increasingly convinced that the best place to begin his investigations would be the village of Sapratian, on the cape to the north. This, after all, was the natal village of Pastor Freddy and this was the place where the statue of Batjameni had once stood. He was certain that the abductions had something to do with this Batjameni about whom the pastor was raving and concluded that the most prudent move would be to make some enquiries first of all in the village that, according to Kruywers, had been at the heart of the Batjameni cult, before heading down through the villages of Amasi Dol and Desa Baru to interview the pastor himself. Besides, the so-called devil was said to be moving north, so by the time they reached Sapratian, there was every chance that they might cross paths with the assailant.

Pak Amukwasi called for six of his finest officers and asked them to make the boat ready for a trip to the north. They departed Bantuk just after sunset. Pak Amukwasi delegated all of his duties to Pak Solo, his deputy, until his return.

# 23

Shortly after noon in Amasi Dol, Pak Wim, Pak Suryono, Damianus Wuluruan and Sam Rivers were eating lunch in the headman's house. They had spent that Friday morning interviewing the villagers, but were no wiser as to where their cargo could be. They were eating in morose silence when they were disturbed by the sound of a motorbike. They looked out of the window.

Pak Talamosu pulled into the village square on an old bike, not wearing a helmet. Riding pillion behind him was a girl. He came to a halt before Damianus Wuluruan's house. 'Pak Wuluruan!' he shouted without dismounting. 'Come out!'

Pak Wuluruan came to the door. 'Pak Talamosu?' he asked. 'What now?'

The man climbed off the bike. 'My daughter,' he said. 'Welly Talamosu.' He pointed to the girl. Her clothes were in a state of disarray, on her face was an enormous smile. 'My daughter has been violated. Last night, in my very own house. The monkey or devil or whatever it is came through the window when my wife and I were asleep. I heard them at it and went to see what was happening. The monkey escaped. I have brought my daughter with me. Ask your monkey experts what they plan to do about it. Ask them if they can restore Welly's virtue.' He spoke the word 'experts' with contempt.

Sam, Pak Wim and Pak Suryono joined Pak Wuluruan at the door. 'Did you see the monkey?' Sam asked. 'If you tell us what you saw, then perhaps we can help.'

Pak Talamosu shrugged and looked down at the ground. His lower lip was quivering and his eyes were damp with tears. 'He was the size of a child. He climbed out of the window and ran very fast into the forest. I followed him with my bow and my arrow, but I could not catch him. What do you say to that, you experts? How can your science restore my honour?'

Welly was still sitting astride the motorbike, gazing into the middle distance, a distracted smile on her face as if she was remembering something incomparably sweet.

The headman of Amasi Da jabbed a finger at Sam. 'My daughter has been taken,' he said. 'Don't you understand? Your monkey took my daughter from me.'

Pak Wuluruan's wife came running from the house. She took Welly Talamosu by the hand and helped her off the bike. 'Come, Welly,' she said, 'let us sit inside.' Dreamily, Welly followed.

'Pak Talamosu,' Pak Wuluruan said, 'we must talk.' He turned to his guests. 'Please, excuse us. We will return.'

They watched as Pak Wuluruan took the headman from the rival village by the arm and led him towards the sea. Pak Wim, Sam and Pak Suryono crossed the village square and sat on the bamboo bench in the shade, hunching over in gloomy silence.

'Another one?' Pak Suryono sighed at last. 'This is not going to make things any easier.'

The two headmen sat themselves down on the topmost step overlooking the bay and shared a clove cigarette. 'We are enemies,' Pak Wuluruan began with fond nostalgia, 'and we have been since the time of the ancestors; but now we both face an even greater enemy. So for now we must be more than enemies. Now we must be friends.'

Pak Talamosu thought about this. The loss of an ancestral enmity is a sad thing. It is like losing one's mother and father, both on the same day. 'For ever?' he asked, sucking on the cigarette before passing it back to his counterpart. 'Do you say that we must be friends for ever? This would dishonour our ancestors.'

Pak Wuluruan laughed. 'No,' he said. 'We must be friends so that we can rid ourselves of the monkey. And we must rid ourselves of the monkey so that we can be enemies once again.'

Pak Talamosu looked pleased by this logic. 'And how do we do that?' he asked.

'My guests will help us. They are experts on monkeys. When they have solved our problem, we can return to being enemies. That is good *adat*.'

Pak Talamosu turned to the other man. 'My friend,' he said, 'I do not believe you when you say this thing is a monkey. I saw it with my own eyes. It was taking its pleasure with my daughter. This thing is like no monkey on earth. Believe me, Pak Wuluruan, there is something horrible happening here.'

'But the experts –' Pak Wuluruan protested.

Pak Talamosu cut him off. 'I do not trust your experts. What do these people know? Things are different in Kenukecil. It is better that we solve this problem in the traditional way. We have no need of experts. Do you want all of the girls of Amasi Dol to be raped by this devil?'

Pak Wuluruan sighed. 'No,' he said.

'The only way is to kill the devil. We must slaughter it and sever the head from the body and we must place it on a spike. Only then will we be free from trouble. Only then can we be enemies again.'

Pak Wuluruan looked uncertain.

'This is the only way, friend,' Pak Talamosu insisted. 'We must be friends so we can kill the devil; and we will kill the devil so we can be enemies again.'

When they had finished their conference, Pak Wuluruan

and Pak Talamosu shared a further cigarette. Then they returned to the village square and walked over to where the three visitors were seated on the bamboo bench in the shade.

Pak Wuluruan gave an apologetic smile. 'It's like this,' he said, squirming. 'We have decided to kill the devil. The people of Amasi Dol and the people of Amasi Da will kill the devil together.'

Sam stood up. 'You can't,' he said. Then, more quietly, he repeated. 'You can't.'

Pak Wuluruan looked from Sam to Pak Talamosu.

'This is no devil,' Sam said. 'This is just a monkey. There is no need for all of this. You must trust us. We are the experts.'

Pak Talamosu broke into the conversation. 'You say you are experts,' he snarled, 'but where were you last night when the devil was fucking my daughter? Where were you when it abducted Lucia Balakana and Bunny Masela? You just sit all day on the bamboo bench and you talk and think fine thoughts, but your science can do nothing here in Kenukecil. Nothing! You are as ignorant as newborn babies.'

Pak Wim spoke up. 'Excuse me,' he said, speaking in Kenukecilese. 'Pak Talamosu, perhaps you do not remember me. My name is Wim. I was born in Amasi Dol. I was brought up here. I am the assistant to these men. You may well remember me. There was a marriage . . .'

Pak Talamosu was wrong-footed by this. He had assumed that all three men were strangers. 'Wim?' he asked, looking at the battered and bandaged man. Then he laughed. 'You are the one who made bad *m'houna*,' he sneered.

Pak Wim did not shift his gaze as he might once have done. 'Yes, I made bad *m'houna*, but I am no longer ashamed. I have lived my life in shame and I will not live in shame any longer. I have returned to help you and you must listen to me.'

'Why should I listen to a man who makes bad *m'houna*?'

'And why should I help a man who permits his daughter to be violated within his own home?' Pak Wim replied sharply. The question provoked a kind of spasm in Pak Talamosu. The headman of Amasi Da seemed to shrink, becoming fragile and weak. He choked back a sob.

This entire exchange being conducted in Kenukecilese, neither Sam nor Pak Suryono was aware of exactly what was taking place. But they could tell from the way that Pak Wim seemed to grow in stature, despite his shame and his wounds, and by the way the fight seemed to bleed out of Pak Talamosu, that Wim had scored a success.

'Please,' Pak Wim continued, 'this is not the best way. The monkey is very rare, maybe the only one. The government want it found and they will be angry if it is killed. As *kepala desa*, both of you, Pak Wuluruan and Pak Talamosu, are the representatives of the government in your respective villages. You are duty bound to help. Not to do so would be treason.'

The two headmen looked at each other.

Pak Wim gave his most sincere and reasonable smile, although it was slightly marred by his injuries. 'I ask only this: that you give us a single day to find the monkey. One single day. Tomorrow you must provide us with three of your best hunters from each village. They will be put under the command of the Englishman and they will do everything they are asked. If by sunset tomorrow we have been unsuccessful, then you can resolve this thing in your own way, according to *adat*. But these are modern times, friends. Perhaps we should find a modern way to solve our problem.'

Pak Wuluruan and Pak Talamosu looked hesitant. 'Perhaps he is right,' Pak Wuluruan suggested.

'One day?' asked Pak Talamosu. 'Is that all you want? One day?'

'Only one,' Wim replied.

Then Pak Talamosu capitulated. 'In that case I agree, but my heart is heavy.' The headman of Amasi Da touched his chest lightly with his fingertips, close to his heart, and then let his hand drop.

'Do not worry, Pak,' Pak Wim reassured him. 'Everything will be good in the end. Let us agree this in the modern manner, by shaking hands.' He put out his hand and shook the hands of the two headmen.

'Now I will explain to my colleagues,' Pak Wim told them. He switched into Indonesian and related the whole story, in brief, to Pak Suryono and Sam. The two men nodded in agreement.

Sam smiled broadly at Pak Wim's display of resourcefulness. 'OK,' he said. 'One day it is. Let us try.'

# 24

That same day, six police officers and the chief of police stepped ashore at Sapratian. While his officers knocked on doors and interviewed all the men of the village, Pak Amukwasi walked towards the headland where the statue of the Virgin stood on a small hill. It was about a mile from the centre of the village and Pak Amukwasi, having spent most of his posting in Bantuk behind a desk, was surprised to find that over the previous few years his vital spirits had diminished a little and that he no longer had the same energy when it came to carrying out investigations in the field. The hill was hard-going. By the time he reached the top his shirt was damp with sweat. The Virgin, her back turned, gazed out over the sea. Pak Amukwasi walked around to the front of the figure. Although he was not sure what he was looking for, when he looked up at the statue of the Virgin he suspected that he had found it. Hanging around the Virgin's waist, tied there by a length of twine, were two objects. First there was a conch shell, hung so that the mouth was vertical; and secondly there was a large, dangling plantain. Man and woman: the Virgin had transformed into Batjameni.

As a pious Catholic, it was Pak Amukwasi's immediate thought to tear these abominations from the Virgin's waist; but as a good police officer he noted that one should not unthinkingly tamper with the scene of the crime. He jogged, sweating, back to the village and called together his men. Then he explained to them what he had seen.

'I want you to find the one who put the conch and the plantain around the Virgin's waist,' he said.

The investigation was largely inconclusive. Nobody in the village confessed, nor could the villagers understand why such a fuss was being made of such a minor matter when terrible crimes were being committed elsewhere. The only thing that people would say was that those responsible must have been from Tanarua, on the unstated grounds that the inhabitants of that village were the ancestral enemies of the people of Sapratian. It was on account of these false testimonies that Pak Amukwasi and his six officers put out to sea just before sunset and headed north for Tanarua. They arrived there at three o'clock on the following morning and in accord with *adat* lowered anchor and waited for the dawn.

It was, however, an error of judgement. As Pak Amukwasi's contingent of police officers was heading north, Sam was in his bed in Amasi Dol, fretting away the hours of the night. His mind, afflicted by insomnia, bobbed just below the surface of full consciousness. Occasionally he submerged into sleep only to find that something – a fragment of dream, a noise, a pang of physical discomfort – pulled him back to the surface. At one point he realized that he was awake and that tears were rolling down his cheeks, but he had no idea why. It was not that there was not reason enough for tears, only that all reasons he could find seemed to be after the fact.

Outside his window, it was a beautiful night. In the bay, Ibrahim was sleeping happily on deck of the *Ratu Mela*, his belly full of fresh fish, eggs and noodles. The sea was flooded with moonlight and a gentle breeze swayed the palm trees. In the village square the hunting dogs were curled asleep, their mottled mongrel fur camouflaging them against the stony ground, so that it was not clear where the shadows ended and where the dogs began. In the moonlight the boundaries of everything became indistinct.

Then a shadow appeared out of the forest, flickering on the border between reality and unreality. Had anybody been there to watch, they might have seen the figure seeming to resolve itself into that of a child, or if not a child a short man. In this light there was only seeming and no certainty. It stood with an air of thoughtfulness. A bird called in the trees, breaking the figure's concentration. It started to make its way across the village square in silence, looking from side to side, heading towards the headman's house. For a moment it stopped by Sam's window and peered through. The Englishman was shifting restlessly in his bed. The figure hesitated and let out a tiny sound, a kind of whimper. Sam glanced up and thought he saw something blocking out the moon; but by the time he had come to his senses, it had gone. He lay back down on his bed.

A little way from the headman's house the figure glanced first left, then right, and slipped back into the forest. It crept between the trees on delicate, experienced feet. Coming to a clearing, it called softly. From out of the trees came another, taller figure. A few moments later, in a pool of moonlight, any who dared to pass through the forest might have seen a pair of buttocks covered with light, reddish hair, rising and falling in that act to which we all owe our existence; and they might have remarked that the body stretched out below this curious figure contrasted strikingly with the russet tinge of these tight, round buttocks. Had they stayed to peer voyeuristically through the leaves, they might have seen a woman with her head tossed back, her open mouth letting out flurries of moans and cries that garlanded the sweet night air as the lovers went about their work.

Perhaps Sam heard these lovers' cries, without knowing

that he heard them; and in hearing them, perhaps his dreams returned to the last time he himself performed this act, that last, sad, time with Fon in his Jogja apartment. And it may be that the other villagers also heard something and dreamed of how the following morning the devil's latest victim would come staggering from the forest, unkempt and smiling with delight.

The night passed without further incident. The peace of the morning was unbroken by cries of 'shame' and blows rained down on another poor village girl. Sam Rivers woke with a heavy head and a heavy heart and breakfasted on sweet coffee and fried bananas. Pak Suryono and Pak Wim, who had already eaten, were seated outside, engaged in conversation. Pak Wim's wounds seemed to be healing well. He had removed his sling for the first time, although he nursed his arm as he sat and chatted to the businessman. Sam noticed that Pak Suryono's distaste for Pak Wim had begun to dwindle: there was between the two men now a glimmer of something not unlike friendship, the kind of friendship that is forged in adversity and lasts only as long as this adversity lasts.

Damianus Wuluruan sat opposite Sam, fidgeting and watching him eat, shooting him occasional, awkward smiles. 'The men will be here very soon,' he said. 'I am praying that you will be able to help us.'

'As am I,' agreed Sam, drinking his coffee. 'I am praying with all my heart.'

# 25

On the evening that followed Lucia Balakana's fall, Mr Liao tightened his tie and slid the knot towards his neck, looking in the mirror and congratulating himself that he was, after all, rather an attractive man. He gave the tie another tug and put his glasses back on his nose. Under his breath he murmured a few mantras. In his pocket he fiddled with his *mala* beads, which had been given to him by a Tibetan Lama back in Taiwan. The Matsya Corporation had funded the Lama's visit on a speaking tour and Mr Liao had drawn reassurance from the Lama's announcement that, due to the corporation's services to Buddhism, all employees, past, present and future, would be guaranteed favourable rebirths, if not into a pure land then at the least into the middle classes.

Mr Gu was due at five o'clock, when the heat of the day had become a little less severe. Tonight they were to sign the contract. The Matsya Corporation was to be awarded exclusive fishing rights in the seas to the east of Kenukecil and around Kenubesar up to a maximum of thirty kilometres from the shore. Mr Gu had brokered the deal and would be taking a percentage of the profits.

The interested parties included, although they were not restricted to, a representative from ABRI – the Indonesian armed forces – Mr Liao and various bureaucrats in Kota Ambon. No Kenukecilese were involved in the negotiations for the simple reason that Mr Liao regarded the local people as ignorant and uneducated, enemies of progress. The contract was for five years and, although it permitted the local people to fish 'within reasonable limits' for their own livelihood, this did not extend to permitting them sale of their catch at a profit, because such would interfere with the commercial interests of the corporation. This implied that, strictly speaking, the children who walked from door to door in the villages with fish strung on a pole to sell for a few rupiah would thenceforth be liable to prosecution, which, in Mr Liao's view, was only right.

His tie straight, Mr Liao left his room and went down the corridor to the cheaper room where Mr Tan was housed. He knocked. The door opened and Mr Tan's bullet head popped out. 'Yes?'

'Mr Tan, let us go.'

Mr Liao and Mr Tan had worked together since they both came to Kenukecil. Mr Liao was the more cerebral of the pair while Mr Tan provided the physical force necessary to drive Mr Liao's more intellectual understandings home. With Mr Liao, Mr Tan was meek and docile, in the way that certain dogs, savage with all strangers, curl up and become as gentle as lambs when in the company of their owners, revealing their stomachs to be tickled and drooling in pleasure. Lacking intellectual refinement, Mr Tan's pleasures in life were simple. He loved two things above all others: administering beatings to Mr Liao's enemies and sleeping with whores. The simple life has many variants: only some of them are swathed in saffron.

Mr Liao and Mr Tan made their way to the jetty at the back of the Lovely Vista Hotel. The contrast between Mr Tan in vest, shorts and flip-flops and Mr Liao in business suit and tie was striking. Mr Gu was already there, dressed in his Armani and looking not at all like the humble shopkeeper he had seemed only an hour before. Even if one was acquainted with the Chinaman who ran the shop in the Hope Market, one would be hard pressed to make the connection between the shopkeeper and this man of elegance with his beard carefully combed and perfumed and his hair tied back. He had drawn up at the entrance of the Lovely Vista in a blacked-out 4 x 4 and slipped into the building smiling the courteous smile of a man confident in his own power as the vehicle pulled away with a purr.

Seeing Mr Liao and Mr Tan approach, Mr Gu rose to his feet and smiled genially. 'Mr Liao,' he beamed, 'tonight is the night we have all been waiting for. I trust you are well. How is your lovely wife? You must again thank her for the time I spent in Taipei. And your children! Delightful!' He shook Mr Liao's hand warmly, but did not stoop to acknowledging Mr Tan.

At the table with Mr Gu was the ABRI officer who had helped negotiate the deal. The military man stood and took Mr Liao's right hand in his two hands, clasping it earnestly. Mr Liao and Mr Tan joined the other two men at the small wooden table.

Thomas brought beers without being asked, and then Mr Gu lifted his briefcase on to the table and clicked open the catches. He pulled out a sheaf of paperwork. 'It is all here,' he said, smiling at Mr Liao. 'I have the remainder of the signatures already.'

'Everything is arranged?'

'Everything. I see that you have agreed with Matsya to have ten per cent of all profits transferred to my account. Thank you for your kind consideration. Of course, I have made sure that this payment is not recorded in the paperwork but I understand that you' – at this he nodded to both of his associates – 'are men of honour, so there is no need for documentation. All we need are your signatures.'

Mr Liao took up the sheets of paper and leaned back in his chair, reading each page through carefully. This took a considerable amount of time, and while Mr Gu appreciated the care with which his business partner was going through the contract, the ABRI officer and Mr Tan found the wait boring. They drank their beer sullenly and ordered several more bottles.

By the time the papers had been signed and put away again, the sun had set and the bare lightbulbs at the back of the hotel were illuminated. The four men shook hands and settled down to a further celebratory drink to seal their deal.

'You will be going back to Taipei to tell them that you have signed,' Mr Gu said to Mr Liao over a beer.

'Indeed,' agreed Mr Liao. 'I leave on the flight on the twenty-fifth of the month. Mr Tan will remain here. I will be away two months. When I return we will be able to begin work.'

'So, Mr Liao, you have time on your hands until then.' He turned to the ABRI officer. 'And you, Pak?'

'I am going nowhere,' chuckled the military man. 'It is my duty to remain here.'

Mr Gu took another drink. 'If this is so, we have time to celebrate our deal properly. I would like to take you all on a pleasure trip, if I may.'

'A pleasure trip?' Mr Liao smiled.

'I have a boat. It is a good boat, comfortable, relaxing. I suggest that we sail tomorrow morning to Makalau in Kenubesar. We can moor just off the coast. I will provide beer. I have whisky also. Several good bottles from Scotland. What they call' – here he lapsed into English – '*single malt.*' Mr Gu reverted to Indonesian. 'If there is a heaven, they drink this whisky in heaven, believe me. And do not worry about expense. I will pay for everything. It is what I like to think of as corporate hospitality. We can spend a week on board, we can do a little sightseeing and we can be back in Bantuk in time for your flight, Mr Liao.'

'We are honoured,' murmured the Taiwanese fisheries officer.

'I will also provide girls, of course,' Mr Gu added, lowering his voice and taking off his glasses to gaze at the other men with every appearance of sincerity. 'I have many fine girls. They are all fresh and clean. I have a new one, who started just this week. Her name is Bunny. I have already tried her out myself – a good merchant tests his merchandise – and I can guarantee that she is the very best quality. I think, Mr Liao, she would be very much to your taste.'

Unconsciously, Mr Liao reached into his pocket and began to finger the beads of his *mala*. He noticed the first stirrings of an erection. A slow smile also dawned on Mr Tan's face. He was having difficulty following the conversation, his Indonesian being basic, but he picked up on this part. 'Girls?' he asked, and then in English he added, 'Fucky-fucky?'

'Fucky-fucky!' said Mr Gu, laughing and slapping him on the back. 'As much as you like!' Mr Gu seemed delighted by the Taiwanese fisherman's use of English.

The men retired each to their separate beds early on the Friday morning and slept until late. When the sun was well risen, Mr Gu returned to the hotel to find Mr Liao and Mr Tan eating breakfast. He told the men that everything was ready for their journey. At noon they boarded the *Lerebulan*, Mr Gu's boat. Bunny Masela sat on the deck at the front, her yellow dress billowing about her in the breeze, laughing coarsely, feeling free in a way she had never felt free before. Mr Liao sat at the back, watching the sea eagles. Mr Tan drank beer from a can, watching Bunny. The ABRI officer lounged on his back in his dark glasses, holding his gun in his hand. And Mr Gu, no longer in his Armani but back in his soiled sarong and string vest, the clothing in which he felt most comfortable, pottered around, making sure that the engine of the boat was in good order, shouting to boys on the pier to bring him this or that for the journey.

The other five prostitutes were sitting and playing cards with each other down below decks, once again all dressed in yellow. They had a guitar with them. The tallest of them – a pockmarked girl known as Flower, in English, because it made her sound exotic – was blessed with a natural facility for music; and although she had never had a single lesson she could pick out a tune and seemed to know instinctively which chords to play to underpin a melody. Her favourite song was 'All You Need is Love', which she liked to play to Western clients, who generally found it charming.

Sitting beside Flower was Amara, from Aru. Petite, with dark skin and a melancholy air, she had been expelled from her family's house for becoming pregnant to a man who worked for a logging company. He had left her and she had then lost the child, eventually finding her way to Bantuk with some Buginese traders. Her melancholy air was attractive in particular to poets: Amara had sheafs of verse written to her beauty, in all the languages of the world, but none of it made her happy, nor did the fact that at the moment she was winning at cards. Susie *Bule*, so called because of her light skin and blue eyes, was losing the game quite badly, while Nenek or grandmother, so called because she was already fifty, was acting as dealer. Nenek's looks were not what they had once been, but there is in the art of love no substitute for experience and for every man who longs for a simpering virgin there will be another who longs for a woman who has touched many men in many ways, a woman who caresses her client as a virtuoso violinist might caress a tune out of a violin. Finally Ayesha, a Muslim girl who had fallen into this life by a series of unexpected accidents and who nevertheless clung to the raft of her faith the way that a woman tossed into the sea in a shipwreck might cling to a single plank, sat watching, having no liking for cards or gambling or, in truth, whoring.

Mr Gu had chosen these particular girls for the expedition – he called them all girls, even Nenek – to cater to the broadest range of tastes. As the *Lerebulan* made its leisurely way out of Bantuk and then turned north, rounding the small island of Kenubesar, already Mr Tan and the man from ABRI had started work on one of the girls each. Mr Liao, however, was taking his time. Mr Gu had assured them that there was time to sample each of the girls if they wished – or even all of them together, if they were up to the task. There was, Mr Liao thought, no great rush.

They moored the *Lerebulan* off Makalau in the late afternoon. Makalau was widely acknowledged to be a wretched village, as Kenubesar was acknowledged to be a wretched island, a place haunted by the spirits of the dead, meeting place for the witches who could be seen flying towards the forests behind the village every night with their paraffin lamps in their hands, home to only a few families who scratched out a living without joy. But it was secluded and out of the way. There was a well in the village for fresh water and it would be possible to buy fruit and meat from the villagers if they needed any further supplies. They were to spend two days and two nights there, fishing, fucking and drinking. Then they would cruise the circumference of Kenukecil, taking in both the inhabited east coast and the uninhabited west coast, before returning to Bantuk. The girls would cook and look after the passengers' every need. They would fetch water and buy food and see to it that the men were all but crippled with pleasure.

By the time they reached Makalau, the party was getting going. Two of the girls were sitting semi-naked on Mr Tan's lap and Flower was playing her own version of a popular Ambonese song: '*Satu Tetes Air Susu, Mama*' – one drop of your milk, mother. The ABRI officer was in tears as he remembered his own mother and the village of his birth. Bunny drew him towards her and gave him a milkless breast to suckle. Mr Liao had an ache at the back of his eyes, something that always happened when he drank beer in the hot sun. He swigged some more to blot it out and leaned over towards Ayesha.

Mr Gu was sitting in the bows with dignified calm, looking towards Kenubesar. From the outside it may have looked as if he was contemplating the beauties of nature but in truth he was wondering whether there were any useful minerals to be had in the soil and calculating how much the timber from the trees would fetch. He turned round to see Mr Liao put his hand on Ayesha's knee. She whispered something in his ear and Mr Liao nodded his head sagely. Then he laughed and she kissed him on the mouth, reaching down with her hand to where the bulge was growing in his trousers.

My trade, thought Mr Gu, is happiness. And with this pleasant thought, he lay back down on the deck and, sheltering his eyes from the sun with his bare arm, fell asleep.

# 26

Sam Rivers had had only a little sleep, so he was not in the best of possible moods on the morning of Saturday, 9 November when six of the finest hunters from Amasi Dol and Amasi Da were to be placed under his leadership to track down the devil that was terrorizing the villagers of Kenukecil.

Rumours concerning the creature were spreading across the island at an astonishing rate. The devil had been seen dancing in the village square at night. He had frightened an old woman who was relieving herself out in the forest. He had tried to abduct another young girl, although this particular girl was known to be of loose virtue and not entirely trustworthy. Two men hunting pigs in the forest claimed to have seen him sitting up a tree, singing lewd songs. In fact there was hardly a single person in the whole of Kenukecil who did not have a devil story to tell. The stories were so various and so lurid that many of the islanders were beginning to speculate anxiously whether there might be not one but rather one hundred or one thousand devils at large, a whole army of agents of sin on the rampage. This view was supported by the startling differences in the stories that were being circulated; some claiming that the devil they had seen was tall, some that it was short, some saying that they had spotted a creature with a single head, still others saying that their devil had many heads, some speaking of a tail with which the devil hung from the branches of the trees, others asserting that, no, the thing was quite tailless and went upright, as a man walks. A number of reports claimed that the devil was, contrary to popular opinion, tall and white, with a mass of curly red hair and – the strangest thing of all – a woman. When the latter reached Sam's ears, he assumed they pointed not to anything demonic but to confused sightings of Dr Aletheia Groeber, who had left Bantuk on foot and was no doubt also heading northwards.

As he breakfasted under the attentive gaze of his host, Pak Wuluruan, Sam wondered whether the Gugu had managed to impregnate any village girls in the night: no cries of alarm had gone up in the village, no messengers arrived on motorbikes to tell of new abductions. Briefly he also speculated on whether the offspring of an *orang pendek* and human female might be viable. Viable but infertile, perhaps, he thought to himself. Like a human mule. He drank his coffee and watched the sun rising. The condensed milk with which the coffee had been sweetened seemed to line the inside of his mouth with a thick film. By the time the sun had set, he thought, either the creature would be recovered, or else he and his companions would have to leave the village, surrendering the Gugu to its fate. The creature would be slaughtered by armies of the Kenukecilese, this being who had looked into his eyes and in whose gaze he had recognized a kind of kinship, this creature he had saved from the taxidermist's implements in Jakarta only for it to be impaled by a hunter's arrow elsewhere, for whom he had risked even his life with Fon, his future happiness. If it were now to be killed, after all of this, what would he do?

He wondered where Fon was. It would be before dawn back in Jakarta. Was she asleep? Was she dreaming of him? Was she awake? What thoughts passed through her head? Sam put down his coffee, leaving half of it in the cup. 'What a fucking mess,' he whispered to himself.

Pak Wuluruan looked at him. 'Mr Samuel?' he asked.

'*Tidak apa-apa,*' Sam replied. It's nothing. 'When will we be ready? There is not much time.'

'Soon, Mr Samuel. I will gather the men from Amasi Dol now,' he said. 'We will be ready soon.'

Sam nodded in thanks, left his breakfast things and stepped outside to wait on the bamboo bench. Pak Wim and Pak Suryono came over to join him. Pak Wim looked more comfortable this morning. 'Today we will know,' said Pak Suryono. 'Today we will know the outcome.'

'Perhaps,' Sam replied. 'But even if we do recapture it, there's the trip to Australia . . .'

'That will not be difficult. If we are lucky, you can leave tonight,' Pak Suryono reassured him.

Sam rubbed his eyes. For a brief moment, he thought he might stand up, shake hands with Pak Suryono, thank him and simply leave: walk back to Bantuk, forgetting the whole business. It was not the money that stopped him from doing so. It was the Gugu. He could not leave this strange cousin to be murdered by the people of Kenukecil. How could he bear the thought of the creature's head being stuck on a pole outside Amasi Dol? No, he had some responsibility. He would have to see the matter through to the end.

Pak Suryono, noting Sam's weary air of distraction, patted him on the arm. 'I am sorry, tuan,' he said. 'I am sorry. This should not have happened. I, too, am responsible. Perhaps I should have used a metal cage. I did not know how strong the Gugu was.'

Pak Wim took no part in the conversation and seemed to have forgotten the purpose of their visit altogether. He looked across the village square. From time to time, old acquaintances from Amasi Dol passed by and, having heard that their village's errant son had returned, bade him a courteous 'Good morning, Pak Wim.'

'Good morning,' Pak Wim replied to each of them. These

simple greetings, over which there was not a shadow of the shame that had pursued him from island to island, eased his heart.

Not long afterwards, the hunters from Amasi Dol arrived, three strong men all of whom could fell a buffalo with a single chop of the machete or spear a pig from thirty paces. They greeted Sam and Pak Suryono and shook hands with Pak Wim. Two of them were old schoolfriends whom Pak Wim recognized although he could not recall their names. 'Welcome back,' they said. 'It has been a long time.'

They brought with them bows and arrows, the arrows laced with poison drawn from the roots of forest plants. The poison, they excitedly explained, could induce instant paralysis, which would last for several hours but cause no other ill effects. While they were discussing the virtues of their poison tips, the jeep appeared from Amasi Da with the second group of hunters. The two groups of men – those from Amasi Dol and those from Amasi Da – eyed each other suspiciously.

Sam noted that all six were armed and it entered his mind that perhaps this joint venture between rival villagers was not the best way forward. He put the thought to one side and stood before the hunters. 'Thank you for coming,' he said. Then he explained the plan: they would track the creature and try to surround it. Once they were within range they would fire a single arrow into the creature's hindquarters. When the creature was thus paralysed, it would be bundled up and returned as quickly as possible to Amasi Dol, from where it would be placed in a dugout canoe and taken to the boat where it could be held below decks. What might happen from that point onwards was hazy in Sam's mind, but it seemed at present such a distant possibility that he did not worry himself unduly about it. What did worry him was the thought of a poison arrow in the creature's hindquarters; but with the resolve of a doctor who knows that he must choose for his patient between a painful operation and death, he recognized that there was little else that he could do.

'Do you understand the instructions?' Sam asked the men.

They all nodded their assent.

'Please, explain what I have just told you,' Sam asked them. One of the hunters – the oldest of the Amasi Da contingent – gave a rambling but more or less accurate summation of what Sam had said. Sam gave a tight, nervous smile. 'Good,' he said. 'In that case, I think we are ready to begin.'

# 27

It was shortly before noon when they set off from Amasi Dol. They had spent two hours haggling over the best direction to go. A number of villagers were called who could testify to seeing the Gugu in the past twenty-four hours. Having sorted the plausible testimonies from the more fanciful, Sam, Pak Wim and Pak Suryono reached an agreement, with the help of a map, about the most likely place that the Gugu might be found. According to the most reliable recent sightings, the Gugu had been seen just to the south of Amasi Dol. It seemed that after its conquest the night before last in Amasi Da it had, for some reason, started to head back in the direction of Bantuk. Between Amasi Dol and Desa Baru, a low and jagged line of cliffs rose up to the landward side of the road, perhaps half a mile into the forest, and the youngest of the hunters from Amasi Dol, a man who had about him an astute and un-ruffled air, suggested that perhaps the creature was using one of the caves in this low line of cliffs as a base. This being so, another of the men added, the best strategy would be to establish first of all whether the thing was in the cliffs. If it was, then they would flush it out and, sealing off the bottom of the cliff, trap it in the southern-most part of the island.

'And if it is not in the caves?' asked Sam.

The hunter grinned. 'At night it fucks our daughters.' He said this without the moral outrage of many of his fel-low villagers, but with something approaching admiration.

'By day it sleeps, by night it fucks. It will come out before sunset, because it will want to fuck again.'

'So,' Sam concluded, 'we go to the cliffs, we search the caves and if we have not found it we think again?'

The men gave their assent.

'All right,' said Sam. 'Let us take the jeep.'

They had use of the jeep for the day, so they would be able to travel at some speed, but as the road stuck resolutely to the east coast, at some time it would be necessary to leave the jeep and make their way on foot into the forest. There were nine passengers in all. Pak Suryono and Pak Wim sat with five of the hunters in the back while Sam sat in front with the driver, a man from Amasi Da. As they pulled out of Amasi Dol, the hunters gave a huge whoop. They headed out of the village singing a warrior song in Kenukecilese.

In the passenger seat, Sam was wrestling with a growing sense of anxiety. 'Can't you tell them to be quiet?' he asked the driver.

The driver turned his head and shouted something in the native language of the islands. There was a pause, then one of the hunters replied. Everyone – except Pak Suryono and Sam, neither of whom spoke the language – laughed.

When they reached the point at which the road turned and the cliff could be seen rising up above the scrubby greenery of the forest, the driver stopped. The hunters got out and squinted towards the low bluff, the rocks rising up towards the plateau at the south of the island. 'We will go and look by the cliff,' they said. 'We will see what we can find.'

Three men – the three from Amasi Da – disappeared into the undergrowth, carrying bows, arrows and spears.

Sam gazed after them into the tangled forest. 'And what do we do?' he asked one of the remaining hunters.

'We wait,' the man said with a kind of shrug, lighting

up a clove cigarette and staring off into the thick green scrub.

They sat down to wait. The hunters were gone a long time. Pak Suryono loosened his tie. One of the hunters offered Sam a *kretek* and, although he never smoked, Sam accepted. He sat by the side of the road, tasting the tobacco and cloves as the smoke filled his lungs.

When the men eventually re-emerged they had grave looks on their faces. They spoke to Pak Wim in rapid Kenu-kecilese. Pak Wim listened, nodding his head thoughtfully. When the hunters had finished, they sat down by the side of the road with looks of defiance.

'The creature is by the cliff,' Pak Wim explained. 'They know it is there.'

'So?' Sam looked at the men. They glared back at him. 'Why have they returned, if they know the creature is by the cliff?'

'They will not go and find him. They are afraid.'

'They are hunters. What are they afraid of?'

'Not the creature. They are not afraid of the monkey or the devil or whatever it is. These are brave men. They are afraid of the cliff.'

'They are afraid of the cliff?' Sam laughed.

'Look.' Pak Wim pointed to the cliff, his hand following its undulating line. 'Do you not see?'

'It is a cliff. What is there to see?'

Pak Wim sighed. 'You do not understand,' he said. 'It is not like your country here. This is a dangerous place. There are many things you do not know.'

Sam stared at the bluff.

'Look again, Mr Sam. You see the shape of the cliff? It is in the shape of a man who is sleeping.'

Sam narrowed his eyes, the detail in the landscape blurring; but he couldn't see it.

'It is the body of a *swangi*, a witch, that has turned to

stone,' Pak Wim explained. 'The men heard the voices of spirits talking in the caves when they got close to the cliff. They were afraid, so they came back here.'

'But they are hunters!' Sam protested.

'They are not afraid of hunting. They are not afraid of buffalo. They are not afraid of being killed by spears and arrows. These are brave men, Mr Sam. The only things they fear are ghosts and spirits and *swangi*. These men are not stupid. They will not go towards the cliff.'

Sam stretched. 'What will it take?'

'It is not about money, Mr Sam,' Pak Wim said.

'Fifty dollars each?'

Sam pointed to the hunters, who were huddled together and seemed to be having some kind of dispute. 'Ask them,' he said.

Pak Wim asked the hunters. They discussed for a short while and relayed their judgement.

'Too little,' Pak Wim said. 'They are taking a very big risk.'

'Seventy?' suggested Sam.

The hunters went into conference again, albeit briefly. When they had finished, they all smiled in shy agreement. 'Seventy,' said the youngest in Indonesian. 'For seventy dollars each, we will take the risk.'

'This is the deal, then,' Sam said. 'If the creature is caught you get seventy dollars each. If it is not caught, you get nothing.'

Once they had agreed the terms and conditions, the three hunters strolled back into the forest, leaving three with the jeep, as well as Sam, Pak Suryono and Pak Wim. Sam wandered round the jeep, watched a lazy monitor lizard ambling through the undergrowth fifty yards away, and sucked in the air through his teeth nervously. Pak Wim was engaged in animated conversation with the hunters, spinning yarns about his years in exile. His stories were punctuated by murmurings of awe – here was a man who had seen the world, who had experienced things that his fellow villagers had never experienced – and by bursts of laughter. Pak Suryono had found a place by the side of the road where he could sit in the shade, and there he sat, immobile and silent, with an air of resigned hopelessness.

After half an hour, a shout came from the forest in the direction of the cliff, seemingly a long way away. Then there was another. Pak Wim broke his storytelling mid-flow. Pak Suryono sat up as if an electric current had been passed through him. And Sam turned towards the woods where, albeit faintly, he could hear the sound of something crashing through the undergrowth. Then he spotted a dark figure on the cliff, just above the line of the trees. From this distance it could have been the figure of a child, scurrying over the piles of boulders that had accumulated over the millennia at the foot of the bluff. Curiously, it was at this precise moment that he saw what Pak Wim had tried to point out to him earlier: yes, the line of the cliff was in the form of a sleeping man, a *swangi* perhaps. Sam shivered.

All six men by the jeep watched in silence as the creature leapt across the boulders. It was the first time that Sam had seen it move. And any thoughts that it might have been a child were dispelled by seeing *how* it moved. Its rapid progress across the boulders was graceful and sure-footed. The Gugu held itself fully upright, not like an ape, but like a man: a man of uncommon agility and strength, compact, lithe, beautiful, tinged with red. The Gugu had reached the cliff-face now and was starting to scale the rock, its movements rapid.

From below one of the hunters appeared among the boulders. The hunter paused, took the bow from his back and fitted an arrow.

'No!' Sam shouted, involuntarily. The creature seemed to pause, hanging to the cliff with the ease of a lizard on the wall of a house and glancing over its shoulder to where, perhaps, it could see the small group of men by the jeep, a half-mile or more away. Did it recognize the Englishman on whom it had been spying the night before? Did it recollect the sound of Sam's voice, the voice it had heard speaking softly to it in the dark of the *Ratu Mela*'s hold, a voice that had not been rough and coarse like many of the others it had heard, but gentle and afraid?

Sam lifted his hand to cover his mouth. There was a silence, followed a few seconds later by a shout from the hunter. The arrow had missed, glancing off the rocks and falling, broken, amongst the boulders. The Gugu resumed its climb, more rapidly now. Two more of the hunters appeared. The Gugu swung itself up onto a ledge, a third of the way up the cliff, and looked down at the hunters, before resuming its climb. Pak Suryono, Pak Wim and the hunters stared at the cliff. All three hunters now took aim. The creature was moving swiftly, zigzagging up the cliff unpredictably, a hard target. The hunters let fly a volley of arrows, but the thing continued to move. Then they lowered their bows and watched for a full three minutes as it climbed the rest of the cliff and, with one more backward glance, disappeared over the lip of the cliff and was gone.

'They missed,' said Sam and then, seeing that the hunters were withdrawing from their positions at the foot of the cliff, he added, 'Why did they not shoot again?'

One of the hunters took him by the arm. 'You do not want the devil to die,' he said. 'If they had shot it then, it would have fallen and broken its skull. We, the people of Kenukecil, would have killed it already, but you say you want it to live. Come, we must get back into the vehicle. We will go towards the south and trap it at the top of the cliff. The Amasi Da people will stay where they are at the bottom of the cliff among the rocks. The devil will not approach Bantuk: there are too many people. So we will be able to trap it. If it climbs down, the Amasi Da people will be able to get it and if it stays at the top, then we people from Amasi Dol can drive it towards the edge.'

The hunters climbed into the back of the jeep. Sam got into the passenger seat. Pak Wim looked at him. 'Who will drive?' he asked. 'Our driver is by the cliff.'

'Do you drive?' Sam asked.

Pak Wim nodded. The keys were still hanging in the ignition.

'Then you drive.'

Pak Suryono joined the hunters in the back of the jeep. It was not as crowded as before.

'We will take the road through Desa Baru and then turn off towards the airport,' Pak Wim suggested. 'From there we will go into the forest on foot and meet the creature at the top of the cliff.' He turned to Sam with a grin. 'Mr Sam,' he said, 'I feel that today we are going to be lucky.'

Then Pak Wim started the engine. The jeep, which had been left in gear, jolted forwards and stalled. Sam looked sideways at Pak Wim. 'Are you sure that you know how to drive?'

Turning off the ignition, then starting it up again, Pak Wim grinned. 'It has been a long time, Mr Sam, that is all. I will remember.'

He put his foot on the accelerator and they headed towards Desa Baru at speed, swerving between potholes.

There were no seatbelts. Sam held on to the window with his right hand and grasped the underside of his seat with his left, biting his lip. The hunters in the back were silent. On the approach to Desa Baru, where the road climbs up a long, shallow hill, they saw a dark shape begin to mass above the trees. 'What is that?' asked Sam. Billows of smoke were rising up into the sky ahead of them. '*Cocok tanah?*' Sam asked.

'No,' said Pak Wim, easing his foot off the accelerator and changing down a gear. 'Not that.' He stuck his head out of the window and looked at the spreading umbrella of smoke. For men such as Sam, smoke is simply smoke; but Pak Wim, raised in a village, knew the difference between the smoke that comes from farmers clearing the land and the smoke that comes from a village being put to the torch; he knew that the smoke from burning houses is not the same as the smoke from burning rubber.

'Tyres,' said Pak Wim, smelling the air. 'Burning tyres.'

'Tyres?' asked Sam.

They reached the brow of the hill. Pak Wim braked sharply and the wheels of the jeep threw up a cloud of dust. In front of them, perhaps a hundred yards off, just before the ceremonial arch at the entrance to Desa Baru, a wall of orange flame stretched across the road from six piles of burning tyres into the shimmering sky. Above the flames bloomed cumulus formations of purple–grey smoke and the air was heavy with the smell of burning rubber. A little way off, Sam could see another column of smoke. In front of the flames wavered thirty or forty shadows, a living *wayang* played with men and not puppets.

Pak Wim opened the door of the jeep and climbed out. Sam cautiously followed suit. Above the roar of the flames he could hear rhythmic chanting, although the words were lost on him. It was a shadow play of warriors, with machetes, bows, arrows and spears. Not all were armed. Some were dancing in time with the chanting. Others seemed convulsed, sobbing and wailing.

Pak Wim walked around to the front of the jeep. He turned to Sam. 'I will go and look,' he said. 'Stay here.'

Pak Wim walked towards the flames. Sam watched his transformation from a man of flesh and blood to a shifting shadow amongst shadows. The hunters jumped out of the jeep and Pak Suryono joined them. They clustered around where Sam stood. The Englishman shivered once.Sweat was breaking out on his forehead. He lifted his hand and ran it across his brow. It came away wet. He rested one hand on the bonnet of the jeep to steady himself, closing his eyes. He felt sick. Through the clamour, he imagined that he could hear the gamelan, somewhere far off. The afternoon breeze was whispering in his ear as Fonny had once whispered that night at the *wayang kulit*, when she had pressed her thin, angular body towards him. Sam opened his eyes. The play of figures in front of the flames seemed no more real than the legends of Rama and Sita, the world nothing other than a flickering of shadow-puppets against a background of fire, a play of illusion and counter-illusion. He tried to make out Pak Wim, but he could not. All the figures seemed the same, playing their part in a drama that had nothing to do with him, projected on a distant screen. If only Fonny was there, he thought, she would murmur the meanings of all this into his ear; but there was only the breeze, which told him nothing meaningful.

Sam shivered again. Sickness began to take hold at the bottom of his stomach. 'Fon,' he whispered. 'Fon. What have I done?'

Then a figure emerged from this shadow-world before him. Uncertain and wavering at first, it gradually took on form and separated out from the incomprehensible drama. It was Pak Wim, making his way back to the jeep. 'Mr Sam,' he said. 'There is no passing.'

'What's going on?' Sam asked.

'They say they are waiting. They say we cannot pass in the vehicle. They have blocked the roads at both ends of the village to protect themselves from the devil. We must leave the jeep where it is.' Pak Wim leaned into the jeep, took the keys out of the ignition and handed them to one of the hunters.

'What are they waiting for?'

Pak Wim shook his head. 'We must walk,' he said. 'Come.'

On any other stretch of road they could have cut through the forest, but the road that led into Desa Baru was caught between the cliffs on the southern side that led up to the plateau at the south of the island and those on the north that plunged down into the sea. The only way forward was through the heart of the village of Desa Baru; then they could round the foot of the landward cliffs and head to the plateau. 'Come,' Pak Wim repeated.

He turned to the hunters and spoke in Kenukecilese. They made approving noises. 'The hunters will accompany us,' Pak Wim said. 'They will protect us. Do not worry. We have the cliff guarded, so the devil will not escape. We will have to go on foot, but there is still time. *Ayo!* Let's go.'

They walked slowly towards the fire: six men, three of them armed. The sound of chanting, the furious roar of the fire became louder. As they approached the flames, Sam felt the heat on his face. The shadows became three-dimensional as they approached, these actors in this strange play of fire and darkness.

One of the men approached them. He wore combat fatigues, his face was blackened with soot, a bandana tied around his head and a rifle held in his hand. He was grinning exultantly. 'Welcome, friends!' he shouted. 'I am the Colonel. You are very welcome. You have come on a happy day.'

The cloud overhead was now seeping its apocalyptic blackness across the sky and blotting out the sun. Sam's shivering intensified.

The Colonel looked at the six visitors. He studied the Javanese businessman's suit and stared for a few moments at the Englishman. 'You have a foreigner,' he said in Indonesian.

'He is a friend,' Pak Wim replied. 'He is an Englishman.'

'Does he have any devils with him?'

'I have no devils,' Sam replied in Indonesian.

The Colonel started. 'The Englishman speaks Bahasa Indonesia?' he asked, directing his words to Pak Wim. 'Ask him if he has any devils.'

Sam held up a hand to prevent Pak Wim from speaking on his behalf. 'Please,' he said, 'I have no devils. I am going to Bantuk with my friends. It is urgent.'

The Colonel gave this some thought and concluded that Sam's command of Bahasa Indonesia was the clearest confirmation of devilry there could be: an Englishman who speaks Bahasa Indonesia, he reasoned, was impossible, for Englishmen speak nothing but English. Yet devils, being crafty, know how to speak in all possible tongues. The Colonel turned his back on the new arrivals and shouted to his fellow villagers. 'We have a devil!' he shouted. 'We have a devil in the form of an Englishman!'

The chanting, dancing and wailing stopped. Several men stepped forward, each one transforming as he did so from a shadow puppet into a figure of flesh and blood.

'We have a devil,' the Colonel repeated. 'The devil has made its home in an Englishman, but it speaks in Bahasa Indonesia.'

Sam glanced round. Five or six men had now surrounded him, cutting him off from his companions. The Colonel took him by one arm, another man grasped the other. A moment more and the rest of the crowd had clustered around this possessed Englishman, some of them armed and some not. Lifting his gun, the Colonel fired a single shot into the blackened sky. 'We have the devil!' he shouted. 'The devil has come to us! We will wash him clean!'

Sam was jostled by the crowd, both arms pinioned. 'What will you do to me?' he shouted

The Colonel did not reply. Instead, in Indonesian, he chanted, 'Kill the devil! Kill the devil!' – a chant that was taken up by the rest of the crowd.

Sam was pouring with sweat, panic distorting his face. 'Pak Wim!' he shouted. 'Pak Suryono!' Then Pak Wim's face appeared. He had pushed his way through the crowd in an attempt to help the Englishman who, after all, still owed him five hundred dollars. 'Pak Wim!' Sam yelled. 'What are they going to do to me?'

Pak Wim shouted something in Kenukecilese and the crowd backed off, although the Colonel and the other man holding Sam's arms did not release their grip. 'They will not hurt you, Mr Sam. You must go with them. Do not worry, we will come with you. You must go with them.'

The Colonel spoke directly to Pak Wim. 'We must not waste any time,' he said. 'The pastor has said that Christ-Batjameni will come. He has spoken many prophecies. When He comes, all devils will be defeated. We will kill the Englishman's devils. Then we will wait together for the coming of Christ-Batjameni. We will give the Englishman a *mandi adat*.'

Sam looked at Pak Wim in alarm. '*Mandi adat? Itu apa?*' What's that?

'The devil speaks!' cried the Colonel. 'We will wash the Englishman clean. We will destroy the devil.'

Then the crowd began to move off again, dragging the Englishman along with it, back towards the flames. Sam glanced up to see Pak Wim's face disappearing into the tumultuous crowd.

# 28

Pak Wim wormed his way back through the crowd to find Pak Suryono and the hunters. 'They are taking Mr Sam,' he said breathlessly. 'We must go with them. They are going to perform a *mandi adat*.' Pak Suryono looked puzzled, but the hunters all made approving noises. On occasions such as this, they thought, a *mandi adat* was not such a bad idea.

The crowd, with Sam somewhere in the centre, skirted the burning tyres and headed under the arch, now black with smoke, into the village. Pak Wim, Pak Suryono and the hunters followed them. Pak Wim took Pak Suryono by the arm. 'Do not worry,' he said. 'Mr Samuel will not be harmed. It will be all right, Pak Suryono.'

But the Javanese businessman was pale with fear. 'What is happening?' he asked. 'What is all this about? Will they kill him?'

'Do not worry,' repeated Pak Wim. 'It is not good to worry. There is nothing we can do.'

The crowd passed through the village, picking up new members as it did so until there must have been one hundred souls accompanying Sam to his *mandi adat*. Weaving through the disorderly village, they came to the Pancasila Hall, Pastor Freddy's church. A newly painted sign above the door – it had been put up only a month ago – read: TRUE CHURCH OF THE COMING OF CHRIST-BATJAMENI (PROTESTANT).

The crowd surged into the church. Pak Wim and Pak Suryono followed. Pak Suryono noted that the hunters from Amasi Dol and Amasi Da had disappeared, having merged into the crowd.

Running with sweat, Sam was half-dragged across the threshold into the church, his head lolling. He looked up to see a crudely painted figure of Christ on the far wall. But this Christ was different. He did not wear a loincloth and between his legs were twin organs, male and female, erect and gaping respectively. His eyes were open. *Christus-Batjemenius Triumphans*. He who has overcome death.

Seated on his throne beneath the painting was Pastor Freddy, his shirt open almost to the belly, his stomach bulging over the waistline of his trousers, attended on either side by a modest village virgin (alas, virgin no more), who had been assigned to attend to the holy man's needs. The hall was already crowded with villagers, dressed variously in T-shirts, torn trousers and shorts. The council of elders sat on chairs, while the rest took their places on the floor. Sam was delivered to the front. Then the crowd fell silent. Very quietly, Pak Wim and Pak Suryono crept into the back of the church and sat down cross-legged.

The Colonel, still holding on to Sam with a tight grip, spoke. 'We have an Englishman who has devils in him,' he said. 'We must make *mandi adat*. We must kill the devils.'

Pastor Freddy rose. 'He must kneel,' he said.

The Colonel forced Sam to the floor. The Englishman was shuddering and seemed only half aware of where he was. Where is Fon? Sam thought. How could he live without her to make sense of this shadow play?

Pastor Freddy dismissed the Colonel with a wave of his hand. The virgins simpered and sat down neatly on the plinth beneath the pastor's throne.

'A devil is taking our daughters away,' the prophet said. 'These are dark days. Now we have the devil, in the form of an Englishman. But the devil's name is Legion, for they are many. We will wash the Englishman clean, but our work will not be done. There are many dark days ahead, friends. We must keep the fires of protection burning outside the village. We must be vigilant.' He closed his eyes and put his hands on Sam's head. Sam could feel a chunky ring pressing into his scalp. 'Christ-Batjameni will come,' the priest intoned.

'Indeed he will come,' the congregation repeated.

The priest smiled and removed his hand from Sam's head so that he might open his arms wide. 'Batjameni is Christ,' he said.

'Christ is Batjameni,' responded the congregation.

Pak Suryono glanced at Pak Wim, as if to say, 'These are your people, not mine: what do you have to say for yourself?' Pak Wim looked away.

'He will come to judge,' Pastor Freddy recited.

'He will come to judge,' the villagers replied.

'Amen,' Freddy said.

And the congregation replied, 'Amen.'

Sam lifted his head. 'Fon,' he whispered. Then the fragile sun of his consciousness shattered as the fever returned.

Freddy was about to speak again when there was a commotion at the back of the Pancasila Hall. A young man – one of Freddy's chief disciples – burst in, drenched in sweat. 'He comes!' he cried out.

Pastor Freddy glared at him across the hall, furious at this intrusion. 'Who comes?' he snapped. This intruder should be punished, he thought to himself. He should be beaten.

'Christ-Batjameni!' the young man panted. 'He comes!'

'Indeed he comes,' Pastor Freddy said, his voice measured. 'We must wait and purify our hearts.'

The young man hesitated. 'No,' he said. 'We must wait no longer. Christ-Batjameni comes *now*!'

Unease rippled through the congregation.

'There is a boat,' the intruder explained. 'Christ-Batjameni comes in the boat. I have seen him with my own eyes!'

For all his prophetic intensity, Pastor Freddy was not equal to the moment. Sam was kneeling before him. The skies outside were filling with dark smoke. Devils were walking abroad. The Last Days were nigh and Christ-Batjameni was coming. But not now. Not today. Not this very instant. He turned to look at his holy virgins, then spoke above the increasing hubbub. 'No,' he said firmly. 'He does not come yet! Please be seated for the *mandi adat*.'

But he had already lost his audience. People were stumbling to their feet, heading towards the door. 'Christ-Batjameni has come!' they were muttering to each other. 'He has come!'

The pastor stood up on his plinth. 'Stop!' he ordered. 'Come back! He has not come yet! He is coming soon. *Soon*, not now!'

Nobody was listening. The people of Desa Baru had heard the Good News. Nothing could stem the exodus from the True Church of the Coming of Christ-Batjameni (Protestant). The congregation jostled through the doorway to see, down by the shore, a small boat, a little way out at sea. It was heading towards land. And lo! on the deck was borne a tiny figure, a figure that seemed to be both male and female, Christ and Batjameni, its arms opened wide to greet the faithful.

Those who had been dozing at home, oblivious to the earlier commotion, came from their houses; those who had been tending the pyres at either end of the village left their posts. Men working in the plantations nearby threw down their machetes. Heedless of the smoke that was filling the sky, the people of Desa Baru ran towards the beach, crying out in joy.

Pastor Freddy trembled as the final few members of his

congregation trickled out of the church. Only Pak Suryono remained. Pak Wim had mysteriously disappeared. At
the front of the church, the two virgins took the priest by
the arms and seated him on his throne, cooing soothingly,
caressing his hair with their long, skilful fingers, kissing the
prophet's cheeks that were becoming wet with tears. Neither
they nor Pastor Freddy paid any attention to the Englishman who knelt, consumed by a feverish relapse, at his feet.
'Not yet,' the priest was saying. 'He does not come yet.'

Pak Suryono strode across the Pancasila Hall and shook
the Englishman by the shoulder. 'Mr Sam,' he said. 'Let us
go.' Sam opened his eyes. For a moment he could not
focus, but then when he saw the hall was empty and that
Pak Suryono was before him he could have wept with
relief. 'Mr Sam,' Pak Suryono said, 'we cannot delay. We
must find the cargo.'

Sam nodded, his eyes blank. 'Help me up,' he said.

Pak Suryono bent down and allowed Sam to put his
arm around his shoulders; he eased him to his feet. 'You
are hot,' he said. 'You still have a fever?'

Sam nodded feebly.

Pak Suryono helped him out of the church. The fresh
air outside revived him a little. 'Thank you, Pak Suryono, I
think I can walk by myself,' he said.

They looked down towards the beach. The sea was
shimmering like a mirror in the afternoon sun, two black
stains of smoke still smudging the sky. Not far from the
shore, a small boat was bobbing slowly in the direction of
the village. The people of Desa Baru were going to meet it,
up to their knees, their thighs, their waists, their chests,
arms held out in supplication, calling out, 'Christ-Batjameni!
He comes! He comes!'

'Where are Pak Wim and the hunters?' Sam asked.

Pak Suryono pointed down the beach. 'We must fetch
them,' he said. 'Time is short.'

Down on the beach they pushed through the crowd: some of the villagers of Desa Baru, those who lacked faith, hovered tentatively on dry land, eyes fixed on the approaching vessel, others were paddling and still others were plunging into the water with baptismal fervour. Thirty metres out from the shore, at the point just before the reef plunged into the depths, stood the Colonel in water up to his chest. He held his rifle high above his head and let out a long, ecstatic moan that somehow could be heard to soar above the hubbub of the crowd. Women were weeping; men trembling with expectation.

Sam and Pak Suryono looked around for Pak Wim. Not seeing him on the beach, they started to wade into the water. It was Sam who saw him first, the waves lapping around his waist, his two hands held up in a gesture of blissful longing, one arm slightly lower than the other on account of his recent injuries. 'That's him,' Sam said. Flailing through the deepening water, half-walking, half-swimming, he approached Pak Wim from behind. 'Pak Wim,' he yelled, tasting salt in his mouth, a burning in his nose where he had accidentally submerged himself. 'We must go.' He took Pak Wim by the shoulder.

Pak Wim swayed, then turned to look at Sam. His eyes were open, but they registered no flicker of recognition, as if Sam was a stranger who had accosted him on a busy street, as if he was about to say, 'I am sorry, but you have the wrong man.'

'Today,' Pak Wim said, 'I will be saved.' A grin dawned on his still-bruised face and his eyes rolled heavenwards. He reached out and took hold of Sam's wrist. 'You too can be saved,' he said, closing his eyes and turning his face towards the sun.

For a moment or two, Sam paused. Pak Wim's grip on his wrist was surprisingly strong.

Pak Suryono arrived, his business suit soaked through,

thrashing through the water with a lack of grace at variance with his character: he was not a man accustomed to getting his feet wet. 'Wim!' Pak Suryono barked, coming between Samuel and the devotee. 'We are wasting time. We must go.'

Pak Wim turned to look at the businessman with a beatific smile. 'Saved,' he whispered. And tears rolled down his cheeks. Salt water mingled with salt water.

Pak Suryono grabbed the collar of Pak Wim's shirt. With a sharp tug he unbalanced him, immersing him in the water. Forcing him under, Pak Suryono held his head for several seconds until a large bubble of air burst on the surface. Then he let go. Pak Wim came up spluttering and blinking, eyes startled and wide open. 'Pak Suryono,' he gasped, 'the boat . . .'

'The boat!' Sam was pointing at the approaching vessel. On the deck was a figure with the build of a man but dressed in women's clothes that shone golden in the afternoon sun. The apparition stood, as if in greeting, arms raised to the sky, a messiah or a saviour.

The water lapping round his waist, Sam stared. *Can it be?* he asked himself. *Can it be him?*

A tremor of expectation shuddered through the crowd. The Colonel tossed his rifle into the water, unknowingly echoing Kruywers's symbolic act more than eighty years before. 'He comes!' he yelled. 'Batjameni comes!'

The arms of the coming god now described a kind of arc, stretching out to either side, as if to embrace the welcoming crowd.

'It's him!' Sam shouted, incredulous. 'It's *him*!'

The bows of the incoming boat rose up on a tall wave. The figure faltered, losing its footing. It reeled on the deck, then collapsed. The devotees hesitated. Gods and messiahs, they knew, should not stumble.

'It's Mr Liao!' Sam yelled. 'In a dress. It's the fisherman, Mr Liao!'

The coming god rose onto all fours and struggled to his feet. As he did so, more figures appeared from the cabin. They were waving their arms: not the gestures of a god and his entourage greeting the faithful, but the panic of mortals. The boat was drifting towards the sharp reefs and Mr Liao – for Sam was right – was now running up and down in panic, his yellow dress flapping. Behind him, Sam could make out the stocky form of Mr Tan, lurching towards the bows of the boat. There was also a girl, dressed in nothing other than a lacy bra and some skimpy knickers. She was calling out in Kenukecilese, 'Help! We're going to run aground! Bring boats! Help!'

'It's Bunny Masela!' one of the villagers shouted. 'It's the girl Bunny Masela. It's the headman's daughter.'

It was this that broke the spell. An embarrassed silence descended over the communion of the faithful. Indeed it was the Masela girl: shamefully dressed in nothing but her underwear, without even the yellow frock she had adopted that morning after the party.

Next to appear on deck was the man from ABRI, stripped to the waist, his belly hanging over his trousers. He held a pistol over his head. Firing a single shot into the air, he roared: 'We are running aground. Bring boats!'

The gunshot brought four more figures onto the deck: Mr Gu, accompanied by three girls clad in yellow.

The Colonel stood paralysed, chest-deep in water, more astonished than he could have been by the arrival of any god. The crowd of the faithful started to break up. Some simply stood and stared. Others waded to shore, shaking their heads. Those who regained their wits more quickly hurried to fetch canoes, for the reefs off Desa Baru could be treacherous and who knew if the passengers could swim?

*

Misfortune, it later turned out, had fallen on Mr Gu's cruise just after dawn that morning, when the all-night party on the *Lerebulan* had at last come to an end. Flower had played 'All You Need is Love' for a final time, the passengers had at last fallen asleep and the sun had climbed the eastern sky out of the sea. When they were dozing, three men from Makalau had silently come on board and siphoned off most of the vessel's fuel. Then they had untied the hawser that tethered the *Lerebulan* to the land and watched with satisfaction as the boat, now surrendered to the wind and the tides, had drifted away from land on an uncertain course, taking with it the Taiwanese fishermen, whose intention of pillaging the waters around Kenukecil was well known to the people of Makalau and equally well resented.

The boat had bobbed northwards, a cradle gently rocking the sleeping passengers. After several hours following the flow of complex currents, with a slight shift in the prevailing wind the *Lerebulan* had started to move towards the south-west in the direction of Desa Baru.

Mr Liao had been the first to awake, the afternoon already advanced, dressed in Bunny Masela's yellow frock (the girl, still asleep, had been lying semi-naked in his arms). The rocking of the boat conspired with the excesses of the night before to bring about a horrible sensation of sickness and he had stumbled onto deck. Only after having thrown up over the side had he noticed that they were adrift and heading towards the reef. He had tried to start the engine, which had spluttered and died. In terror, he had shouted and waved his arms – the divine signal spotted by Pastor Freddy's disciple. The others, drunk, took longer to rouse from their sleep than did the villagers of Desa Baru, but to Mr Liao's bewilderment and alarm when the people of the village came running down to the beach in response to his cry, they did so not to launch rescue boats but merely to shout and moan at him, holding out their arms to him as if he were not a sailor in a state of jeopardy but instead some kind of messiah.

Now that the situation was clear, however, the first dugout canoes were launched, their owners paddling towards the boat to save its crew and passengers from drowning. Sam, Pak Wim and Pak Suryono stood waist-deep in water and watched.

'Pak Wim, Mr Sam,' Pak Suryono said quietly, 'we must go. Let us find the hunters. Our quarry is waiting for us by the cliffs.'

The three men waded out of the surf and back to the beach. Some of the villagers were already trailing back up the hill, muttering with disappointment, cursing Freddy the holy man who had filled them with false hopes. The three hunters from Amasi Dol were standing together on the sand. They too were soaking wet. Sam acknowledged them with a nod, then glanced back towards the village. The smoke was clearing. The tyres must have burned themselves out and the sun was on its descent. Sunset would not be long. 'Let's go and fetch the jeep,' he said. 'Come on.'

# 29

The jeep was where they had left it. A few flames flickered from the remnants of burning tyres. Pak Wim recovered the keys and climbed into the driver's seat. Sam got in beside him. Pak Suryono removed his jacket and wrung it out vigorously, then clambered into the back along with the three hunters from Amasi Dol. His teeth chattered as the evening breeze caught his drying clothes.

Pak Wim turned on the ignition and sat for a few moments, listening to the engine idling, an air of sadness over him.

'Wim,' Sam pressed him, 'we have to go. We have very little time.'

'Yes, Mr Sam,' Pak Wim replied. He eased the jeep into gear, put his foot down and cleared the remains of the burning tyres with ease. They headed underneath the ceremonial arch, through Desa Baru, out through the second arch past the second pyre, and then took the right-hand fork towards the airport, leaving the disappointed faithful of Desa Baru behind.

They had expected the airport to be deserted but, to their surprise, the bamboo barrier at the end of the road was down and Pak Solo, the deputy to the chief of police, stood to one side, wearing shades and chewing gum, as he had seen in American films. He had with him three officers. Pak Wim pulled up in front of the barrier and stopped the jeep. Pak Suryono, maintaining some appearance of dignity despite being both sodden and rumpled, climbed out of the back. He approached the deputy and put out his hand to greet him. 'Good afternoon, Pak Polisi. What is happening?'

Pak Solo examined Pak Suryono with a sneer of contempt. The Javanese businessmen saw himself mirrored twice in the policeman's shades and was embarrassed by what he saw. Never before had he appeared so disgracefully dressed in public.

'The American is leaving,' Pak Solo said. His expression was impossible to read.

'We need to pass,' Pak Suryono said, indicating the hunters, who were getting out of the jeep and preparing their bows and arrows. 'We have business in the forest.'

Pak Solo looked at the hunters. 'For reasons of public safety,' he said officiously, 'the road from here onwards is closed until the plane has departed. If you wish, you may wait in the airport.' He indicated the low building by the side of the runway. 'And who are these men you are with, Pak? Why are they armed?'

Pak Suryono was silent while he considered how to reply.

The deputy turned to his police officers. 'Disarm these men!' he commanded.

The police officers strode over to the hunters and took their bows and arrows. They piled them in the police truck in front of the bamboo barrier. The men from Amasi Dol glowered resentfully, but they did not resist. Pak Suryono started to form an objection, but at that moment both he and the policeman were distracted by the sound of singing coming from the road back to Bantuk. Pak Suryono looked on with bafflement as the ecclesiastical minibus appeared in a cloud of dust, the sounds of joyful song emanating from inside.

'It's the nuns, Pak Suryono,' Sam explained, a clarification that did nothing to alleviate Pak Suryono's confusion.

Suster Elena stopped the minibus by the barrier and leaned out. 'Pak Solo!' she said cheerfully. 'What is happening?'

'The American,' Pak Solo replied. 'She is leaving.'

Pastor Niemann was at Suster Elena's side in the passenger seat. As usual Benny, Ibu Nilasera and the nuns were travelling in the back. Benny opened the sliding door and the nuns climbed out.

When the priest got out of the passenger seat, he recognized the Englishman standing by the jeep from a few days before. The man was soaked from head to toe – as, he now noted, were all his companions. Strange, he thought.

The crowd of onlookers – the hunters from Amasi Dol, Pak Suryono, Sam Rivers, Pak Wim, the nuns, Benny, Pastor Niemann and Ibu Nilasera – now hurried through the airport building and gathered outside by the side of the airstrip. About a hundred yards away, Aletheia Groeber was in the cockpit of her plane, the windshield lifted. The propeller was spinning.

'Who is that woman?' Pak Wim asked.

'Her name is Aletheia Groeber,' Sam said. 'She is American.'

Dr Groeber looked up from the dials in front of her. She saw the gathered crowd and waved at them. Then the plane started to taxi slowly along the runway, ready for take-off. At the end of the runway, Aletheia turned the aircraft through one hundred and eighty degrees. Clouds were massing in the sky above and the wind was stiffening.

The engine started to roar. Dr Aletheia Groeber, PhD, MPhil, FRAS, FAAA, paused for a moment for final checks and adjustments prior to take-off.

Pastor Niemann found himself standing next to Sam, whose clothes were steaming a little in the rays of the afternoon sun. 'I never had a chance to meet her properly,' he said. 'Did you?'

'Oh, yes,' said Sam.

'What was all this business about her looking for a husband?' the priest asked.

'Whatever she's been up to, I guess she's been unsuccessful,' Sam said.

Pastor Niemann blinked. 'Ah,' he said. 'Yes, that is true.'

Then the plane jerked forward and started down the runway. Her hair blowing in the wind, Aletheia skilfully manoeuvred the plane along the tarmac. The crowd watched her approach, the nuns clapping in delight at the spectacle.

The cracking of branches from among the trees on the far side of the runway was unexpected. Momentarily distracted, the spectators turned their heads to see, bursting from the forest further along the runway, the squat figure of what might, at first glance, have been taken to be a child or a short man. He was naked, with a muscular body and a covering of fine, reddish fur. Although the size of a child, three and a half feet tall, four at the most, he nevertheless had nothing of the child or adolescent about him. He was human; but then again not exactly. And he was running along the tarmac towards the approaching plane.

Ibu Nilasera covered her mouth in horror and pointed her finger. 'The devil!' she screamed. 'That is the devil!'

Pastor Niemann's mouth fell open. 'Good God,' he muttered: but it was not a prayer.

Pak Solo took off his dark glasses. He turned to his men to issue an order, but his three officers – all good, God-fearing Catholics who wanted nothing to do with devils – were already running, through the airport building and towards the track that led back to town. The nuns crossed themselves and rattled off their Hail Marys. Pak Suryono, Sam and Pak Wim stood motionless, watching their cargo as it hurtled towards the wheels of Aletheia's oncoming plane. The hunters, taking advantage of the confusion, made a run for their weapons, hauling them out of the police truck.

For a second it seemed that the Gugu would be crushed under the aircraft's wheels, but just before the worst happened, no more than twenty feet away from the spectators, Aletheia Groeber, who had learned her flying skills in the skies above Montana, pulled back on the joystick and took to the air. The Gugu reached up and grabbed at the wheel-struts as they passed over his head. The plane wobbled up into the sky, banking sharply over the trees. Underneath, the Gugu, using his strong arms, swung himself up towards the door of the plane.

'It's going to attack her,' Pak Suryono breathed. 'It's going to steal the plane.'

But Pak Suryono was wrong. At around one hundred feet, circling over the airport building, Aletheia Groeber opened the aircraft door – a delicate manoeuvre – and the Gugu leapt in, onto the pilot's lap. At that moment, the hunters took aim and fired off a volley of arrows. The plane door slammed; two of the arrows fell short. The third could be heard splintering on the fuselage. The hunters prepared to fire again as the plane circled. Aletheia straightened up and the plane climbed sharply out of range. The second volley failed to reach it. The spectators looked up to see the Gugu turn its head to give Aletheia Groeber a brief but passionate kiss. Then the plane arced round towards the north and it was no longer possible to make out the two passengers. It was just an ordinary single-prop plane, hauling itself up towards the clouds, leaving nothing behind but a faint throb and the sound of murmured prayers and curses.

*

A silence fell over the crowd gathered at the airstrip. Tears of vindication were forming in Ibu Nilasera's eyes: there, before witnesses, the devil had manifested itself. Who now could deny her? Pak Solo, furious that his men had deserted him, was the first to come to his senses. He started to yell orders at the crowd: 'Please return to your homes! There is nothing more to see! Please clear the area!' Nobody took any notice.

'Well,' Pak Wim said philosophically. 'Goodbye, Gugu. Mr Samuel, I told you, there are many strange things in Kenukecil.'

Hearing his voice, Ibu Nilasera turned her head. Her eyes came to rest on Pak Wim's thin, lined face, battered by the eunuch Karel, the grey hair above standing up stiffly in a lopsided quiff as the salt water dried.

The woman looked more closely. 'Bapak, do I know you?'

Pak Wim looked at the woman. 'No,' he said, shaking his head. 'You do not know me.'

Ibu Nilasera took a step forward. 'But I do,' she murmured. 'You are Wim. You are Wim.'

It was then that he recognized her. Only one person had ever spoken his name like that, with precisely that tone. 'Anna?' Pak Wim breathed. 'Is it you?'

Overweight, her beauty broken, her flesh sagging – undeniably this was she: Anna, whose breasts once were plump like ripe papayas, whose fingers were cool as the moon; Anna, whose mouth was sweet and tender as a jambu fruit, whose skin was smooth as a shell washed by the waves. The outward husk of her beauty had gone. This was not the girl who had walked from rockpool to rockpool, spearing the fish, singing to the shy boy of low rank who sat on the beach, watching her. Yet this was the very same Anna Nilasera whom he had loved.

'Wim!' she said. 'You have returned.'

'I have returned,' Pak Wim replied.

The sun was sinking and the coolness of evening was beginning to spread over the island. The crowd was milling around in confusion, oblivious to Pak Wim and Ibu Nilasera's conversation.

'You were not there,' Pak Wim said. 'I waited all night, but you did not come. I have lived my life in shame because of this.'

'Ah! Wim, it has been so long . . .' Ibu Nilasera reached out and touched his cheek. Then she withdrew her hand in embarrassment. 'You have suffered, Wim. I see that you have suffered. What has happened to you?'

Pak Wim looked down at the tarmac. 'I waited for you, Anna. I waited in the forest, but you did not come.'

Ibu Nilasera shuffled closer. 'I was there, Wim,' she whispered. 'I waited all night. I waited by the forest pool beside the *kenari* tree. And at dawn I cried.'

Pak Wim looked up, his eyes meeting hers. 'The *kenari* tree? Did we not agree to wait by the pool beside the mango tree?'

Ibu Nilasera reached out and clasped Wim's hand. 'Wim, I too waited all night, and you did not come. Can it be that we waited in the same forest, but by different pools?'

Pak Wim's withdrew his hand from hers. Had his ill fortune hinged on this and this alone? 'What does it matter now, Anna? You have a husband and I am broken.'

Then Anna Nilasera embraced him. Pak Wim's shoulders shook with grief. 'I have no husband other than you,' she murmured. 'Wim, my dear Wim. You are my only husband.'

# 30

Pak Solo was the first to leave, climbing back into the police jeep and heading towards Bantuk without a word. He caught up with his fleeing officers near where the airport track joined the main road. The nuns piled back into the minibus – silent for once – with Benny and Pastor Niemann. Driving with unaccustomed care and thoughtfulness, Suster Elena put the minibus into reverse, turned and headed off down the track. The hunters ran out to the tarmac to collect their arrows where they had fallen. There was no point in wasting good arrows.

Pak Suryono ran his hand through his hair. 'Mr Sam,' he said briskly, 'I must apologize. Your investment has come to nothing.' He smiled. Then he turned to Pak Wim, who was shyly holding Ibu Nilasera's hand. 'Pak Wim,' he said, 'should you wish to return to Ambon, I will be able to pay for your return. I will let the captain of the *Siwalima* know that you will be joining him. As for myself, I will travel back to Jakarta with Ibrahim.'

'No,' Pak Wim said. 'I do not want to go to Ambon.'

Pak Suryono looked round. The three hunters had returned. 'Well,' the businessman said, 'it seems as if my work is finished in Kenukecil. Ibrahim will be waiting at Amasi Dol. I don't suppose you would mind if I took the jeep with these men?'

Sam shook his head. Pak Wim was just standing there, hand-in-hand with Ibu Nilasera and smiling. He said nothing.

'Good. Thank you very much, gentlemen. I will say farewell. *Selamat tinggal.*' He shook hands first with Sam and then with Pak Wim. '*Ayo!*' he said to the hunters. 'Let us return to the jeep.'

'Remember to pick up the folks from Amasi Da,' Sam said. 'They will still be waiting at the foot of the cliff.'

'Of course, Mr Samuel. Goodbye.'

Pak Suryono walked slowly to the jeep with the three hunters. Sam and the two lovers watched as the four men climbed in, slammed the doors and set off down the track into the distance.

There was nobody left at the airport except Pak Wim, Sam and Ibu Nilasera. Pak Wim put his arm around the woman and she snuggled comfortably into his side.

'Pak Suryono has taken the jeep,' Sam said, 'so it looks like we will have to walk. Do you want to accompany me?'

Pak Wim giggled. 'Thank you, tuan. We will say goodbye to you here. We have something we must do. There is a pool in the forest that we must visit.'

Sam smiled. He knew when he wasn't wanted. 'Pak Wim,' he said. 'I owe you some money.'

Pak Wim shook his head. 'No, tuan. We were unsuccessful, so you do not owe me any money.' Sam reached into his pocket, but Pak Wim held up his hand. 'What do I want with money?' he asked. 'I am just a simple man.'

Sam withdrew his hand from his pocket. 'OK,' he said. 'Goodbye, Pak Wim. And goodbye –' Sam paused.

'Anna,' Ibu Nilasera said with a smile. 'Anna Nilasera.'

'Goodbye, Ibu Anna Nilasera.'

Sam shook hands with them both; then he turned to walk back to Bantuk.


That evening in the Lovely Vista Hotel, Sam washed in the *kamar bak*. He shaved and dressed in a clean set of clothes. There was a small mirror in his room. He looked at himself and smiled. *Samuel Rivers* – he said – *you look almost human.*

When he arrived downstairs, Thomas was on the front desk, engrossed in his usual game of minesweeper. 'Thomas,' Sam asked, 'may I make a call?'

Without looking up, Thomas gestured to the telephone.

Sam sat down. 'Thomas,' he said. 'Would you mind?'

'No, of course, Mr Sam,' Thomas said. He got up from the desk and walked away down the corridor.

Sam picked up the receiver and held it to his ear. He gazed out of the door of the Lovely Vista into the night. Then he carefully dialled Fonny's number. The phone rang several times before Fon picked up.

'Fonny,' Sam said. 'It's me.'

Once again, there was silence.

'I'm sorry,' Sam said. Then he started to cry.

Fonny did not put the phone down, nor did she speak. She just listened, waiting for him to finish. Sam sobbed, choking on his own regret and relief and confusion and hope.

'Fon,' he said. 'Fon.'

He wiped his eyes and nose with his sleeve and took a breath. There was still silence at the other end of the line.

'Fonny?' Sam asked. 'Are you still there?'

There was a pause, the lightest of sighs. 'Yes, Sam,' Fonny said. 'I'm still here.'

# About the Author

WILL BUCKINGHAM studied Fine Arts before running away to Indonesia to research sculpture in the Spice Islands. While there he spent most of his time in the Tanimbar Islands, where his research took him into ever stranger territory as he suffered malarial fevers, witchcraft, exorcism and various idiosyncratic forms of folk medicine. He returned to the UK to study anthropology and then philosophy, with phenomenology and ancient atomism among his interests. He now lives in Birmingham, where he is writing his second novel and completing a PhD.